My Heart Belongs in Ruby City, Idaho

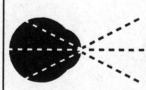

This Large Print Book carries the
Seal of Approval of N.A.V.H.

My Heart Belongs in Ruby City, Idaho

REBECCA'S PLIGHT

Susanne Dietze

THORNDIKE PRESS

A part of Gale, a Cengage Company

Farmington Hills, Mich • San Francisco • New York • Waterville, Maine
Meriden, Conn • Mason, Ohio • Chicago

Copyright © 2017 by Susanne Dietze.
All scripture quotations are taken from the King James Version of the Bible.
Thorndike Press, a part of Gale, a Cengage Company.

ALL RIGHTS RESERVED
This book is a work of fiction. Names, characters, places, and incidents are either products of the author's imagination or are used fictitiously. Any similarity to actual people, organizations, and/or events is purely coincidental.
Thorndike Press® Large Print Christian Romance.
The text of this Large Print edition is unabridged.
Other aspects of the book may vary from the original edition.
Set in 16 pt. Plantin.

LIBRARY OF CONGRESS CATALOGING-IN-PUBLICATION DATA

Names: Dietze, Susanne, author.
Title: My heart belongs in Ruby City, Idaho : Rebecca's plight / by Susanne Dietze.
Description: Large print edition. | Waterville, Maine : Thorndike Press, 2017. | Series: Thorndike Press large print Christian romance
Identifiers: LCCN 2017023034| ISBN 9781432842024 (hardcover) | ISBN 1432842021 (hardcover)
Subjects: LCSH: Large type books. | GSAFD: Love stories.
Classification: LCC PS3604.I377 M9 2017 | DDC 813/.6—dc23
LC record available at https://lccn.loc.gov/2017023034

Published in 2017 by arrangement with Barbour Publishing, Inc.

Printed in the United States of America
1 2 3 4 5 6 7 21 20 19 18 17

For my children, Hannah and Matthew. In the movie *Tangled,* we laugh when the piano guy says, "Go, live your dream." Since I was young, my dream was to write, but you and your dad were also my dream. I'm so blessed to be your mom. I'm cheering for you as you go live the dreams God places in your hearts.

ACKNOWLEDGMENTS

Before Silver City became the seat of Owyhee County in 1867, Ruby City held the honor for four years. Today, little remains of Ruby City except for the cemetery and a few stone foundations, but you can still visit Silver City and view several historic buildings, including the Idaho Hotel.

Many thanks to my editor, Rebecca Germany, editor JoAnne Simmons, and the team at Barbour Publishing, as well as my wonderful agent, Tamela Hancock Murray. Debra E. Marvin, thank you for being such a patient sounding board and generous critique partner; I'm so glad God put you in my life! The ladies of Inkwell Inspirations were always there with friendship, critiques, and encouragement — hugs and chocolate, my friends. Thank you to all who prayed for me as I wrote this story, especially Donna Chaffee, Suzanne Kneale, Jennifer Uhlarik, and the couples in my Bible study: Karen and Al Cartmell, Bitsy and Garrett Ming, and Suzanne and Paul Wagner.

I'm also grateful to Mary O'Malley of the Owyhee County Historical Society, who patiently answered my oddball questions. Any historical inaccuracies in the story are mine alone, however — and a few of them were intentional. I replaced the sheriff, judge, and other county office holders with my own fictional characters, and I took liberties with the stage routes and legal system to suit my purposes.

Karl, Hannah, Matthew, Mom, and Dad, thanks for your prayers, support, and love. You were patient and encouraging, and it means more to me than you'll ever know. I love you!

God setteth the solitary in families:
he bringeth out those which are bound
with chains.

PSALM 68:6

CHAPTER ONE

May 1866, Owyhee County, Idaho Territory
The dimming afternoon sky outside the stagecoach window was thick with flat-topped clouds, but the reverberating crack was no clap of thunder. Rebecca Rice knew a rifle shot when she heard it.

She scuttled across the empty carriage to peer out the far window as the coach skidded to a stop. Men on horseback, four if she counted right, circled the coach, brandishing long guns and pistols. All wore bandannas over their noses and mouths, obscuring their faces.

Bandits.

Lord, You are my guard. Still, she'd prepared for something like this, gartering a bone-handled paper knife to her calf. Her fingers shook when she untied the dainty blade and tucked it up her undersleeve.

Too far — the metal tip poked the inside of her elbow. Wincing, Rebecca curled against the door to hide, her wide bluebell skirt tangled around her ankles. She shoved her reticule beneath the seat, and then her fingertips found the knife handle. If some two-bit bandit thought he could paw at her for the few valuables she possessed —

The door yanked open behind her. She fell out, landing on her backside in the dirt. Dust puffed around her, clogging her throat and sullying her Sunday dress. Some impression she'd make on her fiancé now.

If she lived that long. A sweat-drenched oaf, his head almost too small for his muscular frame, glared at her with close-set eyes. His thick finger rested on the trigger of his shotgun. Behind him a brawny fellow rifled through her valise while a lankier bandit trained a pistol on the coachman.

The smallest of the bandits crawled into the carriage, then hopped out, empty-handed. "Where'd you stash your handbag, lady?" His voice wasn't all that deep. He must be a boy.

Pity he'd started a life of crime so young. "There's nothing in it to interest you."

The coachman, an unshaven fellow of middle years by the name of Mr. Kaplan, sent her a pleading look. "Best do what they say, ma'am. It'll be over soon, and they'll get what they want whether we cooperate or not."

He had a point. Maybe this would be over once they took her bag. The sooner she got to Ruby City, the sooner she'd get married. Then she could get something good to eat. The thought of roast chicken or mashed potatoes or even a stinky tongue sandwich set her stomach grumbling. Even at a time like this.

"Shoved under the seat," she said at last.

The young bandit disappeared back into the coach and returned with her reticule, shaking it to make the coins inside jingle. That was all he'd find, except for a pencil stub and her mother's lace-trimmed handkerchief.

"I hope it's worth it to you." Rebecca's tone was vinegary as a pickle.

"Everything's worth something to someone." The young bandit wandered to where his compatriot emptied her bag, dumping Rebecca's underthings on the dirt. The young bandit pulled out Rebecca's toilet case and then, *oh dear,* the bundle of letters she'd tied with a pink ribbon. Bad enough these criminals mauled her unmentionables and stole her toiletries, but she had no other heirloom to give her future children than the sweet legacy of those letters.

13

"You can't have those." Rebecca lunged. Her hand batted air as the bandit stepped away from her, holding the packet aloft.

The pink ribbon fluttered to the dust as the brigand shook the envelopes. "Any money in here?"

If there was, she wouldn't be this hungry. "Not a dime, so give those back."

The bandit flipped through the letters anyway. Then his gaze lifted to Rebecca's, his eyes narrowed and his forehead furrowed like he recognized her name. Impossible. Her interpretation had to be incorrect, and sure enough, he let the letters fall from his fingers to the ground, like they weren't worth the effort to fling aside.

The muscular bandit hauled the strongbox over his shoulder. "All set?"

"I dunno." The robber with the broad shoulders and small eyes stared at Rebecca. "She could have money hidden under her dress."

Let him try. She'd have her paper knife out before his thick fingers touched her.

"Her clothes ain't that fine and she's lean as a starvin' coyote." The young one tipped his pistol at her. "Leave her be."

The beady-eyed criminal reached for Rebecca's bodice anyway. Rebecca yanked the paper knife from her sleeve and slashed.

The oversize robber jerked back, but he wasn't the one bleeding. A red gash marred the back of the young fellow's hand. Had he tried to protect her by pulling his companion away? He seemed none too happy with her, the way his dark eyes glared at her over his bandanna.

Rebecca's lunch of stale crackers crept up her throat. He'd punish her for injuring him, no question. Her grip tightened on the paper knife.

The beady-eyed goliath rubbed his hands together. "This'll be fun."

"I said let her go. We got what we came for." The boy-bandit scooped the coins from her reticule and then tossed the bag to the dirt. "Let's ride."

Rebecca's boots seemed nailed to the dirt until the quartet of criminals mounted their horses. Then, the moment they disappeared down the sagebrush-scattered hill, she almost fell, crouching to gather her letters. *Thank You, God.*

Mr. Kaplan retrieved her reticule. The tiny purse she'd embroidered with pink peonies dangled off his wrist, an amusing sight, but Rebecca couldn't muster the strength to laugh.

"Those must be important." He pointed at the letters.

15

"They are." She brushed a clod of dirt from one of the envelopes. There, now she could read the return address: *Theodore Fordham, Ruby City, Owyhee County, Idaho Territory*. "They're from my intended. I'm on my way to Ruby City to make his acquaintance."

Her hand flew to her mouth. Why not just tell Mr. Kaplan every embarrassing detail, like how she'd advertised in a newspaper for a husband and Mr. Fordham had answered, and in his fifth missive he'd proposed and she'd agreed? Mortified, she scurried to stuff her petticoat back into her valise.

If the news that she was about to marry a man she'd never met shocked the driver, however, he had the grace not to show it. Instead, he secured her trunk to the coach again. "Sorry we were set upon like that. This can be a wild land in every way, ma'am. Best you know that afore you swap vows."

Wild land perhaps, but she'd not be marrying a wild man.

Rebecca couldn't repress a smile, thinking of the quiet life Theodore described in his letters, a life of safety in the cozy, warm rooms above his mercantile, where he made a sound living selling goods to the miners

16

who flocked here by the score.

A life, he admitted, that could seem boring, with the same tedious routine day after day, returning to the same hearth every night after a full day's work.

She grinned as she climbed back into the coach. Boredom sounded wonderful.

On the remainder of the journey, Rebecca cleaned her face with her hankie and the rest of the water in her small canteen, so she'd be somewhat presentable. As the coach ascended the rugged, uphill road, the sagebrush gave way to fir, juniper, and mahogany — a beautiful sight.

It didn't seem long before she descended from the stagecoach in front of a two-story edifice with a balcony rail on the upper floor. The signage proclaimed it to be the Idaho Hotel. A few men lounging outside the doors eyed her, so she turned away, getting her first full glimpse of her new community. Nestled into a small valley, Ruby City boasted a wide street lined by framed buildings: a barbershop, bank, and a restaurant, but where was the mercantile? She'd like to meet Mr. Fordham first thing.

Movement drew her gaze. A man hurried up the street, shoving a light-colored, flat-brimmed hat on his head with one hand and tugging a coat in place with the other. A few fellows followed after him, patting his back and guffawing, but his gaze fixed on her as he hastened toward her with a sure gait.

It was *him.* Her intended.

Not that she could tell by his looks, of course. They hadn't exchanged photographs. He hadn't minded that she couldn't afford to sit for a *carte de visite,* and considering photographers didn't pass through this way too often, he couldn't send her an image, either. All she had to go on was his description of himself, which had been decidedly slim on details: brown hair, hazel eyes, medium build.

The description hadn't done him justice. His square jaw was clean-shaven, and his smile was wide. From under his hat, coffee-dark tendrils curled over the collar of the dark blue frock coat he'd just donned, which fit well over his lean frame.

But it wasn't his looks that thrilled her. It was the way he'd come out of that door pulling on his coat, as if he took pains with his appearance to meet his bride. To get married.

He was her fiancé. She didn't need a photograph to know for sure. She knew it by the way her heart battered her chest like

18

a wild bird was caught inside her rib cage.

Should she smile? Mercy, she shouldn't. It revealed her crooked bottom teeth and — who cared? He'd see plenty of her teeth throughout their marriage. They'd share tooth powder, after all. Married couples shared such things. Except she was now out of tooth powder, thanks to the bandits. Did Theodore have some? Of course he did. He owned the general store.

Tooth powder? Rebecca shook the silly thought from her head. *I'm babbling like a brook and I haven't even opened my mouth yet.*

Trailed by the gaggle of menfolk, her fiancé stopped a full three feet away, a respectful distance, and removed his hat. "Ma'am, are you just arrived on the stage?"

His voice was smooth and attractive as a polished gemstone.

"I am. Are you Mr. Fordham?" She might be about to marry him, but it seemed forward to call him Theodore first thing.

He nodded, twiddling his hat brim in his hands. "And you're Miss Reese?"

"Rice," she corrected. "Like the grain." The spelling should have made the pronunciation obvious. Maybe he was as nervous as she.

"I'm mighty pleased to meet you, ma'am.

I've been waiting for you for days."

His eagerness sent a little sizzle of heat through her. She hadn't been due to arrive until today, so he must have been counting the moments, just as she had.

Mr. Kaplan tossed her carpetbag at her feet, and the thud dragged her gaze from her intended. Then the coachman thrust out his hand to her fiancé. "Ah, Fordham. This's yer bride?"

"I daresay she is, Kap." Mr. Fordham smiled. There went that sizzle again, right down to the holes at the toes of Rebecca's stockings.

Mr. Kaplan grinned, as if he approved. Then he swiped his nose with the back of his hand. "You should know, we got held up by the Gang o' Four. They took the strong-box but there weren't nothing in it, which they should've figgered since I didn't have a guard with me."

"What?" A grim line replaced Mr. Fordham's smile. He peered down at Rebecca. Then he took her hand, but not in a romantic gesture. Instead, he gently pulled her arm so it extended fully. A red stain the size of a half-dollar blotched the inside of her blue, pagoda-style sleeve. "You're bleeding."

Oh. That. "I hid a paper knife up my sleeve and nicked myself. Nothing to cause alarm." Except that her best garments were now bloodstained. Maybe she could soak both the dress and her undersleeve in cold water before the stain set. Her dust-caked skin and hair wouldn't mind a soak, either. She hadn't bathed in over a week, at one of the stops on the Overland Trail.

She probably still looked better than Mr. Kaplan, whose dirt-streaked countenance made the whites of his eyes look bleached. "When yer bride pulled the knife on the handsy one, I thought we were goners."

Mr. Fordham's jaw tightened. "One touched you? Rebecca — Miss Rice — I'm so sorry —"

His use of her Christian name sent a tiny thrill down her spine, but she'd have time to relish the moment later. She shook her head with vigor. "One tried, but the boy stopped him and I slashed him by mistake."

"There's a boy with them?"

"Not a child, but a youth. He's thin and not much taller than I am, and his voice is still soft. I'm grateful he intervened when the big fellow reached for me, but I didn't realize defending myself could make things worse."

Mr. Kaplan spat a stream of tobacco juice near her skirt. "Just give 'em what they want, nobody gets hurt."

21

This sentiment earned a rumble of approval from the men who'd followed Mr. Fordham up the street. Didn't they have some mining to do?

"No, Rebecca — Miss Rice — I'm glad you defended yourself. Even more glad that you're unharmed." Mr. Fordham's squeeze to her fingers was gentle, but she felt a spark even through her gloves. "This gang has been terrorizing the county for three months, but they've left most of the stagecoaches alone. I hate that this happened, and I hate that I have to leave you alone already, but I should go after the Gang before they get too far."

Mr. Fordham wanted to protect her! Gallant, yet absolutely unacceptable. The last time a man in her family rode off with a posse, he'd never come home. Rebecca's stomach twisted.

"Is it truly necessary for you to go?" Let the local lawmen go. Let somebody, anybody else do it. Not her fiancé, not today, not ever.

Mr. Kaplan shook his head. "No use, Fordham. They're long gone by now. 'Sides, you got more important things to do right now than ride out with a posse." His bushy gray brows wiggled.

Rebecca shivered but not from chill. She

22

was about to get married, after all.

A dry, warm wind tickled her nape and sent a strand of her pine-yellow hair curling into her nose. Her pins had loosened! She shoved the lank tendril behind her ear. If only she could remove her straw bonnet and repin her hair before the ceremony. Except she didn't have a comb or hairbrush anymore —

"I guess you're right." Mr. Fordham expelled a long breath through his nose, clearly conflicted between the twin desires to avenge her and marry her. "Kap, could you do me a favor and take Miss Rice's bags to the county offices?"

"Sure thing, Fordham."

Mr. Fordham smiled down at her. "Miss Rice, would you care to take a walk first?"

"A walk would be agreeable." Her muscles were stiff from sitting in the jostling coach, and the time to get to know him better would be welcome, too. So would the opportunity to speak without an audience. He offered his arm. It felt firm and pleasant under her hand.

"Aw, you can talk right here." An eavesdropping fellow with gray-brown hair and too-big britches hanging from stained suspenders shook a grimy finger at them. "You don't want to lose track of time and

23

miss Orr."

"Orr?" Rebecca couldn't remember if Mr. Fordham had written of the fellow.

"The justice of the peace."

Oh, yes. The circuit preacher wasn't in town but once every season, and no church had been built.

"Thanks, Ulysses," Mr. Fordham said to the eavesdropper.

"Can I come to the weddin'?" Ulysses yelled after them.

"Maybe," Mr. Fordham said over his shoulder as he led her back the way she'd come, past the end of the street and rows of miners' tents to a canopy of junipers. Along the way, he asked about the trip and noted the promise of rain in the thunderheads to the west — nothing too personal. If his intention was to set her at ease, he did a good job, for she almost forgot the awkwardness of the situation. In minutes, they stood by a gurgling creek, where purple wildflowers and white-blooming bushes thrived among the grass.

"Lovely." Rebecca took a deep breath. The world smelled like spring — grass and flowers and the lingering scent of sage. "I can see why you love it here."

"It'll be cold, come winter." He said it like a warning, as if giving her an excuse to back out of their engagement.

But she'd given her word, and she had nowhere else to go. No home or job back in Missouri to return to, and she wasn't sure if her brother Johnny still lived at that California mining camp anymore. Now that she'd met her Mr. Fordham in person, however, she knew this was where she was meant to be. With him, wherever that was.

So she smiled. "You've got access to a stove, don't you?"

"I do, at that." He laughed, a pleasant sound she wouldn't mind hearing for decades.

Rebecca moistened her lips. "I'm fine with it, by the way. Marrying fast, like we discussed. If you still wish it."

"I do." The way he said it was like a vow. He didn't know her beyond their letters, couldn't possibly love her yet, but he intended to be a good husband and provider. And maybe, just maybe, he saw her and liked her as much as she liked him. "But it doesn't have to be today. Orr will be back in a day or two, if you'd rather wait."

She shook her head. "Today is perfect."

Withdrawing a small knife from his pocket, he bent and snipped several clusters of purple and white flowers. For her?

Silly. Who else would they be for?

No one had ever given her flowers.

He smiled. "Anything you want to know about me, beforehand?"

"I already know your age." Twenty-six, four years older than her twenty-two. "And your favorite food." Pork and apples. "And how you came to Idaho a few years ago when your pa and uncle decided to go into the livery business." But his pa was dead now, leaving him lonesome. "I know you love God and want good things for this town, which I admire."

He held a bouquet the diameter of a dessert plate fisted in his hand, but it was his solemn expression which turned her leg bones to jam. "And I know things have been rough on you, but I'll spend my life trying to make you happy."

It took her a minute to gather the breath to speak. "I'll try hard to make you happy, too."

He handed her the bouquet, and when she took it, it felt like he could see straight into her heart. Embarrassed, she sniffed the flowers, finding them sweet and piquant, like orange blossoms. His forefinger brushed the wayward strand of her hair from her cheek. "You're a beautiful bride, Miss Rice."

She was in desperate need of soap and he was a sweet talker. But she liked it and couldn't hide her smile.

His mischievous grin drew out his dimples again. "I'll take us around back so we don't have an audience for our vows, unless you want Ulysses to come after all."

"No, a quiet wedding suits me fine."

He took her hand and they ran, laughing like children. He led her behind the row of buildings and stopped at a back door. Without knocking, he ushered her inside.

Rebecca blinked, adjusting to the dim after being out in the sun. Slowly, the office came into focus: four tidy desks with chairs, filing cabinets, and little in the way of decor. A door to her right opened onto what looked to be a closet with crates in it; a door to her left held two jail cells. Ah. The justice shared space with the sheriff, then.

Before she had time to blink, a black-haired fellow with a paunch under his vest and an impish gleam in his eye strode around one of the desks, extending his hand.

"Ahab Orr, Justice of the Peace." His grip was firm and his southern accent was thick as molasses. "Nice to meet you, Miss Rice."

"You know my name?"

"Ever'body knows. This groom o' yours has been most impatient. Y'all ready, now? Hate to rush you, but I've got to be in Silver City before sunset."

"One minute, Orr." Mr. Fordham took her bouquet and leaned into her ear. "I meant it, you're pretty as you are, but if you need a moment, there's a washstand through that door."

She cast him a grateful smile and disappeared into the closet with the crates while Mr. Orr said something about needing a witness for the ceremony. Half the tiny room stored cartons and boxes, but the other half boasted a cot, a washstand, and a blessedly full pitcher of water. She made use of the bar of soap, washing her hands and face and blotting the bloodstain on her sleeve. She removed her bonnet, combed her hair with her fingers, and repinned the bun at her nape. Then she poured a cup of what water remained in the pitcher. Maybe it was the dust on the trail or her overwrought nerves, but it was the most delicious water she'd ever tasted. When she returned to the office, a lanky youth rocked on his heels by the door — the witness to her wedding.

"A lovely bride." Mr. Orr waved her over. "Do you go by a nickname, ma'am? Becky or anything? Because I like to use the name folks call you when I officiate your marriage. Makes it more real to you."

It made sense. "No one's ever called me

Becky. Rebecca is fine."

"And your middle names, folks?"

"Mary."

"Percival. My maternal grandfather's name," her groom explained with a smile.

"I like it." It sounded chivalrous. Wasn't Sir Percival one of King Arthur's knights?

"Stand here." Mr. Orr pointed.

She set her bonnet on a desk. They took their places as Mr. Orr picked up a book and she took the bouquet from Mr. Fordham. After a few words, Mr. Orr stared down at her with a solemn expression. "Do you, Rebecca Mary Rice, take Tad Percival Fordham to be your lawful husband —"

Tad? Oh — Mr. Orr must have said *Ted*. A common nickname for Theodore, and one her groom must go by. It just sounded off because of Mr. Orr's thick accent. A flutter of nerves flurried up her spine. *My Ted.*

"I do."

"And do you, Tad —"

Ted.

"— take Rebecca Mary Rice, for better or worse, for richer or poorer, in sickness and in health, keeping yourself only unto her, so long as you both shall live?"

"I do." There was his dimple again.

Ted pulled a ring from his pocket, a pretty opal nestled atop a gold band, and placed it

29

on the fourth finger of her left hand. It slipped off-center of her finger, a bit too large, but it was the most gorgeous thing Rebecca had ever seen, much less hoped to own.

"Then by the power vested in me, I pronounce you man and wife." Mr. Orr talked over her amazement. "Go on, now, kiss yer bride."

Ted's hands went to her shoulders and he leaned in to kiss her. The pressure of his lips against hers was gentle, but firm, as if sealing a promise. He pulled back. A perfectly decent, chaste kiss, but she couldn't help feeling disappointed it was over.

Then he kissed her again. Just as gentle, just as sweet, but this one sent a jolt of lightning through her bones, from her skull to her toes. When he pulled back this time, his eyes were wide.

So the kiss had affected him, too.

"Come on, then, sign the register. Sun's goin' down."

Ted blinked. "Sure thing."

Rebecca giggled. She was married! To him! She may have been robbed and threatened a few hours ago, but she'd actually forgotten it during the ceremony.

Ted led her to Mr. Orr's desk. His scrawl was inelegant; all she could read was the *Th* of his first name and the *F* of Fordham. His mark didn't resemble his signature when he signed his correspondence to her, but there was often a difference between one's penmanship and one's official mark. He handed her the pen, and she dipped it into the inkwell and signed her name in her precise hand.

Then the lanky witness took up the pen. "Congratulations, ma'am. Deputy."

She almost missed it, so dazzled was she by her new husband's smile. But once the word settled into her brain, it echoed like a yodel off the mountains. "Deputy?"

"What's that, my bride?" Ted was shaking Mr. Orr's hand.

"You're not a *deputy.*" Her throat gurgled on the word.

He opened his coat, revealing a broad chest clothed in a plaid vest. A golden star-shaped pin was fixed over his heart. "You don't remember?"

"I'd remember a thing like that." And she would've turned down his proposal of marriage, flat as a flapjack.

How could this be happening? Not ten minutes ago, she'd known she was home at last — here, with this man. But she'd never been more wrong. Her chest ached. Everything ached. She stepped back. "You never told me. Or — I didn't get that letter."

"Uh-oh," the witness murmured.

"I mentioned it in every letter I wrote." Ted's jaw clenched, as if he was unhappy to have their first argument in the hearing of others. "You didn't seem to mind."

"You did not tell me. You lied in your letters, and you're lying now."

"Wait up, ma'am." Mr. Orr smiled. Didn't he understand how terrible the situation was? "Our deputy's as good as they come."

Ah. Cronyism. Or a conspiracy. She was the newcomer against a corrupt city government. Well, she'd not be swept into this — whatever this was. "I have been deceived. If you represent the law, Mr. Orr, I demand you help me or direct me to someone who will. This marriage is invalid, due to fraud."

"I didn't mislead you." A flash of anger darkened Ted's eyes. "But you're singing a different tune than you did in your letters. You told me you thought my being a deputy a noble calling. See?" He pulled a few letters from his inner coat pocket and held them out. As if they were tainted with arsenic, she held them by the edges, just enough to read the envelopes, which were all the same. Addressed to Mr. Thaddeus Fordham of Ruby City, from Miss Rebekah Rhys of Kansas.

So that was why he'd asked if she was Miss *Reese.* When she corrected him, he'd probably thought Rhys was pronounced Rice . . . and she and this other woman shared the same Christian name. Just a different spelling.

Her extremities went cold. He was indeed *Tad,* not her Ted. She handed the letters back. "I am sorry I called you a liar, D–deputy, but there seems to have been a mistake."

"A what?" It wasn't a question. He folded his arms.

"I'm not your Rebekah. Those aren't my letters. I'm supposed to marry Theodore Fordham. Do you know him?"

Mr. Orr hooted, but something like loss softened the edges around Tad's hazel eyes.

Someone smacked the front door. "Orr. Need your services. Heard tell my bride came in on the stage. Orr?"

"Come on in," Mr. Orr hollered, sounding like he was enjoying himself.

A sick sensation swirled in Rebecca's empty stomach as a gentleman in a tidy coat strode into Orr's office. Brown hair. Medium build. Hazel eyes. And when his gaze found her, he smiled — a dimple-free smile — until he saw the man standing beside her.

"Tad, what're you doing here?"

"That's a fine howdy-do for your intended," Tad grumbled.

"So it's you?" The man looked back at her. "Rebecca Rice?"

"Allow me to introduce you." Mr. Orr stepped between them and grinned. "Theodore Fordham, cousin of Thaddeus Fordham and owner of Fordham Mercantile, meet Rebecca Rice. Or Mrs. Tad Fordham. Y'all are kissin' cousins now."

Before Rebecca could faint from mortification, Theodore lunged at Tad.

CHAPTER TWO

Tad dodged a half step to the right, just out of the path of Theodore's fists. He didn't brawl with strangers, and sure as his new Stetson Boss hat, he wouldn't fight with kin. "Come on, now, Cousin. Let's talk this through."

"Seems a little late to talk, *Cousin.*" The word dripped from Theodore's tongue with more venom than a rattler's fangs.

Tad raised his hands in a gesture of peace, one that'd served him equally well working with horses and belligerent miners. "This is not what it looks like."

"Seems I heard that from you before."

Were they really going to do this, here, now? Tad's gut sank. Behind Theodore, both Orr and the rangy fellow who'd witnessed the vows wore twin expressions of glee, as if they'd swap wagers if they weren't in the presence of a lady. Rebecca's mouth popped open as if she wished to speak but was waiting for something. Maybe for Theodore to really look at her, rather than glare at Tad. He dropped his hands. "This is all a misunderstanding."

"You took my bride. How else am I supposed to understand that?"

"I had no idea you had a bride coming. Just as I did." If they spoke once in a while, they could've awaited their brides together.

"Yours wasn't good enough, and you had to steal mine?" Theodore shook his head in disgust, but at least he wasn't trying to tackle Tad anymore.

Mr. Orr leaned toward Rebecca. "Ever had two men fight over you before?"

"Whatever they're fighting over, sir, I am confident it is not me." Rebecca, stranger though she was to them, had already figured it out. And she shouldn't have to see the two of them act like this.

"You're right." Tad met her gaze. Such pretty eyes, clear as the creek on a windless day. She had pretty features, too, with a sprinkling of freckles over her nose and cheeks like gold dust, and a delicate frame that looked like she could use a few square meals. Her dainty lips, however, turned down in a frown. Some impression the Fordham boys made on her. "I'm sorry, ma'am."

Once she nodded, he turned back to Theodore. "This is all a mistake. One we're still trying to figure out. You can ask Orr and . . . your name's Jones, isn't it?" Tad tipped his chin toward the miner.

"Yessir, Jeroboam Jones, I rented a mule from you a few weeks back to haul wood." He focused on Theodore. "It's true, Mr. Fordham, sir. When yer bride found out she got hitched to the deputy, she 'bout near demanded a dee-vorce."

Theodore's scowl relaxed a pinch, but Rebecca's posture didn't. She folded her hands over her middle like a schoolmarm. "Not a divorce. An annulment will do when the marriage is invalid."

Jeroboam leaned toward Orr and hid his mouth behind his hand, as if about to impart a secret. "Seemed valid to me." The whisper wasn't discreet. "That kiss was a scorcher."

Theodore's glower deepened. Then he snuck an abashed look at Miss Rice — but now Mrs. Fordham — oh, just Rebecca.

"All right." Tad tossed Jeroboam two bits and gestured toward the door. The fellow had witnessed more than enough for today, and the story would no doubt be the talk of Ruby City by morning. "Thanks for your services."

Jeroboam's face fell. "You're sure you don't need me no more?"

"Quite." Rebecca's smile was polite.

As the door shut, Orr patted Theodore on the shoulder. "They didn't plan to marry the other. I mean, they did, and willingly too, but not the who — oh, I'm muddling this."

Rebecca stepped forward. "I thought I was marrying you, Theodore. When Mr. Orr said Tad, I thought he said *Ted,* and well, it sounds ridiculous now."

Theodore straightened the lapels of his coat and took a deep breath. "Maybe I'd better hear the whole story."

Tad leaned back against Orr's desk. Did he look serene? He tried to, but inside, he was coiled tighter than an untried rope. "My intended, a gal by the name of Rebekah Rhys, was supposed to arrive a few days back. The second I heard there was a woman on the stage, I assumed it was she. And she had the right name." Rebecca had looked right, too, blond, blue-eyed, and in her early twenties. As well-spoken as her letters, and his insides had gone soft as mush when he saw her. He'd thought —

It didn't matter what he'd thought or felt when he'd first seen her. Rebecca was claimed. And he had his own intended to think about now, too.

Rebecca bit her lip. "I arrived and he was there to greet me, a Mr. T. Fordham waiting for a Rebecca."

Which begged the question, why hadn't Theodore come running? The whole town would've known a gal stepped off the stage within five minutes. Where had Theodore been when Rebecca arrived, or in the hour since? Probably making a profit. There must've been a miner, flush with success, spending a wallop at Theodore's store.

Chiding himself for his uncharitable thoughts, Tad pushed off from the desk. "So what do we do now?"

"We see the judge about an annulment, as Miss Rice said." Theodore couldn't meet Tad's eyes. Intolerance still poisoned him, after all this time. "And then, if Miss Rice is still willing after the dreadful scene I've caused, I should like to marry her."

His look was contrite, Tad would give him that.

"Yes. I think it's best." Rebecca resumed her schoolmarm pose. There wasn't a trace left of the blushing bride he'd kissed not ten minutes ago. "Mr. Orr?"

The justice waved his hands. "Don't look at me. I'm no judge."

"Then let's find one." For some reason,

Rebecca looked to Tad, not Theodore.

"He's in Wyoming for some government meetings." Tad rubbed his forehead. "Won't be back for a full month."

"July." Theodore's head tipped.

"Then let's go to another judge. Or to Wyoming." Rebecca's lips pressed into a grim line.

Tad laughed. "Wyoming's a ways, ma'am. I won't stand in the way of the annulment, but we're going to have to be patient."

Theodore moved to Rebecca's side, at last. "I hate to admit it, Miss Rice, but he's right."

"And in the meantime?" Had she looked so stiff when she'd stood by Tad?

Orr took his hat from the peg by the door and set it atop his head. "I'd better head out but I think I can trust you fellas to see to Mrs. Fordham."

"I'll care for *Miss Rice,* thank you," Theodore corrected as Orr took his leave.

"Why don't you both call me Rebecca? I think it's acceptable to use our Christian names under the circumstances." Engaged to one, married to the other. Tad nodded his agreement but then noticed Rebecca's pale face. She must be exhausted.

And hungry. If she'd been on the stage all day, she'd had nothing to eat but cold hog meat and hominy at the station. "Come on, Theodore. Let's talk this out while we get a warm meal."

He'd been not-really-married for only five minutes, but it still felt wrong to let Theodore escort her out the door.

A fine howdy-do. Rebecca shuddered.

The gentle beginnings of a cool rain pattered her shoulders as the small party exited out the front of the building, where she turned to catch the sign: COUNTY OFFICES. Under the listings for the JUSTICE OF THE PEACE, SHERIFF, AND ASSESSOR was the name T. FORDHAM, DEPUTY.

If she and Tad had come in through the front, she'd have seen the sign and none of this would have happened.

They strode three across, back up the street. Pity she hadn't donned a larger-brimmed bonnet this morning, but she'd wanted to wear the finest of her hats to meet her intended. She stifled the urge to snort. Some story this would make for her brother Johnny, if she found him again. *Lovely wedding day,* she imagined writing to him. *One wee thing. I married the wrong man.*

She'd imagined retiring to the mercantile after the wedding, but now, where was she to go? "Will I stay at the hotel?"

41

"I know for a fact it's full up." Tad rubbed his brow. "I've got an idea, but let's eat first."

She wanted to protest, but the smells of meat, onions, and coffee wafting from the restaurant lured her like a trout to a baited hook. She might not have been able to resist going in if she tried.

Lit by glass-globed kerosene lamps, the restaurant lacked decor, except for the red-checked tablecloths spread over square tables, a third of which were occupied. Not a single female joined the menfolk sitting for their meals.

"Deputy and — *oo-wee,* Mr. Fordham! Both of you together, now, isn't that a wonder?" A gray-haired woman with a stained apron over her ample midsection waved a dish towel. "Sit on down. Who's your friend?"

Theodore held out Rebecca's chair. "This is Miss Rice, from Missouri. Rebecca, this is Mrs. Croft, owner of Ruby City's best restaurant."

"How do you do, Miss Rice? Hungry for supper?"

"Oh, yes." An understatement if she'd ever uttered one. "Thank you."

Mrs. Croft lumbered off, leaving an awkward silence, and not just at their table. The other customers turned in their chairs to stare. Was it because she was a woman, or did they stare at the feuding cousins, sitting together to dine? Whatever had caused bad blood between Theodore and Tad was deep-rooted, and she couldn't help but feel a twinge of sadness for them. Curiosity, too.

But when Mrs. Croft returned bearing a jug of milk and steaming plates of food, Rebecca's appetite superseded her curiosity. Pot roast, simmered with carrots and potatoes in thick gravy, had never tasted so rich. Tender peas and onions were a mild contrast to the plate of pickles, and the hot yeast rolls warmed her hand and melted in her mouth.

Be dainty eating. Your intended is watching you.

And so was her husband. Her gaze caught Tad's over her milk glass. He looked away before she did, releasing a deluge of embarrassment in her chest. There had been that crackle of something with Tad, and their kiss was — oh, it didn't matter. He was a deputy. And more important, she'd agreed to marry Theodore. It was he who deserved her attention now.

She turned toward him. Everything about her fiancé seemed tidy, from the crispness of his starched collar to the way he cut his meat, into precise squares. His mercantile was probably neat, too. In looks, he resembled Tad, although his eyes were rounder, his build softer, and he wasn't as tall.

"Are you two the same age?" The question blurted out.

"Theodore's eight weeks older." Tad's tone was clipped, as if surprised Theodore hadn't told Rebecca of his existence. "We went through every milestone together, it seems, including the loss of our mothers in a wagon accident when we were four."

Rebecca had lost her own mother when she was eight, and she was about to express sympathy when Theodore grunted. "Speaking of regrettable incidents, I behaved poorly earlier. Responding with violence, well, it's unconscionable. I beg your forgiveness, Rebecca. Tad. I just — it was not what I expected to see when I walked in."

His tone turned strained when he said his cousin's name, but at least he'd apologized for his behavior. Rebecca nodded. "None of us anticipated things to turn out as they did."

A handful of men entered the restaurant. From the smell of them, they'd already consumed a quantity of whiskey. One, a good-looking fellow, loudly ordered steaks for the table.

"We need to decide where you should live until we see the judge." Tad sat back in his chair, a picture of contentment, except for his fingers, which were tight on his coffee cup. Though he spoke to Rebecca and Theodore, his gaze fixed on an older man whose tiny frame was dwarfed by an enormous gray beard. The fellow's mouth worked, like he was speaking or chewing, but he was alone and Mrs. Croft had just cleared his plate.

Tad spared Rebecca a glance. "I think the boardinghouse is just about the only proper option in town."

"A boardinghouse." Rebecca could have clapped. Except — how would she pay for it?

"Absolutely not." Theodore glared at Tad. "You live there, and I'll not let my intended live with you."

Rebecca's supper clustered into an indigestible lump in her stomach. Even the delectable cinnamon smell of the apple pie Mrs. Croft brought to their table didn't tempt her. *God, please let me end this day somewhere safe.*

"Be sensible, Theodore." Tad's words might be for his cousin, but his gaze returned to the bearded man across the room. "She needs a decent place to stay for an entire month until Judge Harris returns, and I can't think of a better spot. Besides, the boardinghouse is full, so she can have my room and I'll sleep on the cot in the county offices. I could take advantage of Pa being in Idaho City and sleep at the livery, but he'll be home within the week and I don't cotton to being relegated to the hayloft when he comes back."

Theodore leaned toward her. "You may recall Tad and his father run the livery business that brought them, and my father and me, to Ruby City three years ago."

She nodded, but her mind whirled with the idea of sleeping in a real bed tonight. The situation was so awkward, though, it was hard to accept Tad's offer. Theodore seemed none too pleased, either. Still, where else was she to go? She peeked at Tad. "Are you certain I can stay at the boardinghouse? The proprietor won't mind?"

"She'll be delighted to have another woman around the place." Tad chuckled, but then his face fell.

She recognized the look. Her Pa had worn it far too often. "What is it?"

Theodore crooked his neck to look behind him. "Bowe Brown is at one table and 'Longbeard' Pegg's at another. They get along like oil and water." He turned back to his pie.

Rebecca chewed her lip. Feuds seemed rather frequent in Ruby City. She glanced at each of the fellows. "Does Longbeard have a real name?"

"Nobody knows it." Theodore forked another bite. "He doesn't talk to folks much."

Tad dropped his napkin onto the table. "Take her out, Theodore. Quick."

"What for?" Theodore's fork hovered over the pie. "There's no trouble."

"There will be in a minute." Tad scooted back his chair. "Longbeard isn't drinking his coffee with his gun hand. I'd say that fight he's promised Bowe Brown might be brewing tonight."

Theodore's brows knit, but he didn't move. When Tad stood, Rebecca did, too. If Mr. Longbeard Pegg's left hand was around his cup, there was only one place for his right hand to be — around a pistol.

A flash of lightning lit up the dim room, but Rebecca didn't want to stick around for whichever followed first: thunder, or the report of gunfire.

"Let's go, Theodore." She tugged his sleeve. "Now."

She didn't like the skeptical look in his

eyes when he dropped his fork and took her hand, following her out.

CHAPTER THREE

Rebecca hurried to the restaurant exit, stumbling on an uneven patch of flooring. Theodore's hold on her hand didn't lessen, nor did he falter in gripping her arms and pulling her upright —

That wasn't possible. Theodore couldn't grasp her fingers and at the same time secure both her arms in his two hands. That meant someone else had hold of her.

She twisted, coming face-to-face with the object of Longbeard Pegg's grudge, the one Theodore called Bowe Brown. She wrenched her arms, but he held fast. Green-eyed and young, he had the sort of square-jawed good looks that would make her school friends back in Missouri swoon. But the telltale odor of alcohol seeped through his pores, and the gleam in his eyes seemed more roguish than friendly.

"Howdy, ma'am." He grinned as if he were flirting. Or comfortable being on the business end of a gun.

Neither appealed to her. "Unhand me."

His smile didn't falter. "In a minute. You just stand here in front of me until Long-beard holsters his gun, an' then we can part ways."

Bowe used her as a shield? What a coward.

This was monstrous. Why didn't Theodore do something? She followed his gaze, which fixed on Bowe's free hand, resting over the Arkansas Toothpick sheathed at his waist. It would only take an instant for Bowe to pull the straight blade. So that was why Theodore held still and kept his mouth shut.

Her supper crawled up her insides.

She'd wanted a safe haven. Security. No more fear or want. *I thought You told me to come to Ruby City, Lord.* Well, somebody had been wrong, either her or the Almighty. Her head knew which, but it didn't stop her weary flesh from accusing Him. *You should've stopped me, Lord. At least in Missouri, I was safe.*

Well, that wasn't true. Her safety there was debatable. But at least in Missouri, no one had used her as a buffer against being shot.

Longbeard boggled, looking at her as if for the first time. "I don't know you. You're new."

50

"She sure is." Tad's tone was gentle, as if he spoke to a child.

"Welcome, ma'am." Bowe squeezed her arm. Oh, this one was trouble.

"You could welcome me fine from over there a ways." Rebecca tipped her head toward the far side of the room.

"I ain't moving till the deputy tells me Longbeard's gun is holstered. He won't shoot me if I'm standing by a pretty lady."

Ha. Pa had called her sweet in spirit and face, but she was no beauty. Aside from her crooked bottom teeth, she was too lean and freckled. Her brothers insisted she was built like a bird and speckled as an egg.

Maybe they didn't have high standards of attractiveness here in Ruby City.

"Bowe." Tad didn't turn around but kept his gaze fixed on Longbeard — the greater threat, since he seemed to hold a gun under the table. "Let the lady go."

"Not yet." Bowe's breath was hot on her neck.

Would he let her go if she stomped on his foot? Every fiber of her being was taut, ready for some action she couldn't take, caught as she was by Bowe's firm grasp. Theodore's grip tightened, too. She felt like the flag tied to a rope's center in tug-of-war. No matter who yanked the hardest,

51

she'd end up bruised.

"Do something for me, Longbeard." Tad held up his hands at the miner with the waist-length beard the color of ash. The peaceful gesture was the one he'd used when facing Theodore at the county offices. "Show us your hands and we can all go home."

"Just do it so we can get back to supper." The proprietress, Mrs. Croft, held a platter to her midsection like a breastplate.

Longbeard's watery eyes blinked. "If'n someone shot that ne'er-do-well, the world'd be a better place."

Tad inched closer. "And if that someone was you, you know what'd happen."

One of Bowe's friends slashed at his throat with his forefinger.

"He stole my ma's fur collar, and now he's tryin' to jump my claim." Longbeard's waist-length beard wiggled as he spoke.

"I didn't steal your stupid, mangy pelt. I borrowed it to see what all the fuss was about with you and that thing, and I can't help it if the Gang of Four took it when they robbed me."

Borrowed, her eye. Rebecca had seen her share of bullies. Bowe no doubt took the collar to upset Longbeard Pegg, who clearly had a strong attachment to it.

Bowe pulled her closer. "Come to think of it, Longbeard, you should be mad at the deputy over not getting it back yet, not me. And while we're at it, Fordham, I want back the other stuff that Gang stole from me. An eagle coin and a carte de visite of my dear old ma and grandmammy. Can't replace that."

"They must be proud of you, using a woman as a shield." Rebecca tugged again.

"I want my collar back and you off my claim." Longbeard seethed.

"I don't have your collar, and I don't want your stupid claim," Bowe insisted. "I walked into it in the dead of night. A body can't see where he's goin' with a new moon. Looked just like my spot."

"A fool story." Spittle flew from Pegg's mouth.

Theodore squeezed her fingers. With the hand that didn't have hold of her arm, he reached behind him, slowly, for the door. All the while Tad crept closer to Longbeard, his motions fluid as a cat's.

Tad took another step. "Bowe didn't dig on your claim, did he?"

"Not yet." Venom shot from Pegg's glare.

"You're a simpleton," Bowe said, laughing.

Tad's body was now between the old

miner and Bowe. And Rebecca, too. Her heart filled her throat.

"Why don't I come out tomorrow with some rope and stakes?" Tad suggested. "We can set up a perimeter around your claim. Then nobody can wander in by mistake."

"Sounds fair," Theodore announced.

Mrs. Croft harrumphed. "Never thought you'd agree with anything the deputy had to say."

A few of the men seated at tables chuckled. Rebecca felt a frown pull at her lips. The feud between the Fordham cousins was grave, indeed.

But Theodore was right. Tad's idea was a good one. Simple, effective, and kind. Tad could have overpowered the frail, older Longbeard Pegg, but he'd weighed the cost and determined to try compassion first. Something wasn't right with Longbeard, and he needed help — she didn't need to spend more time with the miner to comprehend that. But Tad took it into consideration and found a way to settle the matter peacefully.

Her opinion of her accidental husband rose.

After a minute, Longbeard nodded. His right hand lifted, revealing a flash of metal in his fist.

A fork.

Longbeard hadn't held a pistol. He'd thought to defend himself against a bully with a utensil.

A whoosh of breath left Rebecca's parched lips. Bowe released her arm, and Theodore yanked. They were outside, dashing through sheeting rain, before she could take another breath.

Gratitude filled her chest when Theodore pulled her under an overhang and unlocked a door, ushering her inside a storefront and setting off a bell over the doorjamb with a *ding-a-ding.* The odors of kerosene, wood shavings, and damp met her nose, and she shuddered as the warmer temperature hit her wet skin. "Your mercantile?"

"Soon to be ours." With the strike of a match and a whiff of sulfur, Theodore lit a lamp, brightening the space and illuminating shelves of goods. To the right of the door spread a display of buckets, ropes, pickaxes, shovels, and boots — good sellers here, no doubt. To the left of the door, fancy glass and crystal glittered in the lamplight, expensive items that might not sell as well out here, but they were certainly lovely. Fabrics and premade items were at the back, but near the squat wood-burning stove to her right stood neat rows of canned goods, food sacks, and barrels. She may have just eaten a full meal, but her mouth watered at the thought of their contents. Crackers? Oats? Sweet pickles?

Once she married Theodore, she'd cook the most wonderful things for him. They'd eat like royalty, and she'd never be hungry again.

He watched her, a tiny smile playing at his lips. Her cheeks heated. Perhaps instead of admiring the goods in the store, she should have been admiring him. Her gaze dropped in embarrassment, which only heightened when she caught sight of the puddle encircling her as her skirt dripped onto the floor. "I'm sorry. Have you a rag?"

"I'll get it." He reached behind the counter for a cloth. Then he knelt at her feet and mopped the wood planks, but not her skirt. He must think dabbing her clothing to be too personal, even if he was her intended.

They'd be married right now if things had gone the way they were supposed to, but she couldn't help feeling Theodore was a stranger. As if she didn't belong here.

Rebecca shook off the gloomy thought. This had been an extraordinary day. She was tired and overwhelmed, that was all. "What a fine store."

"I do all right. Well, I have Corny to help,

too." He stood.

"Corny?" What a funny nickname. At least, Rebecca hoped it was a nickname.

"My employee." He tossed the rag behind the counter. "I'm sorry I wasn't there to meet you at the stage."

If he had been — well, what was done was done. She should choose to see the potential of the situation. "Now we have time to get to know one another before the wedding." She blushed so hot, it was a wonder a fog of steam didn't mantle her dress.

He looked about to speak when the bell over the door rang behind her. She spun.

Rainwater dripped from Tad's hat as he rushed inside, carrying her bags — oh yes, they'd been stowed at the county offices. "I am so sorry, Rebecca. What happened with Longbeard was bad enough, but Bowe grabbing you like that? I hate that he touched you. Are you hurt?"

If bruises had formed, she couldn't feel them yet. "No."

Relief lightened his eyes. "I hope you sleep better, knowing I locked him up."

She hadn't thought of it, but yes, it did ease the knot in her belly a bit.

"You arrested Bowe but not Longbeard?" Theodore's brows knit.

"Longbeard clutched a fork. No crime in

57

that. Bowe held Rebecca hostage. Didn't help his case any when he swung a punch at me, too. See, I'd be sleeping on that cot tonight anyway, since I've got a prisoner and the sheriff's not in town." His eyes were soft when he turned back to Rebecca. "I'm sorry."

His gaze held hers until Theodore gave a discreet cough. "I'm sorry, too, Rebecca. What a day you've had."

Suddenly, fatigue weighed her down, as surely as her wet dress did. "I would like to end it. Start fresh tomorrow."

"Need anything from here before we go to the boardinghouse?" Tad turned back to Theodore. "The Gang of Four took some of her personal items."

"By all means, take what you need." Theodore turned up the lamp to brighten the space.

"I don't have the funds," Rebecca demurred.

"I've got it. Let me see here." Tad fished in his coat pockets, placing their contents on the counter: a key, a derringer, and some coins, which he left on the counter when he repocketed the rest.

"You have a gun," she said without thinking. "But you diffused the situation without it."

He looked startled and then laughed. "I prefer to handle things by talking, I suppose."

Which he'd done, and rather well, too.

"Put your money away, Tad." Theodore waved his hand. "Rebecca, you're to be my wife. I don't think anyone would dare accuse us of impropriety if I provided for you."

And she did need some tooth powder, so she wouldn't argue. She picked that up first, and then selected a plain, inexpensive comb and brush set, but Theodore insisted she take a silver set instead. After a minute, she'd chosen a few more necessities. Theodore handed her a bar of rose-scented soap. "None of the miners use this brand, but they'd smell a lot better if they did."

His quip coaxed a smile, but when she turned to the door, Tad was frowning.

"Come on," he said as Theodore extinguished the lamp. "Let's get to the boarding-house."

Mercy, how good it sounded. Proper or not, it seemed she'd be sleeping in her husband's bed tonight. And she was so tired, she didn't care.

Light spilled from the windows of the two-story house, beckoning Tad inside. Mrs. Horner's place was simple, but it was warm and comfortable — and sheltered from the downpour. Still, a trickle of unease snaked through Tad's gut as he ushered Rebecca and Theodore through the front door. Would it be too simple for Rebecca? Too rough-hewn?

His intended, Rebekah Rhys, would be thrilled to have a roof over her head, but Rebecca Rice? Tad shook off the concern like water drops from the brim of his Stetson Boss. Rebecca's impressions, thoughts, and feelings were none of his concern. They couldn't be. She was Theodore's.

Tad led Rebecca to the hearth in the parlor and excused himself to look for Mrs. Horner, all the while shaking his head at himself. In all the fuss, he'd forgotten about Rebekah. What would he do when she arrived? He'd told her they'd stay in the boardinghouse until the cabin was finished. Now there was no room for her, and since he was already technically married, he couldn't marry her and carry her over the threshold of — where? The cot at the county offices was no bridal bower. He rubbed his forehead. Maybe she could bunk with Rebecca until the marriage was annulled.

His wife and his intended, sharing a room. Lord, have mercy.

"Mrs. Horner?" He poked into the

60

kitchen. Sure enough, his short, slender landlady was busy with the kettle and a tin of tea. Dressed in her usual calico frock and apron, her gray-tinged chestnut hair neat in a bun at her nape, the widow was as predictable as the moon and sun.

"Good evenin', Deputy. Tea?"

He didn't care for the huskiness in her voice. It seemed like she couldn't yet shake the sickness that took hold near a month ago.

"For four, please. You, me, Theodore, and someone I'd like you to meet. Here, let me help." He took the cups and saucers out of the oak hutch.

"I'm sorry, but did you say Theodore?"

A snort escaped his nostrils. "You think that's astonishing, wait until you meet Rebecca."

Mrs. Horner's gray eyes bugged. "Your lady-friend? She finally came? Congratulations!" A racking cough overtook her, but she waved away his outstretched hand. "This calls for cake."

"No, I'm sorry. I shouldn't have said it like that. She's not my Rebekah. This Rebecca is marrying Theodore." He patted her bony shoulder, offering as quick an explanation as he could. His landlady tsked at the mention of the stage robbery and the tussle

61

with Longbeard and Bowe, but her mouth went slack when he told her about the wedding, which he mentioned last, even though it was out of order. "She's my wife, but not for long. And in the meantime, she's got nowhere to stay. I thought she could take my room while I stay at the jail."

Her brows knit. "Bless her heart. A holdup, the wrong husband, and scrapping miners. What a day she's had."

He carried the wooden tray of tea things to the parlor. Before he'd set them down on the low table before the horsehair sofa, Mrs. Horner had introduced herself and taken Rebecca's hands and proclaimed them icy as January. "Longbeard is harmless. I can't say the same for that Bowe Brown." She dropped Rebecca's hands and started pouring tea. "Or that Gang of Four. I ordered fine lace for curtains and they stole it from the cargo wagon. You and Sheriff Adkins have a lot on your plate, Deputy, between the shenanigans in town and the Gang of Four."

"Don't I know it." Tad didn't care much to talk about it now, though. Rebecca looked about to fall over.

Theodore led Rebecca to the chair by the fire and handed her a cup of the warm beverage. "This will help, dear."

The endearment nipped at Tad. Theodore had known her a few hours and already called her *dear*?

Mrs. Horner sat across from Rebecca. "I've got four bedrooms — all taken. Not a big house, of course, but you'll be snug as can be in the deputy's room. Sheets are clean. Today was laundry." She broke off, coughing with such force that Tad cringed.

Tad sat on the stiff sofa with Theodore, thankful some of the fire's warmth extended this far. His shirt was soaked from the rain. "Have you seen the doc in Silver City about that cough?"

She shuddered. "I don't like him. I'll ask Wilkie for more tonic, next time he's sober."

"Tonic can only help so much, and Wilkie's a barber. Good for pulling teeth but not for treating coughs." And he was rarely sober these days. Tad frowned. Some impression Rebecca was getting of Ruby City. Feuding cousins, a hostage-holding ne'er-do-well, a simple-minded, fork-wielding miner, and a drunkard barber.

Mrs. Horner coughed again but then caught his eye. "I'm fine, Deputy."

Tad glanced around, seeing the house as Rebecca might view it. Dust thick on the furniture. Rug in need of beating. His meticulous Mrs. Horner was not fine.

63

Rebecca shifted in her seat. "You have a fine home, Mrs. Horner, but I can't stay. I can't pay for the room."

"Send the bill to me," Theodore insisted.

"Thank you, but no. You're not yet my husband, and I'm not certain it's seemly for you to pay for my keep."

"Then I'll pay you a wage. You can work in the mercantile."

After a moment, Rebecca nodded. Weariness lined her clear eyes, but her spine was straight when she faced Mrs. Horner. "If it would be of any assistance, I could help around the house, too. I worked as a maid in Missouri for a respectable lady."

"I don't need a lady's maid," Mrs. Horner said before coughing.

"While I know my way around a needle and basic coiffures, I cooked, cleaned, and shopped for my employer. For a time, her house also served as a Confederate hospital. Every hand was needed, so I know about nursing, too. Not that you require a nurse. All I mean is, I could help out however you saw fit, to thank you for taking me in under such unusual circumstances."

Tad's estimation of her rose even higher. She knew how to work and she didn't wish to be a burden. She also seemed to understand Mrs. Horner was a prideful woman.

He tipped his head. "Sounds like a fair trade, Mrs. Horner."

"I think something could be arranged," Mrs. Horner said after a minute. "I'd knock off part of the rent if you tidy and help cook."

"I'd be delighted." A ghost of a smile played at Rebecca's lips as she sipped her tea.

"Finish your tea then, gentlemen, and shoo," Mrs. Horner ordered. "Can't you see this woman's been through an ordeal?"

"I'll just get my things." Tad mounted the stairs to his — now Rebecca's — room. *Thanks for settling this matter, Lord.* With the burden lifted, he whistled. Everything would work out. Rebecca would be safe and warm tonight and fed again in the morning. He didn't know a lot about females, but it was obvious this one hadn't eaten in some time. Mrs. Horner would see to fixing that.

His whistle died on his lips. Was Rebekah Rhys warm and safe tonight? Praying for her, he stuffed his clothes and incidentals into a carpetbag and headed back downstairs.

Tomorrow he had more work to do than roping off Longbeard's claim or going after the Gang of Four. He'd better start looking for Rebekah. She should have arrived days ago. Had she missed a connection? Fallen ill?

Or changed her mind?

Best not jump to conclusions. He'd find her. Meanwhile, he had another wife to care for, and he should hurry and get out of her bedroom.

CHAPTER FOUR

Alone at last in Tad's vacated room, Rebecca unpinned her soggy straw bonnet. Oh, to wash her hair, but Mrs. Horner was bringing up a pitcher of wash water, not a tub. A sponge bath would suit just fine, tonight. Besides, she could make a little water go a long way.

She hung her bonnet on a rack by the door. Did it rest on the same peg where Tad's hat perched at night? Mercy, what a ridiculous thing to think about when she had unpacking to do. Theodore had placed her carpetbag on the foot of Tad's bed —

No, it was her bed now. Just because Tad Fordham was the last person to sleep under the white quilt with ringed blue-and-apricot fabric pieces didn't make this his room. Still, the bedroom held a faint trace of his scent, the soap-and-man smell she'd caught when he'd bent down to kiss her at the end of their wedding ceremony.

Warmth suffused Rebecca's face. It would not do to dwell on that particular memory. Nor on the irony of the wedding-ring pattern of the quilt spread over the bed, reminding her she received such a token of Tad's pledge — oh goodness. She'd forgotten to return the opal to him. She slipped Tad's ring over her knuckle.

Such a pretty ring. Turned this way, the stone glittered whitish blue with sparks of pink fire. Turned thataway, green glimmers joined the palette, the colors so rich and deep it seemed the opal served as a window into the depths of the earth. Had Tad purchased it for his bride, Rebekah, or had it belonged to his mother? With care, she set the ring on the oak dressing table. Its pale shimmer reflected the flickering glow of the coal oil lamp, spark and fade, spark and fade, as if it winked at her.

Foolish thoughts after a long day. She turned her back on it and tested the mattress with her palm, sighing at the pleasant give under her hand. And the width of the bed — she could spread out tonight, if she wished. Roll from one side to the other. How long had it been since she'd slept in a bed like this?

Since Pa died, of course. She and her older brothers, Johnny and Raymond, couldn't afford their place and had to rent a room above a wheelwright's shop. She'd slept on a narrow pallet so the boys could share the lone bed they'd been able to keep. Even that arrangement hadn't lasted long, though, and she'd tolerated worse beds. But tonight she'd sleep in comfort.

Her fingers traced the quilt's pretty fabrics and fine stitching, lingering over the hand-sewn design. This past winter, she'd been caught touching her former employer's bed. Well, not touching, exactly. She'd knelt to tuck in the sheet and, so weary her thoughts had jumbled like dreams, she'd rested her head on the edge of the mattress. Just for a second or two, or ten. Long enough to get caught.

That night, her supper withheld, she'd been too hungry to sleep despite her fatigue. Her stomach had cramped, the ache spreading to her back and chest. But it was no excuse for what she'd done the next morning —

Halting the memory in its tracks, Rebecca's hands clutched at her midsection. *Thank You for not holding my sin against me, Lord. Even when I can't forget it.*

Mercy, the sun would be up before she ever unpacked. The package from Theodore's store still waited, bulging with her replacement toiletries. She loosened the string and wound it around her left forefinger and thumb like thread on a bobbin. Next she folded the brown paper into a neat rectangle, setting the materials aside for future use. Only then did she sigh over the contents of the package. The bristles of her new hairbrush made a soft *shh* under her fingers.

She set her toiletries on the dressing table and the opal ring twinkled again, as if the inanimate thing wanted her attention, or wanted her to think about Tad. Well, of course she thought of him. He was kind, and his smile did strange things to her insides. But that was neither here nor there. Tad's kiss, like the memory of her empty nights in Missouri, was something she shouldn't mull over, not when she had a future with Theodore. She rotated the ring, so its opal could twinkle and wink all it wished at the whitewashed wall.

With a wheezing cough, Mrs. Horner bustled into the room bearing a steaming pitcher, which she set on the lower shelf of a barley twist washstand. "Everything look decent to you, Miss Rice?"

The owner of the boardinghouse couldn't be much more than forty, but her illness had clearly worn her to flinders. Her calico frock was a flattering shade of rose, but it hung loose on her slender frame, and dark circles shadowed her brown eyes. Gray streaks tinged hair the color of earth, pinned carefully at her nape. She was a pretty lady — widowed young, it seemed, and making a way for herself in the Owyhees. Rebecca took inspiration from her new landlady's gumption.

"It's wonderful." So was the thought of that hot water in the pitcher and lathering with the fragrant soap Theodore gave her. But it wouldn't do to rush Mrs. Horner from the room, so she tipped her head toward the door. "How many other guests live here?"

"I sleep next door." Mrs. Horner crooked her thumb toward the wall. "Across the hall are two gentlemen from back East hoping to make their fortune in the mines. They won't stay long; they never do, but there's always a list waiting on a vacancy."

Rebecca's brothers popped into her mind again — especially Johnny, who'd set out for the California mines. Last she'd heard from him, he hadn't found a place as nice as this house to stay in. It had been difficult to tell him good-bye, but then the war started and Raymond enlisted. Even before he died, she'd felt thoroughly alone in the world.

Mrs. Horner coughed again, waving her hand over her face. Heavens, the woman wasn't coughing blood, was she? Consumption was a horrible thing. Poor Ma had suffered so. Thankfully, no dark spots or flecks marred the handkerchief Mrs. Horner pulled from her sleeve, a good sign. Still, the situation bore monitoring. "May I be of assistance tomorrow morning?"

"Sleep in, dearie." Mrs. Horner patted the moisture from her eyes. "I serve breakfast at seven, but you've had an ordeal. I'll keep a plate in the oven for you."

"You're too kind." Her stomach growled at the thought of breakfast, despite the fine meal she'd eaten at the restaurant. Rebecca pressed her hands to her belly to hush the rumbling.

Over her coughing, Mrs. Horner didn't seem to hear the noise. "Good night then, dearie." She shut the door behind her.

Rebecca twisted the simple lock on the door, undressed, and washed both her skin and the bloodstains on her undersleeves and the dress's pagoda sleeves, luxuriating in the warm water and rosy scent of the soap. What a kind gift from Theodore.

What was it Ma used to say about the

kindness of strangers? It had always been a counterpoint to Pa's words about the dangers in the world. Dressing in her nightgown and crawling beneath the line-crisp sheets, it was impossible not to think about how right he'd been, considering today she'd met stagecoach robbers and feuding miners.

But as she snuggled deeper into the fresh-smelling sheets, Ma's voice was stronger than Pa's. *The kindness of strangers.* Mrs. Horner. Theodore. Tad. They'd all shown her care. She thanked God for each act of grace she'd received today, ending with Tad giving her this room and this bed. How would he fare in that cot in the closet at the jail?

Theodore's disapproving scowl replaced the image of Tad bunking on that cot, his long legs extending over the end. And really, Theodore's image in her head was preferable. She had no business thinking of Tad.

Rebecca rolled over with a huff. If she kept thinking about her husband and husband-to-be, she'd never get to sleep.

Tad sat up to darkness and a sense of unfamiliarity. The window was in the wrong place. His hip ached from the lumpy mattress. He blinked. It wasn't Mrs. Horner's

73

mattress but the cot in the jail. He'd come here because he'd arrested Bowe, but he would have slept here anyway because the Tuesday stage brought Rebecca —

The memory roused him like a splash of cold water. Rebecca. And Rebekah. A wife that wasn't his and another who hadn't come yet. Theodore in the middle of it all, and things between them still cold and ugly as winter slush.

Tad abandoned the thin blanket and made up the cot in the dark. He fumbled for the matches and lit the kerosene lantern at his bedside so he could dress and wander over to the livery — his main source of income, and a responsibility he shared with his Pa. A quick check on the snoring Bowe assured him his prisoner was sleeping soundly, but he dare not leave for more than a minute without finding a watchman. He found one on his way to Mrs. Croft's restaurant.

"Jeroboam Jones, is that you?" He held up his lantern.

The rangy wood hauler's grin reflected the light from Tad's lantern. "Yessir, Mr. Deputy, sir."

"Up early before a full day of woodcutting?"

"Yessir, I am — up early, that is. But my day is wide open, a benefit to bein' a carefree gent-ilman like me. Say, care to join me?"

"I can't today, but I could use a hand with something. I'll pay for your breakfast if you're willing to eat it at the county offices and feed the prisoner while I see to my livery chores. It won't take me long."

Jeroboam's chest puffed out. "I won't let you down, sir."

"Not as long as you keep the cell door shut and locked." Tad laughed. "I'll ask Mrs. Croft to send the tray shortly."

He did just that, and once again outside, the brisk morning air hit his skin. Last night's rain had awoken some sort of fragrant plant. What was it? Almost flowery. A bit like Rebecca when he'd bent down to kiss her yesterday —

Stop it right there. No more of that. Not with chores and a dozen animals in the barn, which reeked, as it always did first thing in the morning. The anticipatory shuffles and snorts of twelve beasts greeted him. "Morning, all," he said, hanging the lantern on a hook.

Madge, his favorite of the mules, leaned her thick head over the stall door and gazed at him. "Hungry?" Her long ears were soft as silk to his callused fingers. She held still, enjoying his attentions. "Nice to know there's a lady in my life after all," he mused.

A snuff escaped her large nostrils.

Tad grinned. "You think I'm being melodramatic, do you?"

Madge dipped her head.

Tad rubbed her nose. "I don't think you understand how complicated things are, sweetheart."

How would he find Rebekah Rhys? Scratching Madge's neck, he saw no option other than to retrace the stagecoach's route. Inquiring after her would take time, but if Rebekah had come to trouble, it was his obligation and privilege to help her — even if it meant leaving Ruby City unprotected while the sheriff was on his circuit of the area mines.

Tad's jaw tensed. Hopefully the Gang of Four wouldn't cause any more trouble while he was gone, but the Gang seemed to take a few days' break between robbing cargo haulers and miners, so things should be quiet for a few days.

The horses and mules in his care, however, were unable to feed themselves or rent themselves out. He couldn't leave the livery unattended until Pa returned on Saturday. Even if Tad paid someone to feed the stock for the interim, he and Pa needed the income from renting out the animals, and they couldn't trust just anyone to handle that end of the business. Especially now. Money had been tight since a piece hauler drove one of their wagons into a crevasse — and left it there, with a busted axle and two injured horses. Poor ol' Grady was fine now, but Red's leg had broken and he hadn't made it. Tad had entertained harsh thoughts about the long-gone miner for mistreating a creature like that.

Tad's lips compressed. *God, I feel like that plate-juggling clown from the circus that passed through town last month. Something's going to slip through my fingers, and when it does, the crash will make a mess.*

Madge shifted her weight from one hoof to the other, drawing Tad to the present. There wasn't time to dwell on things he couldn't control. He gave Madge's bony skull a final pat. "All right, let's get everyone fed."

After seeing to the horses and mules, Tad scrubbed in the pump's brisk water and entered the door connecting the livery to the kitchen of the small house he and Pa built. He lit the stove, helped himself to the coffeepot, and scrounged for breakfast fixings while the coffee brewed. In little time, he sat down at the scratched table to eat. The bread was stale and the coffee scalded his tongue.

"I miss you already, Mrs. Horner."

Truth be told, though, he was blue about more than missing his landlady's cooking. He couldn't help thinking about what the morning after his wedding should have been like, how he planned to take his bride on a ride to show her the area he loved and the beauty to be found under the jagged shelter of the Owyhees.

But he'd just decided not to dwell on things that weren't meant to be. He had other tasks to accomplish. Marking off Longbeard Pegg's claim, searching out stagecoach robbers, and checking on his wife all had to be done today — in addition to looking for his missing fiancée.

Rebecca's stride up the street was a combination of walking and hopping over mud puddles, requiring her to watch where she stepped. Perhaps that's why she almost walked into a mule.

The gray beast stood in her path beside a round-cheeked fellow who wore a shirt that had probably once been white but had yellowed with time and use. With his weatherworn features, he appeared old enough to be her pa. His expression wasn't particularly fatherly, however. His gray-brown brows wiggled in a manner that was almost flirtatious.

Mrs. Horner had warned her there weren't many females in town and masculine attention was to be expected. Rebecca resolved to be courteous while not giving her new neighbor a hint of encouragement. "Good morning, sir."

The fellow doffed his wide-brimmed hat, revealing a shock of hair that seemed a perfect match to the shaggy forelock tufting atop his mule's head. "Mornin', ma'am. Delighted to see you again."

Again? Ah, yes. She recognized the stained suspenders holding too-big pants up to his small paunch, and the eager grin revealing gaps in his teeth. He was the man who'd told her and Tad yesterday that Mr. Orr was about to leave town and they'd best hurry and get married. What was he called? Eustace? No, that wasn't right.

She was about to ask his name when his head inclined toward her with a conspiratorial bent. "I couldn't help overhearin' when you got off the stage that you'd been set upon by the Gang of Four. I had the misfortune to meet them, m'self. I didn't have a coin to scratch with so they took the gold tooth right out of my maw." He stretched open his lips and pointed.

"Oh, my." The sudden glimpse into his mouth was not pleasant, and her first instinct was to recoil. In an instant, however, indignation rose within her chest. What sort of people took a poor man's tooth right out of his mouth? "They're bullies, that Gang of Four."

"Robbin' and terrorizin' for pleasure, that's what they do." His clear eyes opened wide. "Say, it won't make up for what they took from you, but I got a weddin' present for you."

Silver? Gold? A kiss? "Oh no. The deputy and I aren't — married after all." It seemed easier to say that than explaining the whole sordid affair.

He stopped digging in his pockets to gape. "The deputy wasn't to yer taste, then?"

She'd liked the deputy just fine, until she learned he was a deputy. "It's complicated."

"He's nice to look at, I s'pose, and that hat o' his is a thing to behold, but if you say so." He shrugged. "I'm still givin' you a present. Call it a welcome gift." He dug back into his pants pocket, withdrawing a clump of used handkerchiefs, which he balanced atop the mule. Then he sifted through his stash, plucked something out, and reached for her hand. "Don't peek."

At least it wasn't a kiss. Still, the last time

someone put something in her hand and told her not to look, she'd received an unpleasant surprise from her brother Johnny. She could still feel the baby snake, and still wished she'd had the presence of mind to calmly return it to the earth rather than screaming, just as Johnny had wanted her to.

She squeezed her eyes shut. *Don't scream this time.*

Whatever the fellow — whatever his name was — deposited on her hand, it didn't seem to have feet. He curled her fingers like a protective cage over the object. "Here you go."

She opened her eyes and her hand to see a rock the size of a dove's egg, rough and reddish brown. "Thank you."

"It's jasper." He hitched up his pants. "Not much to look at on the outside, but get it cut and polished, and you'll see. The inside's glorious."

A bit like some people. Maybe even this fellow here. Perhaps it was the effect of a good night's sleep on a real bed, the sun warming her back, or the gift of the jasper, but a sense of protectiveness grew in her chest for the man with the mule. He was probably lonely, something she could certainly understand. And he seemed as harmless as his mule. "You are most kind, sir. I don't know your name."

"Ulysses Scruggs." He bowed. "This here is Madge."

"Lovely to meet you, Mr. Scruggs. Madge." She patted the mule's neck. "I'm Miss Rice."

"It's Ulysses. Mr. Scruggs was my pa." He laughed at the old joke. "He stayed in one spot, rooted like a tree, but you never could tie me down. No sir, I follow the breeze, chasin' one adventure after another, minin' hither and yon. But I might be willin' to reconsider my bachelor ways, should the right female come along."

Madge hung her head, as if she was embarrassed by such talk.

She wasn't the only one, but Rebecca wouldn't bite Ulysses's bait. "You've got Madge."

"She's a rental from Fordham and Son. Works best for me to hire out animals for minin' ex-pi-ditions, since I'm somethin' of a roamer."

"Since you're on your way to the mines, then, I won't hinder you." She smiled and held up the jasper. "Thank you for my welcome gift."

"Aw, I don't mind talkin' further." He didn't budge.

"I'm sure we'll see one another soon, but I'm expected at the mercantile."

Madge nudged him with her nose, as if to prod him along.

Rebecca stifled a laugh and strode around him and Madge. "Good-bye, Ulysses."

"But if you ain't married to the deputy, does that mean you're lookin' for a man?"

"No, Ulysses." She waved farewell. Maybe she should be irritated, but she couldn't help but feel amused.

She was hopping over another puddle on her way to the mercantile when a figure jogged alongside her. My, Ulysses was persistent.

But it wasn't Ulysses. Tad, grinning, tipped his hat. She'd stopped walking without thinking about it, peering up at her accidental husband. His clothes were less fancy than yesterday's. Then again, so were hers. Her red-sprigged calico skirt, fraying at the hem, looked tired and worn. So did Tad. Bags pouched under his eyes, indicating he hadn't slept nearly as well as she had, but a spark glinted in his gaze despite his obvious fatigue, and his dimple flashed in his clean-shaven cheek. "I see you met Ulysses."

"And the mule. He said she's yours?"

He laughed. "Madge, yes. Smarter than

me, and better looking, too."

Ha. Tad was the best looking — oh, never mind.

"So," Tad continued. "Did everything go well last night?"

"I was so tired, I could have slept on a plank, but the bed was much nicer. Thank you for giving up your room to me."

"Mrs. Horner will keep a good eye on you." His boot toed the squishy earth. "Are you off to visit Theodore?"

"I thought I could help him in the mercantile." Lest Tad think she'd forgotten her promise to Mrs. Horner, Rebecca rushed on. "I found the feather duster so I could clean the house, but it was ragged as a half-plucked turkey, so I asked if she had another one and she said never mind cleaning house today. I hope she didn't think I was being persnickety. I could've used a rag." She was babbling, so she lowered her head. "Anyway, I convinced her to let me start pea soup for dinner."

"Thanks for trying. She's a proud woman."

His gaze shifted so suddenly that hers followed, and she met the wide-eyed stare of the lanky young man from yesterday. Jeroboam Jones. "Howdy, ma'am. Pardon me for intrudin', but this is official county business."

He certainly looked proud to be conducting it, too, the way he puffed out his chest and nodded at Tad. Rebecca bit back a smile. "It's no intrusion."

Jeroboam stuck his thumbs through his belt loops. "The prisoner is still secure, Deputy. Orr has returned early and relieved me from my post."

Jeroboam must've kept watch at the jail so Tad could see to his chores. Rebecca appreciated Tad's diligence in guarding the town's prisoners.

Tad tipped his hat. "I'm grateful for your service. You get enough to eat?"

"Did indeed." Jeroboam rubbed his stomach. "Getting a dee-vorce today?"

Hopefully it wouldn't take an entire month for Jeroboam and the rest of the town to lose interest in Rebecca, Tad, and Theodore's private affairs, but she might as well set the record straight. Her hands clasped at her waist. "Not a divorce. An annulment is an altogether different thing."

"Speaking of," Tad said, nodding at Jeroboam. "The lady and I have to discuss a few things, if you don't mind."

"I'll leave you to it, then. I need some supplies from your other husband, ma'am."

85

Jeroboam nodded knowingly at Rebecca before he turned away.

"I do not have two husbands," she called to his retreating form. Too late. He was already in the mercantile.

"About yesterday." Tad's eyes were the softest mixture of green and brown, like looking into the depths of a lake. "I shouldn't have rushed you into marrying."

"You didn't. I was agreeable to the notion, remember." What an understatement. Heat flooded her cheeks. "If I'd spoken up when Mr. Orr called you *Tad,* we could've figured it out, and it would've spared us both the inconvenience." Although that didn't seem the right word. It wasn't as if she'd purchased the wrong color of thread.

He shrugged. "It'll be easy as pie to set things right."

That old adage stuck in her craw, in a funny way, and she laughed. "Pie isn't so easy, for me, at least. Crust and I don't get along. Lots more work than a cobbler."

He joined her in laughing. "I'll try to make it easy as cobbler, then. Probably won't be as tasty."

My, that dimple of his went as deep as the fire in that opal he gave her. At the thought of it, she gasped. "I still have your ring. Not on my hand, of course." Her fingers flapped

86

as if to show him their bare state, but she wore gloves anyway. "Would you like me to fetch it now?"

"No. I won't be using it until the judge comes back, at least." He must be worried about his Rebekah, the way his mouth twisted.

Something in her chest twisted, too. "I suppose I should go see Theodore now."

"Me, too." He extended his left arm, indicating she should precede him up the steps to the mercantile. "I need some rope before I visit Longbeard Pegg."

"A man who keeps his promises. Rebekah Rhys is blessed to have you."

Oh, she shouldn't have said that aloud. It sounded like she admired him in a way a woman shouldn't admire her fiancé's cousin.

"Deputy!" A short fellow poked out the door of the post office. "Mail just arrived. Letter for you."

"Maybe it's from your Rebekah." Rebecca tried to smile.

"I hope so." But he looked more anxious than happy. "I'd best read it before I go into Theodore's."

"Until later, Deputy." It felt odd to part from him, but it was only fitting. She had another life to start, one she'd chosen.

The mercantile door stood wide open to allow the morning breeze inside, she supposed. She sauntered in. And stopped cold.

Theodore stood behind the counter, face-to-face with a red-headed woman, her hands on his shoulders, his hands clamped about her waist.

CHAPTER FIVE

Rebecca's heart jumped to her throat and stifled her tongue, preventing her from giving voice to the words locked behind her teeth: *I beg your pardon* and *have you no decency?*

She did not come all the way to Idaho to see her fiancé snuggling another woman. She did not condone, appreciate, excuse, or tolerate such shenanigans. The minute she could speak again, she'd let loose with every word in her arsenal.

Then the strangest thing happened. Gratitude. She didn't know where she'd go now, or how she'd live, but thank God she'd walked in and seen Theodore and this other woman with her own eyes so there'd be no doubt. If he had affection for someone else and wasn't the husband for her, it was best to know now, before she married him. Before she loved him.

Yes, this was a good thing indeed.

Her tongue loosened, but she didn't make a sound other than to clear her throat.

Theodore looked her way and inexplicably grinned like she'd brought him a birthday cake.

"Rebecca." He hoisted the redhead to the ground and then bent, rising again with a step stool in hand. Now that the young lady's feet were firmly planted on the floor, the top of her head reached Theodore's shoulder. Rebecca gulped. The young lady had been standing on the stool. Theodore was simply helping her down.

What sort of person was she, jumping to the conclusion she did? And then feeling grateful about not marrying the man she had come here to marry? She forced a smile. "Is something amiss, Theodore?"

"Corny lost her balance, and once I righted her, lace from her sleeve snagged my collar." Theodore chuckled good-naturedly. Corny, the employee Rebecca had assumed was a man, glared. Who wouldn't be embarrassed, though?

Theodore's introduction of her by her first name indicated that she was still a child, but despite her dainty build, thin frame under a dress that fit her like a sack, and the youthful look of the looped braids pinned over her ears, it was obvious Theodore's employee was no longer a schoolgirl. Rebecca strode toward the young lady and started to extend her hand, before realizing she still held the jasper. She slipped it into her bag. "Nice to meet you, Corny. I'm Rebecca Rice."

"My name isn't Corny. I prefer Cornelia." The scowling redhead's handshake was limp as a rag.

Cornelia may not be a child, but she still acted a little like one. Why the hostility? Did she expect to lose her job now that Rebecca was able to help in the store? Rebecca would have to mention it to Theodore so he could set his employee at ease, reassuring her he still needed her or informing her of changes to her schedule or status.

"How long have you worked at the mercantile, Cornelia?"

"Since my pa started mining on War Eagle Mountain." However long that was. Cornelia disappeared through a gray curtain to a room off of the store, giving Rebecca a glimpse of crates, a desk, and a broom stacked against the far wall before the curtain fell again. She spun to chat with Theodore, but he gestured toward the lone customer in the store, Jeroboam Jones, who stood staring at two brands of coffee with a confused look on his face. "Pardon me."

"Of course." There'd be plenty of time to talk later. He had a job to do. But it might have been nice to swap pleasantries, at least.

Well, this was to be her store, too. Perhaps she should become better acquainted with it. She sauntered behind Jeroboam and Theodore, who pulled down a tin Jeroboam hadn't been scrutinizing. "This one here is from the Pioneer Steam Coffee and Spice Mills in San Francisco. Costs a little more, but get a gander at the beans."

He opened the tin and Jeroboam peeked inside. "They ain't beans at all."

Theodore chortled. "These are beans, in fact, but they're not green. They've been roasted and ground for your convenience."

Already roasted and ground? Amazing. The coffee smell wafted around Rebecca's nose, making her mouth water for a cup. With cream and sugar, something she hadn't had since Pa was alive.

"How much?" Jeroboam's eyes went wide at Theodore's answer. "I don't got enough, Mr. Fordham."

"That's what credit is for." Theodore's arm went around Jeroboam.

Rebecca bit her lip. Theodore knew his job, and by selling more to his customers than they needed, he'd make money and keep a roof over her head for the rest of her life.

But the look on Jeroboam's face tugged at something in Rebecca's chest. Had she borne the same forlorn expression when she was on the journey from Missouri, counting coins before she ordered meals? Or when she worked for that old pinchpenny Mrs. MacGruder and went to bed hungry, fantasizing about her employer's food?

She stepped closer and smiled up at Jeroboam. "The Pioneer coffee will be here next time you come in. Maybe by then you'll be ready to give it a try."

Smiling, Jeroboam pointed to a different tin. "I'll keep it in mind, Mr. Fordham, sir, but I'll jus' take this today."

Theodore's smile was strained. "Need a new grinder? This one here is a beauty."

"No thanks, sir. Not on credit, anyway."

Theodore didn't smile anymore. His hand waved at Cornelia, who must've slipped out of the storage room. "Corny? Mr. Jones is ready for payment."

"Sure thing." Cornelia was all smiles for him and Jeroboam.

Rebecca turned to Theodore. Maybe now they could talk. "How are you today, Theodore?"

"A little upset, to be frank." He didn't

make eye contact. "I was about to make a larger sale, but you talked the customer out of it."

Her lips popped apart. "He couldn't afford that ground coffee."

"You don't understand the business, Rebecca. Folks wheedle and fib to get a lower price. If I lower my standards, I won't make a living."

When he put it that way, hot shame welled in her stomach. "I'm sorry."

He looked at her then. "You didn't know. But best leave the workings of the store to me, until you learn how it's done."

She was about to nod when the hairs at her nape lifted, and she turned. Tad paused at the threshold, removed his hat, and strode toward her and Theodore.

"Tad." Theodore's tone was crisp.

"Theodore."

So much for a thaw between them. Then again, maybe this was an improvement in their relationship, if they hadn't spoken in months.

"Shopping for Longbeard?" Rebecca smiled and indicated the front window where the rope was before she remembered she wasn't supposed to help sell products yet. Her hand fell.

Tad held up a letter, as if unsure what to

do with it. "I heard from Rebekah Rhys."

"Wonderful." Theodore sounded friendly now. "When's she coming?"

She wasn't. It was obvious in Tad's hollow-looking eyes. Rebecca's chest ached for him. "What happened?"

He held out the letter to her. "Maybe you'd better read it."

Rebecca didn't want to, and at the same time her fingers itched with curiosity about his Rebekah. What had made him propose to her? Her charm? Her wit?

Her penmanship was stunning, to be sure. But Rebecca couldn't read past the first line.

Mr. Fordham, please do not hate me, but I find I am of a changed mind.

She read ahead, just to be sure. Then felt her jaw go slack as she gazed up at Tad.

"Rebekah married someone else?"

Tad laughed at himself. Rebecca grasped in thirty seconds what it had taken him several read-throughs to comprehend. "That's what she says."

One line of information amid repetitive apologies — Rebekah met a banker on the train two days after she started her journey west.

"Impossible." Theodore snatched the letter.

Clearly it wasn't. "Maybe she felt more confident marrying a stranger she'd seen in person than one she'd never glimpsed." Either way, she'd gotten off the train with the banker, married, and had the courtesy to tell Tad she wasn't coming.

Rebecca's hand hovered midair, hesitant, but at last she patted his bicep in a gesture of comfort. "You must be devastated."

Was he? To be truthful, he was more aware of the warmth of Rebecca's palm through his sleeve than his disappointment over Rebekah. Sure, he'd made plans. Sure, he'd committed to her. But he didn't love her, not yet. "I'm relieved she's well. I worried something had happened to her, since she hadn't yet arrived. I expected her days ago."

"You're a generous man, Tad." Rebecca's eyes filled with tears. For him? Her heart was as big as the territory. It wasn't hard to smile at her.

Theodore thrust the letter against Tad's chest, breaking the connection of his gaze with Rebecca's. "Maybe you can check the advertisements for another bride. Need a copy of the newspaper? I have a few on the counter."

Did his cousin try to encourage him or make a sale? Tad's laugh was mirthless. "It's a little soon, Theodore. Besides, I'm a married man at the moment."

He shouldn't have said it. It was like rubbing salt in the gaping wound of their relationship, reminding Theodore he was legally married to Rebecca. But it was true. Tad had no business reading the matrimonial papers in search of a wife when he hadn't settled his current state of affairs.

Rebecca nodded. "It's sensible to wait. The heart needs time to heal, too, of course." Her glance flicked at Tad.

So it did, and now it had to heal from his minute-long marriage to Rebecca, too. Learning she wasn't his Rebekah hurt, more than he hurt right now. Strangely, losing Rebecca after that minute had hurt him even more than when he and Theodore drove Dottie away —

No use thinking such maudlin things. He pocketed the letter and forced a smile. "Just thought you all should know."

"You're still going to get the annulment promptly, aren't you?" Theodore folded his arms.

"Yes, Theodore." But right now he didn't want to talk about it. "I'd best get that rope for Longbeard's claim. Pardon me."

He glanced at Rebecca again and his heart gave a little flip over the expression of pity on her face. Corny and Jeroboam watched with ill-concealed interest from the counter as he selected and paid for the rope. There was no use thinking about Rebekah or Rebecca or anything but his job right now.

When Tad returned to the county office, Orr sat in Tad's chair, his feet propped on Tad's desk. "You look comfortable, Orr. Problem with your desk?"

Orr chortled. "I like the view from yours."

Funny. Tad's desk faced the room that served as their jail. He repaid the favor by leaning against Orr's desk. To think, yesterday afternoon he'd signed paperwork on it, just after marrying Rebecca. The spot where they'd swapped vows was lit up with a beam of sunshine from one of the front windows.

He forced his gaze away. "Bowe eat yet?"

"I'm hungry!" The cry carried from the jail. "Ham and eggs ain't enough for a man like me."

"He ate." Orr rolled his eyes.

"Then let's escort him out of town."

"Is it true he punched you and took your wife hostage?"

"She's not my wife." He realized a beat too late Orr teased, because of course, he already knew. "I'd keep him in there until the judge comes back, but Sheriff Adkins's instructions were clear. Unless we have a murder or armed robbery, I've got to send 'em out of town. Now if Bowe comes back again, that's another story."

Letting Bowe go went against everything Tad stood for, though. Not because Bowe had struck out at him, but because he'd laid hands on Rebecca. Just thinking about it made Tad's fists curl.

Escorting Bowe to the edge of town didn't take long. "You're free to go, but if you return, the sheriff won't hesitate to lock you up until the judge comes back."

"Fine." Bowe held up his hands. "Sorry I touched your woman."

"She's not —" Tad mentally kicked himself. "Go on, Bowe."

Once the deed was done, Tad jogged back to the livery. To his surprise, a handful of mules clustered in the front paddock — including two he didn't recognize — and the Open sign hung on the door. Who'd opened the livery?

He strode inside. Finding no one, he poked into the small office. A familiar lean figure with a cowlick at the back of his head of salt-and-pepper hair bent over the scratched desk, entering information in the stock ledger.

"Pa, you're home early." Tad embraced his father. Gifford Fordham clung hard to his only child, thumping Tad's back in such a way that communicated both affection and strength — and almost made Tad choke. Pa might be of slender build, but his shoulders and arms were as strong as a young man's. He could hoist and toss feed bags as easily as Tad.

Or tease like a young fellow, which he did often. At the embrace's end, Pa flicked Tad's hat off his head to the floor. "That fancy hat of yours still making you smile, Deputy Dandy?"

Tad scooped up his new hat, brushed it off, and hung it on a peg by the door. "It's called a Boss, Pa. And you'd order one for yourself if you'd try this on."

Pa put the hat on his head. "Nope." He replaced it on the peg, laughing.

"You come home early to poke fun at my Boss?"

"I came home early because I found what I wanted right away. Did you see the new mules? Sure-footed and fair." Pa pointed in the direction of the paddock, beyond the wall.

"I didn't get a close look."

"I didn't look close in the house, either, but I could tell you cooked in my kitchen." Pa's bushy brows rose. "Isn't Mrs. Horner feeding you anymore?"

Tad took a deep breath. "About that."

"Hmm?" Pa gathered a clean rag and brushed past to the main barn.

Tad followed, wondering how to start. Maybe the end of the story would be best. "Rebekah isn't coming, Pa. I got a letter this morning. But yesterday, a gal named Rebecca got off the stage and I thought she was my Rebekah, and, well, we got married."

The rag fell from Pa's hand in time with his gaping jaw. "Beg pardon?"

Tad related the whole story. "So Theodore's still none too friendly —"

"Nothing new there, since Dottie."

"— and I'm bunking at the office until the annulment gets worked out and Rebecca can marry Theodore." Tad picked up a curry comb. Patches, the gentlest horse in the stable, needed a good brushing, and it was easier to focus on something so he wouldn't have to look at the pity in Pa's eyes right now.

Pa clasped his shoulder in a kind gesture. "I'm sorry, Son. I know you had high hopes for your Rebekah, and, well, I was looking forward to having a daughter. But it wasn't meant to be, and now we'll be two bachelors, starting fresh in Silver City."

Tad's brushing stopped. "What do you

mean by that?"

"Silver City attracts more newcomers than Ruby City." Pa squatted with a jar of grease beside the wagon. "It's a mile closer to the mines and it's out of the winds. I'd settle there, if I was new to the Owyhees."

"But we're not new."

"The folks who run the *Avalanche* newspaper are talking about moving to Silver City. Not just the paper but the literal building, walls and all. They asked me about renting mules and sledges. I said we'd be delighted — and as Ruby City's only livery, they don't have much choice but to give us business, eh? Looks like we'll make some money when others move their buildings before we have to move ourselves."

Pa had come back this morning and heard gossip about the newspaper moving to Silver City but not about Tad's mistake of a marriage? Huh. Tad wasn't sure whether to feel relieved or offended. "Doesn't mean we need to leave Ruby City, too."

"We're businessmen, Son." Pa worked grease into the wagon's axles. "We follow the crowds."

That's how things had been done with the Fordhams since Tad was young. When Gifford and his brother, Theodore's father, Stanley, lost their wives in the carriage accident outside Sacramento, they determined a change of scenery would help them and their boys, Tad and Theodore. Giff and Stan started a livery business in a neighboring mining town, and when it dried up, they moved to another California town. Then Nevada. Now here, where Uncle Stan died and Theodore decided he'd had enough of mules and wagons and started a mercantile.

If business was the driving factor, Theodore would probably move to Silver City, too. But Tad had no desire to follow. "I'm tired of moving, Pa."

"Not like you to complain, Son. You're just plum tired, is all." Pa chuckled. "I was thinking, if most of the businesses make the trek, the county seat will probably move, too, and you're the deputy. Maybe you'll be sheriff with one of these elections."

"That's never been my aspiration, Pa. You know that."

"It could be. You've got leadership potential, Son. A good sense of vision, folks listen to you, and you're always one to lend a hand, like you did during the war. Then when you came home, you agreed to help the sheriff, and he relies on you so much that he leaves town with you in charge. I know I can leave, too, and the livery will be in good shape when I get back."

"Thanks, Pa." The praise felt good, but at the same time, Tad couldn't help feeling his pa was not proud as much as he was trying to steer Tad in a particular direction.

And like a mule seeing a rocky path ahead, he wasn't sure he liked this course.

Pa nodded. "I don't see any reason why you can't be sheriff and continue to be a partner in the business, until you take over."

But Tad didn't want to be sheriff, and he wasn't so sure he wanted to take over Pa's business —

The realization pierced him like an arrow, ripping through his chest with excruciating speed. Tad's fingers shook when he put the comb back in its place. *Of course you want to stay in business with Pa. You wouldn't betray him by leaving the livery.*

And that's what it would be. A betrayal. He stayed turned away from Pa, the better to hide his conflicting thoughts.

"Rebekah's news has shaken you," Pa said from behind him. "Lick your wounds today, and tomorrow you'll be as eager as I am to start fresh."

Tad led Patches outside to the corral, thinking and praying. Maybe his wild thought about leaving the livery business was no more than fatigue after sleeping on a narrow slab of a cot and pain over Rebekah, and Rebecca. But maybe it was something more. He returned inside with a pain in his gut and more questions in his head than bees in a hive.

"I've — if you don't need me, Pa, I should go make a cursory look for the Gang. They're long gone, but I want to see if they left any tracks."

"Of course, Son. Everything's fine here."

Tad retrieved his Boss hat and saddled Solomon, his favorite riding horse. He wouldn't take a posse with him, since it was unlikely he'd come across the Gang. Besides, he was going out to think and pray as much as to look for signs of the Gang.

"I'll be home by dusk, Pa."

Pa didn't look up from greasing the wagon's axles. "With a clearer head over Rebekah and ready to start fresh in Silver City, I'd bet."

Not likely. Tad rode off, grinding his teeth over Pa's remark. It wasn't fair of Tad to be upset with Pa, who only wanted the best for him: a stable job with family, and a position in the community among people he cared about. That was what made a town a home, wasn't it? The people, not the place? If all his friends relocated to Silver City, then that would be where home was.

He didn't want to relocate there, though.

The knowledge stiffened his spine and worked its way out through his grinding molars. He desired to please his father and his community, but he sure felt like he wanted something different than what they wanted.

He shouldn't crave anyone's blessing but God's, but Pa's would sure be nice.

A flash of red caught his eye when he passed the mercantile, and his head turned.

Rebecca crossed the small mercantile porch, broom in hand. She looked up at him, waved and smiled.

He waved back and settled in for the ride.

It wasn't until he'd ridden long past the edge of Ruby City that he realized his jaw didn't hurt anymore, and he'd started smiling again.

CHAPTER SIX

The next morning, Rebecca poured boiling water over the tea leaves she'd measured into a stout brown teapot. At once, steam fragranced with the delicate leaves wafted around her, eliciting a sensation of calm. There was something soothing about tea, and Rebecca hoped Mrs. Horner would feel the same.

She carried a tray with the pot, two cups, and the sugar bowl into the sitting room, where Mrs. Horner perched on the horse-hair sofa, attending to her mending. Or at least, she would have been if she hadn't been overtaken by coughs.

Rebecca set the tray on the dusty table in front of the sofa and patted her landlady's back. "May I fetch anything for you?"

Mrs. Horner shook her head, waving off Rebecca's hand while she continued to cough. After a minute of hacking, she sat back, weary and flushed.

Rebecca poured a cup of tea. Pity there was no lemon. Mrs. Horner's throat might benefit from the acidic juice. Rebecca would have to ask Theodore if fresh lemons ever came this way. For a steep price, probably. "I've finished the breakfast dishes. How about a spot of tea?"

"How thoughtful." Mrs. Horner dabbed her lips with a hankie and took the cup Rebecca offered. "Sleep well, dearie?"

"Once I went to bed. I stayed up late writing to Johnny, my brother. He's two years older than I am, and he's mining in California. I told him I was coming out here, but I wanted to let him know I'd arrived. Then I allowed my thoughts to get the better of me, I'm afraid."

"Thinking about your two menfolk, you mean?"

Menfolk, as if she collected them like a child pockets pretty rocks. Although, now that she thought of it, two pretty rocks sat atop her dresser, and both were gifts from gentlemen: the jasper from Ulysses and the opal ring from Tad, which she really must return. What a ridiculous mess she was in. Something of her befuddlement must have shown on her face, because Mrs. Horner's brows were raised in expectation.

"There's no protocol for this . . . situation

I find myself in." Rebecca set down her tea and rubbed her forehead. "Is it proper for a woman to sleep in the bed that was last rented by the husband she wasn't supposed to marry? Should I be pledged to another when I'm married, or should Theodore and I break the engagement until I'm single again?"

Mrs. Horner's laugh was raspy from her illness. "This sort of thing doesn't come up in etiquette lessons much, does it? You're caught in a situation beyond your ken, dearie. It doesn't help matters that Theodore and Tad have such a grudge betwixt 'em, making this whole thing even harder than it needs to be."

"Why don't they get along?" Maybe Rebecca shouldn't have asked, but she couldn't restrain her curiosity any longer.

"A woman, o' course. Dottie Smalls. Theodore and Tad were inseparable until she played 'em against each other. Both of 'em thought they had a shot at marrying her, but high on nine months ago she up and ran off with a miner named Ralph White. Her granddaddy died of a broken heart, I'm sure of it, but she didn't come back for the funeral or anything. That Ralph was something else, especially when he spent time with Flick Dougherty — but that's another story." Mrs. Horner squinted. "Does it bother you, hearing your menfolk had another lady before you?"

"Of course not." But once she spoke, she recognized it wasn't quite true. The thought of Tad and Theodore loving the mysterious Dottie Smalls nipped at her skin like a flea. Rebecca scratched through her sleeve as if that would make the sensation disappear, but it only spread.

"Everybody has a past, you know. You, me, and your menfolk, but I'm sure Theodore doesn't love her anymore, so don't you fret."

Maybe not, but did Tad still love Dottie Smalls? It didn't matter if he did or didn't, since he was no one to her, but it seemed likely that he'd forgotten Dottie since he offered marriage to Rebekah Rhys. Rebecca rubbed her itchy arm. "I'm recognizing how little I know about this family I'm marrying into."

"Well, you know Theodore from his letters. He's stable and steady. I'm sure you can guess Tad is a kind man and a good deputy. He rode out after the Gang of Four yesterday."

So that was where he'd been headed when he rode past the mercantile. "Alone?"

"He knew he wouldn't catch up to them but wanted to scout out their direction, if he could. At least, that's what Giff said." Mrs. Horner pinked. "Giff is his pa."

Tad thought he wouldn't catch up to the Gang, but what if he had? He wouldn't have stood a chance alone. Her trembling fingers covered her mouth.

"Are you worried about meeting Giff, dearie?"

Rebecca's gaze drew up with a start. She dared not admit she'd been worrying about Tad, not the awkward first meeting she'd no doubt have with his father. "A little."

"He's a good fellow." Mrs. Horner took a sip of tea. "I imagine you're meeting all kinds of folks in town."

"I met Ulysses Scruggs yesterday. Do you know him?"

"Biggest flirt in the territory, but to be fair, there are so few women here, even I receive a proposal a week. And I'm old enough to be half the fellers' ma. They just want three square ones a day, is all."

Rebecca doubted it. Mrs. Horner was as pretty as she was kind. The pink that appeared in her cheeks at the mention of Giff brightened her illness-pale complexion. Rebecca determined to help put roses back in her landlady's cheeks.

She started to clear the tea things. "I'll be back to help prepare supper, but I thought

I'd go to the mercantile to help Theodore, if that's well with you."

"You go on and enjoy yourself."

"I'd like to help tidy today, too, if I may."

Mrs. Horner's brows knit as she drained her tea. Maybe Mrs. Horner was proud, or didn't understand that Rebecca needed to feel useful — and earn her keep. Then Mrs. Horner eyed the thick dust on the table. "Tidying up, and a hand with supper and breakfast, too. I'd say that's a fair exchange for your room."

"Thank you, ma'am." Rebecca gave in to the urge to kiss her landlady's cheek. "I hope you don't mind, but I'll bring a new feather duster from the mercantile. Anything else we need?"

"I don't think so —" The rest of her words were lost to another coughing fit.

Rebecca ensured her landlady would be well on her own and then hastened to the mercantile with a bounce in her step. Cornelia stood behind the counter, busy with a task, and Theodore, neat in a blue plaid shirt, string tie, and clean apron tied around his waist, held back the gray curtain to the storage area.

"Good morning." Rebecca's smile encompassed both of them.

Theodore didn't release the curtain.

"Good morning. I was just about to unpack something before the buyer arrives at nine, and since there are no customers right now, this seems a good time."

Since he didn't walk over to greet her, was this his way of inviting her for some privacy? "I'll help."

She followed him, passing Cornelia. With her glower, looped braids, and too-large dress of faded yellow calico that hung off her like a sail, Theodore's employee had the look of a pouting child. Rebecca would have to reach out to Cornelia later, but right now, she wouldn't waste a minute with Theodore.

They'd talk. Maybe he'd notice the hue of her dress was the same as the pale blue stripes in his shirt, and they'd share a laugh. Instead, he set to work with a hammer claw and a large crate. "You don't need to help, Rebecca. You can visit with Corny, if you want."

Why visit with Cornelia, when she could spend time with her fiancé? She leaned against Theodore's desk, which sat perpendicular to the stove, where a pot of fragrant coffee kept warm. "I was hoping we could talk."

"About what?" Theodore's brow furrowed in suspicion.

Anything. Their future, her journey, their

wedding, but he seemed to be waiting for a specific subject. Very well. She dried her damp palms on her skirt. "I was speaking to Mrs. Horner this morning, and I realized it might not be proper for me to be engaged to you while I'm not legally a spinster. Would it bother you if we temporarily suspended our betrothal, for the sake of propriety?"

"It does seem less than ideal for a woman to be engaged to one man and married to another." He uttered the last word like it was distasteful. "Once the annulment's granted, we can resume our plans?"

"Of course." They might have been discussing ice delivery, rather than an engagement.

He nodded. "Now I'd best get to work."

She leaned over his shoulder. "What can I do to help you? Sort items? Clean the packing straw?"

Theodore brushed the hair from his brow. "No thanks, but maybe Corny needs help."

With a sigh, Rebecca returned to the storefront, where Cornelia straightened bottles of tonic. "Anything I can do?"

"Nope." The diminutive redhead didn't even turn around.

The temptation to make Cornelia look at her, by tugging one of her looped braids maybe, made Rebecca squeeze her hands behind her back. "I don't wish to get in your way, but —"

"You're not in my way. I just don't need the help."

Rebecca would create something to do, then. After donning an apron, she organized yesterday's receipts, dusted the counter, and polished the candy jars with a rag. After that, she wandered to the cleaning section to hunt for a new feather duster for Mrs. Horner. Cornelia eyed her with one orange, quirked brow but didn't say a word.

Rebecca had selected a puffy duster and a tin of waxy polish when Theodore reappeared from the storage room. He moved behind the counter and leafed through the paperwork stacked by the cash box.

"Looking for something?" Rebecca set her items on the counter.

"Yesterday's receipts."

"I organized them alphabetically, so they're ready for filing."

"Where'd you put them?" Theodore's lips compressed.

"Right there, by the cash box like I'm supposed to." She peeked around him. "Oh, I don't see them now."

"That's because they're not here. Did you throw them out?"

"No, I left them by the cash box." As she'd already said.

"Oh my." Cornelia scooted one of the candy jars to the side. "What do we have here?"

Theodore brushed past Rebecca. "How did the receipts get here?"

"She cleaned the jars." Cornelia smirked. "She must have brought the receipts with her. Not intentionally, of course."

Indignation rose hot in Rebecca's chest. "I left them by the cash box. I couldn't have cleaned the candy jars with receipts in my hand."

Theodore shook his head. "You're new to storekeeping, and it's understandable that you'd hop from one task to another without thought, but you have to be careful with the receipts. They're private and important to our record keeping."

"I know all that." She wasn't a dolt. "But I didn't do it."

Theodore didn't appear to have heard. He patted Cornelia's shoulder and returned behind the counter. "Alphabetize these, will you, Corny?"

The high lace collar of Rebecca's blue dress tightened. Or maybe her throat swelled from holding back all the choice words she'd like to heap on Cornelia, who'd obviously hidden the receipts and "found" them again. To impress Theodore, perhaps? Or just to sabotage Rebecca?

Either way, the receipts were alphabetized because Rebecca had done it already.

At last, Theodore gazed at her with a tender smile. "Don't be embarrassed, Rebecca. No harm done."

Harm had indeed been done, against Rebecca. She took a deep breath. High time to have a talk with Cornelia.

The bell sounded over the door, indicating the arrival of a customer. As Theodore wandered to greet the miner, Rebecca turned away. Clearly, it was no longer the time or place to discuss the matter, but Rebecca couldn't stay here and pretend all was well. Or that she'd misplaced the receipts by the candy jars.

"I'm going to the post office to mail my letter to my brother," she announced to the mercantile. Theodore smiled at her from where he attended to the customer but didn't wave. Cornelia started to polish the already-polished candy jars.

Rebecca reclaimed her embroidered bag from under the counter and stomped out of the mercantile.

Straight into Tad's broad chest.

■ ■ ■ ■

"Whoa, there." Tad jerked backward on the mercantile porch, yanking back his hand from the door that had suddenly flung open on him, spilling Rebecca into the circle of his arm.

Flushing a pretty pink color, she stepped back, her gaze fixed on the shiny star pinned to his vest. "Sorry. I wasn't looking where I was going."

"No, it was me. I almost trampled you." He lifted one boot off the ground in an exaggerated display, which made her smile. A warm, gratified sensation filled his chest. "Where are you off to?"

"The post office." She tipped her head in its direction. "I wrote a letter to Johnny, my brother, to tell him I got here safely, but I need a stamp."

So she had a brother. Wonder what the fellow would think of Rebecca's plight? Amused? Protective? Couldn't be the latter, considering Johnny wasn't much for providing for his sister. It seemed she was alone in the world.

As for a stamp, Tad had a few to spare in the desk at the livery. He could give one to Rebecca, but Theodore probably wouldn't appreciate Tad giving her anything more than a *howdy-do.* Tad shrugged. He wanted to reconcile with Theodore, and if letting Theodore pay for her stamps preserved his cousin's pride and helped their family heal, so be it, but that didn't mean Tad couldn't be Rebecca's friend. They were to be family, after all.

Tad gestured toward the post office. "I'll walk with you, if you don't mind."

Her head tipped back at the mercantile. "Didn't you need something from the store?"

"Just you."

Her eyes widened in shock, and Tad could've kicked himself for the way that came out. "I mean, I came looking for you."

"You did?" She looked up at him, her pale yellow hair burnishing gold in the sunlight. "I confess, I've been thinking about you, too. Mrs. Horner said you went after the Gang of Four yesterday."

"Not them, just their tracks. Shall we?" He tipped his head toward the street. They fell into step. "I didn't see a thing, by the way. Much as I'd like to catch the Gang, they're good at avoiding capture. Say, your eyes match your dress. Mighty pretty."

"Thanks," she whispered, her gaze fixed to her toes. Oh no. He should *not* have said that aloud. Shouldn't have noticed her eyes or her dress or that she was pretty. It didn't matter how drawn he'd been to her, how glad he'd been to marry her. She was not his wife and wouldn't ever be, and if he didn't stop thinking and saying such foolishness, he'd make things a hundredfold worse for all of them: Rebecca, Theodore, and himself, too.

But she wasn't too mad. On the contrary, her lips quirked in a shy smile. And her appreciating his compliment seemed more dangerous than him giving it, because it made him want to compliment her again and again.

Clearing his throat, he forced his gaze to the passersby on the street. "I came looking for you on official business."

"Oh?" There, she met his gaze again. Official business was nice and safe.

"I sent Bowe Brown out of town last night. He deserves a longer stay in jail for grabbing you like that, but the sheriff's policy is to expel most of the lawbreakers."

"Where is the sheriff?"

"Checking on a situation at one of the mines. He'd do the same with Bowe if he was here, though. But Bowe is not welcome in Ruby City. I'm sorry he's not in jail, but at least he won't be here to bother you again."

"I'll sleep better knowing I won't see him again." Relief smoothed her features. "And I understand why you had to send him out of town. My father used to do that, too."

Tad stopped walking as understanding hit him like a mule kick to the gut. Now her reaction on their wedding day made sense. It wasn't just the thought that he, or rather, Theodore, had lied to her about being a deputy.

She was upset because he *was* a deputy. Because she had been hurt by one.

"Your father was a lawman, then?"

Rebecca nodded. "A sheriff."

He took her elbow and led her to the old log bench outside Wilkie's barbershop. He sat, keeping a full two feet between them out of respect for Theodore. "And something happened? You don't have to tell me, if you don't want to."

"No, I don't mind. Just before the war started, a pair of cardsharps came through town. Pa escorted them out, the way you did Bowe, but they came back, and before Pa knew they'd returned, one of them killed a town councilman over a game of poker. Pa rode after them with a posse, and — well." Her words had thickened, as if tears

121

clogged her throat.

"He didn't come home," Tad finished for her.

"His passing was quick, according to the men with him. Pa didn't even know he was in peril. That's the thing about danger. It has a way of sneaking up on the unsuspecting." She swallowed. "It was a long time ago."

Not that long. It was just before the war, she said, and Fort Sumter was five years ago. A long time in some ways, yet still fresh and painful to her heart.

"Hey." A slurred voice startled Tad. A lean man with sharp cheekbones and brown hair curling on his shoulders leaned heavily against the doorframe, glaring at Tad and Rebecca with watery eyes. The stench of whiskey emanated from his unkempt clothes. "That bench is for customers, which you two ain't."

"That's no way to speak to a lady, Wilkie." Tad propped his hands on his knees, indicating he'd stand if he had to, but Wilkie wouldn't like it if he did. "And you don't own this bench."

"It's outside my store." Wilkie blinked. "Who are you, lady?"

She's my wife. The words almost blurted out, and they would make Wilkie scuttle back into his barbershop. But it wasn't correct, exactly. Tad sighed. He would have to deal with Wilkie, but now, with Rebecca here, wasn't the best time.

To his shock, Rebecca hopped to her feet and extended her hand. "I'm Rebecca Rice from Missouri, sir."

Wilkie eyed her dainty hand before grunting and re-entering his barbershop. Rebecca turned to Tad. "Something I said?"

He burst out laughing. Then he stood and led her from the barbershop. "Sorry about that. Wilkie's our barber, as you guessed. He's —"

Unhappy. Lonely. A drunk.

"Troubled," Rebecca finished for him.

"It's been tough for him since his wife and baby died, not that I'm excusing his behavior. In fact, I'll have words with him once I escort you to the post office."

"Not on my account."

"Well, I'd like to see him sober for his own sake. He's missing out on a lot, living the way he is, but while I can encourage and support him, I can't change him."

He'd learned that lesson the hard way, thinking his affection could heal Dottie's brokenness and win her to a life away from the wildness she'd shown.

Her head tipped. "You're kind to help

123

such a troubled man. Him, and Longbeard, too."

"And you're kind for showing such patience, considering Wilkie was rude and Longbeard almost started a gunfight."

"With a fork." She sighed. "Thanks for listening to my story about my father, Tad, and for understanding."

"We're family." Cousins, once she married Theodore. "Friends, too, I hope."

"Friends." There was her pretty smile again. "Speaking of family, though, I'd best mail this letter to Johnny."

He nodded and bid her farewell. It was good that they'd be friends. Maybe it would help resolve things between him and Theodore. Once they got out of this marriage, that is.

It's not like Rebecca would ever have chosen Tad. Even if he, instead of Theodore, had been the one to answer her advertisement in the matrimonial magazine, she would never have married him because of his profession.

He'd known she was going to marry Theodore, but still, the realization settled into a clump in his stomach, like cold oatmeal. Had he harbored a hope he hadn't admitted to himself, that their accidental marriage hadn't really been a mistake after all, that maybe he and Rebecca —

No use thinking of it. It was over before it ever began. Tad returned to work.

CHAPTER SEVEN

After the post office, Rebecca returned to the boardinghouse, prepared dinner, cleaned the parlor, and started a savory lamb stew for supper. Then she made her way back to the mercantile.

Theodore looked up from behind the counter and grinned. "Rebecca, am I glad to see you."

"You are?" A quick glance assured her the store was empty of customers, and Cornelia wasn't in sight. Maybe now she and Theodore would chat. When he untied his apron and hung it on the peg, indicating that he was leaving the store or closing it, her heart skipped a beat.

"Now that you're here, I can collect on a bill. You'll watch the store, won't you?"

Oh. She'd thought he was happy to see her because she was his intended, not because he needed a pair of hands. It was no small thing to mind the mercantile, however, and it indicated his trust in her. Off came her bonnet. "Of course. Thank you for showing faith in me."

"You shouldn't have any customers, but remember, money goes in the till. Receipts in the stack, alphabetized if there's time."

That was like saying shoes went on her feet or the sun traversed the sky. He must still be sore over the earlier receipt incident. That made two of them, although Rebecca was trying not to think uncharitable thoughts of Cornelia. She forced a smile. "This will be my store, too, remember. I have to be alone here sometime."

"What a wise woman I'm marrying." Theodore stood before her, smiling, the space between them charged, like maybe he wanted to squeeze her hand or even kiss her.

Rebecca was thinking *maybe* a lot, trying to determine Theodore's motives. It would be such a relief to know him better and not second-guess his every action or lack thereof. "Go on. Everything will be here when you come back. Unless it sells, of course."

He chuckled. "Money in the till, receipts in the stack."

There was no *maybe* going through her mind at that one. Where else would she put the money? Her ears? And those receipts would never go anywhere but the stack, especially after earlier. She nodded, biting her lip.

Rebecca circled behind the counter for an apron. She was tying it in a bow about her waist when the bell over the door rang. A reed-thin young blond crept inside, her gaze darting about as if she expected the place to be stocked with snarling guard dogs. Two small girls clutched at her faded skirt, their eyes wide, their cheeks hollow.

"Good afternoon." Rebecca smiled, hoping she looked professional yet welcoming. "How can I help you?"

Everything about these females was pale: their cheeks, their bloodless lips, and their wash-worn calico dresses. The mother's bony fingers clutched a tattered shawl and a torn basket. "I need a pound each of corn and rice and a half pound of dried fruit, whatever kind is most reasonable."

Good, inexpensive choices for someone with little funds, as Rebecca well knew. She'd dined on similar fare the past few years. "Certainly."

She loaded the items into the woman's basket, pricking the side of her finger on a jagged piece of straw. Rebecca held back her grimace of pain. The woman clearly couldn't afford a new basket, and it would only insult her to draw attention to it. Gathering the receipt pad, Rebecca looked up. "I'm new to town, so pardon me for not knowing your name. I'm Rebecca Rice."

"Evans is the name."

Rebecca wrote it down. Then she checked Theodore's chart, written in the neat penmanship she'd come to admire from his courtship letters, which stated the prices. She spoke them aloud as she wrote. "Ten cents for the rice, fifty for the corn, and twenty for a pound of dried apples, so half of that is ten cents. Seventy cents."

Her mouth dried, uttering that total. The apples were double what she'd paid in Missouri for dried fruit. True, it cost more to transport food to Ruby City, but she'd no idea it would cost that much.

"I only have sixty cents."

The younger of the two girls hopped to her toes. "That gang took her purse that had five dollars in it."

"The Gang of Four?" Rebecca dropped the pencil.

"Met 'em about a week ago when I was off gem hunting. It was foolish of me to wander off alone like that, but I just thought — well, it doesn't matter." Mrs. Evans blinked. "Put back the apples, please."

"But you said we could get somethin' sweet." The older girl's voice was thin and high.

"Not today, dumplin'." Mrs. Evans met Rebecca's gaze for the briefest of moments.

The girls didn't protest further. Their gazes swooped back to the ground.

Rebecca removed the fruit from the basket, wishing she could do something to help the family, who clearly didn't have much. How could she get them the fruit? She could say she added sums wrong and quote a lower price, but that would be a lie. She could offer a discount, but Theodore would be angry if she did that.

What about offering a tab? Theodore had offered credit to Jeroboam Jones for the coffee. Rebecca's chin lifted. "I met up with the Gang of Four, myself, and it caused me a heap of trouble, so here's what I'll do. I can set up an account for you. Pay the sixty cents, and you can pay me another ten by the end of the month."

Mrs. Evans looked up. "I could do that?"

"Sure." Rebecca didn't know Theodore's policy, so she had best get some information, to be safe. "What's your address?"

"One of the mining camps up yonder."

"War Eagle? Florida?" Rebecca had overheard snippets of miners' conversations about the mountains, but she still knew little of the area.

Mrs. Evans shook her head. "Not quite. But Donald, that's their pa, he or I will be back next week with your dime."

Rebecca jotted down Donald's name on the receipt and returned the apples to the basket. "See you then."

The littlest girl skipped out of the store. Rebecca felt like skipping, herself. Her first customer, and she'd not only found a way to keep from losing a sale but to get a little more nutrition into those girls' bellies. She was still smiling when Theodore and Cornelia entered the store together, sharing a laugh.

Rebecca joined in, clasping her hands under her chin. "What's the joke?"

Cornelia spun to gather her shop apron, her red looped braids flapping over her ears. "You wouldn't understand, Mrs. Fordham. I mean, Miss Rice."

"Why not?"

Theodore tied his apron on, too. "Corny's mother just offered me a *prairie* that Corny made, instead of a *pastry*. But I'd eat a prairie anytime, if it had that cherry filling. You make good pastries, Corny."

Cornelia chuckled. "I think you still have some cherry on your chin, Mr. Fordham."

131

"Do I?" His fingers swiped his jaw, laughing when they came away clean. "You're teasing me."

"Just a little." Cornelia settled behind the counter.

Rebecca's hands fell. "I thought you went out to collect a bill."

"I stopped at Corny's on the way back. There's always something delicious in the Cook kitchen. Your surname is apt, Corny."

Another round of giggles filled the mercantile, but Rebecca didn't join in this time. When Theodore glanced at her, his laughter subsided. "I should have thought to bring you a pastry, too. Sorry."

"That was the last *prairie,* anyway." Cornelia smirked.

Rebecca didn't appreciate Cornelia's attempt to keep the laughs going. All of a sudden, she wanted to get out of the mercantile. Her fingers busied with her knotted apron strings. "I should check on Mrs. Horner —"

"What's this?" Cornelia held up a receipt.

Rebecca had placed it on the stack, as Theodore requested. "I made my first sale."

"What's wrong, though, Corny? Didn't she put the receipt in the stack?" Theodore dashed to the counter. "Is the money in the till?"

She was right here and capable of speaking for herself. "Everything's where it's supposed to be."

"Not quite." Cornelia showed the receipt to Theodore and pointed.

"You started a line of credit, Rebecca." Theodore frowned. "For a miner."

Rebecca tugged off her apron. "Did I set it up incorrectly?"

"That's not what I meant." Theodore rubbed his forehead. "We don't offer credit to miners."

"You offered it to Jeroboam Jones."

"He's a wood hauler, but he has a history with us. Miners are transient. They move a lot," he added, as if she didn't understand the word.

Cornelia rolled her eyes. "Miners up and leave town, dodging bills all of the time."

Wasn't Cornelia's pa a miner up on War Eagle? Rebecca's arms folded. "I was trying to find a way to keep the sale and help them at the same time. She and the children were hungry."

"Folks tell you that to get you to feel sorry for them." Theodore's pitying look unspooled something in Rebecca.

"I know what hungry looks like, and I know twenty cents a pound is too high for dried apples."

Theodore dropped the receipt back on top

of the stack and held up his hands, as if imitating Tad's tactic to keep peace. "Remember how hard it was for you to get here on the stagecoach? Up hills, lonely roads, bandits? Imagine hauling food over those same roads — some of them toll roads. I pay extra for what I sell on account of the difficulty, Rebecca. I need to make a living on top of that, too."

"I know that." But he'd told her in his letters how he padded things to take advantage of the miners. It was one thing to make a profit but another to charge such exorbitant sums that a parent couldn't afford to feed her children. It was no use arguing the point anymore, though. "Add the price of the apples to my tab, then."

Rebecca didn't think anyone would take her seriously, but Cornelia picked up a pencil. "Ten cents to Mrs. Tad Fordham's tab," she said as she wrote. "I mean, Miss Rice's tab."

Rebecca brushed past Cornelia to hang her apron, stuffing down more uncharitable thoughts about Cornelia's gleeful smart talk. One day soon, Rebecca might not be able to hold back a retort. She should quietly speak to the young woman about her attitude, before she snapped.

But not now. She was too angry to open

her mouth. Muttering about returning to Mrs. Horner's, she marched to the door. And stopped at the window.

Longbeard Pegg lumbered up the street, stooped and bone-thin. His mouth worked, like he told a story, but he had no companion as he shuffled past. His tattered boots and lonely manner ached her heart. She should go talk to him —

A brawny man shoved Longbeard's shoulder as he passed, knocking him sideways before he jogged into the bank across from the mercantile. The moment her foot lifted from the ground to hurry to Longbeard something clicked in her brain and her muscles froze, locking in place. The big man was familiar, frighteningly so. His shoulders were so wide, his head looked a pinch too small for his body.

Just like that member of the Gang of Four who'd reached for her, the one she'd tried to stab with her letter opener.

"Help."

She didn't think she'd spoken aloud, but the prayer must have left her lips because Theodore came up behind her. "Something wrong, Rebecca?"

Her muscles thawed and anxiety thrummed through her veins. She had to move. Now. She spared Theodore the briefest of glances over her shoulder. "I need Tad."

It wasn't until she was out the door, gripping handfuls of her skirt so she could run to the livery, that she understood why Theodore's face had purpled at her words.

It was unfortunate that she'd given him the wrong impression, but she'd explain later. This was urgent, and only one person in Ruby City could help her. She couldn't help it if the deputy was also her temporary husband.

Tad finished wiping down a bit with a rag and was about to set it on the workbench when he heard movement from the livery's wide doors.

"Tad?" Rebecca stood in the threshold, blinking as if she adjusted to the dim light of the barn after being out in the bright sun. Clearly, she couldn't see him yet.

He stepped toward her. "Right here, Rebecca."

"Oh, there you are." Rebecca rushed forward. "That member of the Gang. Remember, I told you about him?"

On their wedding day, right after she got off the stagecoach. "He's a boy, you said."

"No, I mean the biggest one." She took a deep breath. "I'm not being clear. The one who tried to touch me? I think I just saw him walk into the bank."

His blood iced. "He's here?"

"Maybe." Rebecca's hands curled to her chest, in fear or embarrassment, Tad wasn't sure. "The Gang wore bandannas over their faces, but it could be him. I need to see his eyes to be sure."

Here, in Ruby City — could it be that easy? Rebecca could have been mistaken, but Tad would rather err on the side of caution than let the opportunity slip away. He brushed past her, grabbing his Boss and his gun belt. "Stay here."

"Be careful, please, Tad. I'm so sorry."

"What's this?" Pa leaned out of the office, a sandwich in his hand and his gaze on Tad's gun belt.

"One of the Gang might be in town. I need you to keep an eye on — sorry, this is Rebecca Rice, Pa. Theodore's intended."

Pa's eyes widened, but he clearly understood Tad's need to hurry, as well as his desire for Rebecca to be protected. Pa set down the sandwich. "I'm Giff Fordham, your father-in-law for the time being, but you can call me Uncle Giff, since that seems more suitable for the long term."

"Hello." Rebecca smiled, but her repeated glances at Tad were fearful.

"Stay here with Pa. I'll be back."

She offered a tiny nod.

"Have lunch yet, Becky?" Pa asked as Tad dashed outside. Becky? Rebecca didn't go by it; she'd said so at their wedding. Tad shook his head, clearing his thoughts. The brawny fellow in the Gang could be finished at the bank by now, but he couldn't have gone far.

Tad kept his pace casual, his posture relaxed, but his gaze fixed on the faces of folks he passed. While it was true that Silver City attracted more folks of late, Ruby City stayed plenty busy. The discovery of gold and silver a few years back brought investors and prospectors hoping to make their fortunes out of the hills, as well as those who made their livings off of them: gamblers, reporters, soiled doves, and businessmen of all types, including the Fordham family.

Not that Tad hadn't tried his hand at mining. He'd done his share of gem hunting, and the best he'd found was the opal he'd had set into a gold band and given to Rebecca on their wedding day.

His gut jumped into his rib cage, just like it always did when he thought of Rebecca. He hated that she felt unsafe. Maybe today, God willing, he'd get a start at stopping the

Gang of Four once and for all, and she'd be able to rest easy knowing they couldn't hurt her or anyone else again.

Tad pushed open the door of the bank, allowing his eyes a moment to adjust to the dim. It didn't take long to make out the mahogany desk by the window with its green-shaded lamp and inkwell, or the long counter separating the bank in two. Two male customers stood at it — neither of them particularly large. Ebenezer Cook, the father of Theodore's employee, Corny, was a short fellow with a paunch and fading red hair. Donald Evans stood behind him, waiting his turn. He was a widowed miner with two girls and a sister to feed, but by the skin-and-bones look of them, he hadn't fared too well in the mines.

Neither of them was the man Rebecca had seen.

Bilson, the banker, perched behind the counter, stamping a paper for Eb Cook with the sort of precision he applied to his fastidious appearance. Bilson slicked back his goose-gray hair with pomade and kept his clothes pressed and free of lint or dirt, making him the fanciest gander in Owyhee County. He looked up with a professional smile. "Good afternoon, Deputy. I'll be with you in a moment."

It couldn't wait that long. "Actually, I have a question. Was there another customer here a minute ago? No need for alarm, but I'm looking for someone."

Bilson tipped his head to the side. "Banking is a private business, Deputy. I couldn't possibly say who conducts transactions here."

"I ain't no banker, so I can say, Deputy," Donald Evans said. "Wilkie was here makin' a deposit. So was that hauler you hired to sit at the jail."

Bilson cringed. "Mr. Evans, please show some discretion."

Tad rubbed the back of his neck. Neither the town barber nor Jeroboam Jones were in the Gang of Four. "The fellow I'm looking for is big. Broad shoulders."

Eb Cook pocketed the paper Bilson had just stamped. "Orr was here. He's a big fella."

He was, but the justice of the peace wasn't it, either. "Anyone else?"

"A few fellas left when I came in," Evans added. "And Flick Dougherty."

"Dougherty?" He'd been thick with Ralph White, the man Dottie ran away with nine months ago. Dougherty hadn't been around much lately, but miners came and went. Nevertheless, Dougherty was muscular and big boned, which fit Rebecca's description.

The thought that someone he knew — not well, but nonetheless was acquainted with — could be in the Gang of Four soured his stomach.

"Dougherty was all smiles." Eb Cook rocked on his heels. "He withdrew two dollars to send to his mother."

Bilson purpled. "Mr. Cook, banking is a private matter!"

"I can't help overhearing," Eb protested.

Tad stepped forward. "Where'd he go? The post office, maybe?"

The men all shrugged.

"What about the other customers you mentioned? Were they big? Did you know them?"

Bilson sighed. "Since they weren't customers, I suppose it's acceptable to inform you they were inebriated and wanted to exchange small coins for larger denominations, but I wouldn't call them *big,* per se."

And they'd been together, not alone. Flick must have been the man Rebecca saw. Whether or not he was in the Gang of Four or just resembled one of them had yet to be determined. "Thanks, gentlemen. Much appreciated."

On the way to the post office, Tad's gaze assessed everyone on the street, but none looked like Flick Dougherty. No one at the post office had seen him, either.

Tad stopped in at the mercantile, the tanner's, Wilkie's barbershop, Modine's saloon, and the Idaho Hotel before returning to the livery, shaking his head.

Rebecca was still inside the barn, brushing Madge's gray coat. Pa stood at her shoulder, nodding. "You're a natural. You must have grown up with animals."

"I had a sidesaddle before the war and drove the wagon a few times, but I was never the one to feed or care for the horses."

"You could've fooled me. You're doing fine. Now try short strokes, ear to her backside. She likes that."

"Is that good, Madge? You like that?" She smiled at the creature. Then her gaze lifted and met Tad's. "Anything?"

"The men in the bank said a local fellow, Flick Dougherty, stopped in, and he possibly fits your description. I looked all over town for him but couldn't find him."

"You don't think it's him. I can tell."

Tad puffed out a breath. "He withdrew two dollars to send to his mother, which isn't much cash for a man who robs cargo wagons and stagecoaches."

"I don't imagine he'd bother with a bank, either." The rhythm of her brushstrokes slowed. Madge leaned into Rebecca, reminding her to keep going.

"He may not be in the Gang — he might look like the one who . . . was familiar, but if Flick shows his face in town again, I'll question him."

Pa's gnarled hand landed on Rebecca's shoulder. "Don't fret, Becky. Tad'll find the Gang sooner than later. Now, I need the smithy to look at some mule shoes, but when you finish with Madge there and go home, tell that landlady of yours howdy for me, will you?"

"Will do, Uncle Giff. Thanks for the company." She waved as Pa exited.

"Becky, huh? I thought you didn't like being called that." Tad shoved his hands in his pockets.

She resumed brushing, and Madge shut her eyes under Rebecca's ministrations. "It's just that no one's ever called me Becky. But I don't mind your pa having a special name for me."

"So you don't want me calling you Becky, then?" He was teasing, but Rebecca's face looked about to crumple.

"I'm sorry I sent you on a goose chase."

"It wasn't any such thing. You're a witness and your information is invaluable. In fact, when Flick comes through, maybe you could give him another look."

When her eyes watered, he took the brush from her hand, tossed it to the straw, and enveloped her hand in both of his. "Hey now, are you worried if the Gang sees you they'll remember you? They don't know you or where you live, though. They just wanted your cash."

"They might remember me. The boy read the envelopes of Theodore's letters, so he saw my name. It wouldn't be hard to find me." She swiped her eyes. "But that's not why I'm teary. I'm grateful you believe me, is all."

Tad's gut squeezed into a ball. He wanted to pull her in for a comforting embrace, but instead, he clutched her fingers, an action he hoped was comforting but cousin-like. "Of course I believe you."

Rebecca gazed up at him with moist eyes.

Madge leaned into them, warm and heavy. Rebecca released his hands and bent for the brush. "She's not done being brushed, I guess. Sorry, Madge."

Thanks a lot, Madge. You interrupted a tender moment, here.

Except Madge had actually done him a favor. She'd saved him from making a fool of himself. Holding Rebecca's hand, *cousin-like*? Sure. Nothing questionable about him

144

holding his accidental wife's hand and wanting to hug her. All he needed was for Theodore to walk into the livery and take another swing at him.

A form darkened the door. Theodore? No, someone squatter. "Ulysses? Howdy."

"Deputy. Why, Miz Rebecca, I didn't expect to see you today." Ulysses bent at the waist, as if he were a knight of old greeting his lady on a field of honor.

All traces of her tears were gone. "How are you, Ulysses?"

Bless her for not shrinking from Ulysses's antics. The miner was lonely, and sometimes he gave the ladies too much attention. Tad knew something himself about how loneliness influenced a person's behavior. Chasing Dottie those months ago, for one. Answering an ad in a matrimonial magazine, for another.

But that had been different. He was ready for a wife, family, and a home with roots, and the way he'd been drawn to the matrimonial magazine that day, it was like it was part of a bigger plan. Clearly not, though, because he was standing in the barn wanting to hug a woman who was not-really-his-wife, with Ulysses watching like a contented pup.

"I got news, Deputy." Ulysses's smile fell.

"Piece haulers just rode in. The Gang o' Four met 'em about two miles down the way. The fellers were armed but no match for the Gang."

Again.

Could Flick Dougherty have had time to rob folks and then patronize the bank? It was possible, if he hurried. Two miles went a lot faster on a horse than a loaded wagon.

Then again, it was unlikely. Visiting the bank to make a withdrawal wouldn't achieve anything, except giving Flick an alibi.

Tad could figure it out later. He tossed a saddle over Solomon's back.

"You're going after them." Rebecca chased him.

The Gang had to be stopped. She knew it as well as he did, but the tense set of her shoulders and her white knuckles spoke to her fear.

"Their tracks will be fresh." He kept a saddlebag of rations ready just in case something like this happened, so he grabbed it and secured it to Solomon's saddle. "Ulysses, wait for my pa to return, tell him where I am, and then escort Miss Rice home, will you?"

"Sure thing, Deputy." Ulysses saluted. "Forgot to mention, a few fellers are ready to go with you, seein' as the sheriff's not back yet. Ahab Orr and Jeroboam Jones are gatherin' at the hotel."

Tad nodded at Ulysses and smiled at Rebecca in a way he hoped comforted her, cousin-to-cousin. His foot was in the stirrup when Rebecca reached for his sleeve.

"Be careful."

Her lips trembled. So did the fingers that clutched the green plaid of his shirt. Tad yearned to reassure her everything would be well, to squeeze her hand again, but he hadn't the time — or the right. That was Theodore's job.

And this was his.

"I will. Don't fret, Rebecca." He mounted Solomon and smiled at her again, but his face fell the moment he was out of her sight. He didn't like thinking about Theodore comforting her. Not with his words, nor his arms.

And that put Tad in a whole heap of trouble.

CHAPTER EIGHT

It had been two whole days since Tad rode out with his small posse, and there hadn't been a word. Rebecca wandered to the mercantile, where Theodore and Corny bent over a bolt of heavy wool fabric. The warm-looking material reminded Rebecca that Tad had ridden off without a bedroll — a clear indication he'd planned to return before nightfall.

But he hadn't. Her mind slipped to fearful thoughts while she prayed and battled to trust God, finding little distraction in her chores. Twice a day, she'd marched to the livery seeking news, but Uncle Giff didn't seem concerned at the lack of information. Just now, he'd patted her hand and said, *"Don't fret, Becky."*

But she couldn't help it. She strode to the mercantile counter. "He's still not back."

Theodore glanced up from the wool. "Who's not back yet?"

Rebecca stopped midway through loosening her bonnet strings. Tad's name died on her lips as she recalled Theodore's face when she'd run out of the mercantile when she saw Flick Dougherty. "The posse."

Cornelia glanced up. "Still out chasin' tracks, I guess."

Theodore turned to the shelves of fabric. "Say, Corny, these haven't sold. Any idea why?"

"This one is too expensive, I think, but it's so wonderful someone will take it, I'm sure." With reverent fingers, the dainty young woman touched a bolt of cobalt and robin's egg blue striped satin. "But the yellow calico is rough and makes me itch whenever I take it down for a customer. One touch and no one wants it."

Rebecca froze, still as ice. Tad was in the wilderness hunting armed robbers, and Theodore and Cornelia talked scratchy calico? Didn't they care about their neighbors or the danger they placed themselves in to protect the people of the county? She was about to say something when the bell over the mercantile door sounded. She spun, praying it was Tad.

Mrs. Horner shut the door behind her and smiled. "Good afternoon."

Rebecca drew closer as coughs racked

Mrs. Horner's slender frame. Her landlady hadn't been out of the house since Rebecca moved in, due to her lingering illness. "Should you be out, Mrs. Horner? I can get whatever you need."

Mrs. Horner swiped her watering eyes with a lace-edged hankie. "I couldn't stay cooped up any longer. I needed a walk."

Rebecca understood the woman's need for fresh scenery. She wouldn't mind one now, and she'd only been in the mercantile two minutes — but that had to do with Theodore and Cornelia's lack of concern for the posse more than anything else. In the past two days, she'd explained about seeing a man named Flick Dougherty who looked like one of the Gang of Four, but had little opportunity to speak to either Theodore or Cornelia about anything of substance.

And she really must have a talk with Cornelia, assuring Theodore's employee that Rebecca was not going to take her job and wished to be friends. It would have been nice to talk to Theodore, too, but the past two evenings, he'd dined with Cornelia's family since Rebecca "was taken care of at the boardinghouse."

If he'd come calling, she would have been thinking about the posse, anyway. Rebecca took her landlady's arm. "I'll join you, unless you need me, Theodore."

"Not in the least."

And he clearly didn't, the way he and Cornelia adjusted bolts of fabric and returned to talking about texture and pricing. Rebecca led her landlady to the porch.

Mrs. Horner eyed Rebecca like she was wearing her bonnet backward. "Why'd you drag me back outside? What's the matter?"

"Tad, of course. I just checked with Uncle Giff, and he's still not back. That's what you came to find out, isn't it?"

"Well, no. I came for salt."

Rebecca rubbed her forehead. Didn't anyone care about Tad? "He should be back by now. I mean *they*. The posse. Uncle Giff doesn't seem concerned, and Theodore cares more about his calico."

Mrs. Horner frowned. "You didn't go to Theodore with your concerns, did you?"

"I told him the posse isn't back. Everyone wants a report, don't they?"

Mrs. Horner burst into laughter, which turned into another coughing fit. Rebecca patted her landlady's back but couldn't help the prickles of irritation needling her flesh. What was so funny? She'd ask, once Mrs. Horner recovered. "Need a fresh handkerchief?"

"What I needed was a good laugh, and you gave it to me. Showin' Theodore you're worried about Tad? That's a good one."

Rebecca's arms folded. "Why wouldn't I apprise him? He and Tad are family."

"They're cubs fightin' for their place in the wolf pack, is what they are. Put a female in the mix and whoo-ee!" Her hands waved in the air. "First Dottie, now you."

Ulysses paused on the street below the porch, drawn by Mrs. Horner's enthusiastic waving. He must have mistaken Mrs. Horner's wave for a greeting, because he offered a sly smile and tipped the brim of his hat. "Howdy, l-adies."

The way he said it, drawing out the *l* sound, set Mrs. Horner laughing again. "Aw, go on, Ulysses. I told you already, I ain't marryin' you."

He didn't seem bothered. "How 'bout you, Miz Rebecca?"

"I've already got one husband too many, thank you," she said through clenched teeth.

Ulysses was laughing so hard he had to clutch his belly. Mrs. Horner swiped her eyes again but not from coughing. And Rebecca's face heated like a griddle.

Mrs. Horner made a tutting sound with her tongue once Ulysses moved on. "No harm meant, dearie. Don't be angry."

"At that? — whatever it was with Ulysses? Hardly. But Tad being missing after riding after four armed criminals is not amusing. Nor is your suggestion that I'm like Dottie. I'm not. I'm not trying to play cousins against one another."

Mrs. Horner tipped her head down and blinked up at Rebecca.

Rebecca's anger curdled in her stomach, and a fresh wave of heat suffused her face. Had she made things worse for Tad and Theodore's relationship? She'd wanted to make it better, to be a bridge of peace, but she'd dashed off to Tad without explanation when she saw that Flick Dougherty, who resembled the member from the Gang. She'd later clarified what happened to Theodore, of course, but she could never take back the fact that she'd caused Theodore distress and fed his insecurities. Nor did it help that she kept announcing her thoughts were on Tad and the posse.

She rubbed her forehead. "You're right. I made a mistake. Several mistakes, I think. It's been difficult in the mercantile. Cornelia hasn't been welcoming —"

"Who?"

"Cornelia Cook. Redheaded employee, just now complaining about scratchy calico?"

153

"Oh, you mean Corny."

"She likes to be called Cornelia."

"Does she now?" Mrs. Horner's brows rose. "Well, she's frustrated, is all."

"Why? Theodore shows no signs of planning to let her go from his employ."

"Keepin' her job might not be what's stuck in her craw. She's not the little whippersnapper she used to be. She may be feeling things she doesn't know what to do with yet, like the itch to start her own life. Maybe she's sweet on someone who doesn't know she's alive, and that can make a woman ornery. Don't take it personal-like. It's better to assume people's antics have nothing to do with you unless you have the facts, or you'll be shouldering the weight of the world." Mrs. Horner patted Rebecca's arm. "Now, I'd like to get that salt and go home, so I can put my feet up."

Rebecca escorted her back inside. While Theodore assisted Mrs. Horner, Rebecca removed her bonnet and tied her apron around her waist. She'd made a commitment to Theodore. She needed to show she was invested, so she set about tidying the store.

After Cornelia had gone home for lunch and no customers milled the mercantile, Rebecca cleared her throat. "Theodore? I'd like to apologize."

"About the line of credit you started for Mrs. Evans? No need. She paid half of it this morning before you came in, so now she's only in debt for a nickel."

"That's not it." Maybe she should be sorrier about giving Mrs. Evans credit, but she couldn't regret finding a way for the family to eat. "I'm sorry I ran to Tad without pausing to explain. I was in a hurry, you see —"

"You wanted him to catch the man you thought was in the Gang. Time was of the essence. You already explained everything." Theodore turned away to shelve coffee cans.

"But what I didn't tell you — what I should have told you — is that my pa was a sheriff, and he was shot dead while out on a posse."

She held her breath until Theodore turned around.

At last she had his full attention. He stared at her, brow furrowed in concern, as she told him about Pa's final posse ride. "Lawmen going out like this? It sends me into a state, especially since I know Tad. I've been panicking, but you couldn't know why. I'm sorry if my actions confused or hurt you."

Theodore looked back at the coffee display. "Don't give it a second thought."

Was he unwounded by her confession, or

did conflict make him uncomfortable? Either way, they needed to work through this. "I have to think about it, Theodore. I don't want to cause strife —"

"I'm more concerned about you." His words made her relax. "I knew all your people were dead, but to relive your pa's murder must ache something awful."

"Yes, but I still have people. One, anyway. My brother Johnny is somewhere in California. I just sent him another letter, remember?" She'd announced it to the mercantile. Hadn't he been listening to her?

"Oh, that's right." Theodore shrugged. "I'm glad you told me about your pa. We haven't had much time to talk since you arrived, what with the store and you helping Mrs. Horner and all."

Rebecca nodded. Maybe now that they'd had this discussion, they'd spend some time together courting — a benefit of their delayed wedding. "What about a picnic tomorrow? We could close the store for lunch."

"Oh no, I could never close it. But maybe when Corny comes back from her break —"

Ding-a-ding. The door flung wide, startling Rebecca. Two dirt-caked men paused inside the doorway, one supporting the other by the waist. Jeroboam Jones held up the other man, who clutched his gut and whose downcast face was hidden by his Stetson Boss hat.

She didn't need to see his face to know his identity. Her heart beat triple-time.

It was Tad, his green plaid shirt soaked in blood.

It hurt to lift his head, but Tad pushed through the sting so he could meet Rebecca's gaze. "It's not as bad as it looks."

Then his knees gave way, completely contradicting his words.

Rebecca rushed forward, her weight gentle against him, but the touch still made him wince. "You need a doctor."

"Wilkie ain't at the barbershop, or he ain't answerin' the door." Jeroboam shifted to better hold him upright.

"I meant a real doctor." Rebecca tutted.

"All I need are bandages." His gaze met Theodore's, and his cousin reached for a spool of white gauze.

"You might need more, depending on what happened." Rebecca bent, inspecting him.

"Gunshot, o' course." Jeroboam's grip loosened. "We caught up to the Gang o' Four, and they started shootin'."

Tad winced but not from the pain of his

wound. Rebecca lost her father in a similar fashion, and a quick glance assured Tad her jaw clenched. "That's enough, Jeroboam. It's just a flesh wound."

"Flesh wound or not, you need to get this sewn up. Can you make it to the livery? If not, I can try to attend to you at Theodore's desk in the stockroom."

"The livery." He and Theodore said it in tandem.

Maybe he should be insulted that his cousin didn't want his mercantile turned into a makeshift hospital for his sake, but right now, all Tad wanted was a bed.

"Let's go." Rebecca took the wad of bandages from Theodore and asked for a bucket of other items, including a needle and astringent. "I assume you have soap at the livery."

"We try to stay cleaner than the animals." His attempt at a joke made her fist her hands on her hips.

"Doesn't look like it today. I've seen hogs cleaner than you two." She jutted her chin at the door. "Let's go."

Jeroboam's strides were longer than hers, but the trio managed to hobble to the livery. Jeroboam shook his head. "Never before been so glad Ruby City's small."

Small enough for word to carry. Pa was

already waiting in the wide livery door with Orr and the horses. At least Orr's presence meant Tad didn't have to explain everything. Pa took Rebecca's place and helped him through the door to the house by the livery office, through the kitchen and parlor, to the lone bedchamber in the house.

"Not your bed, Pa. I'll bleed on the quilts."

"Take off his shirt," Rebecca ordered.

Pa didn't obey. "I'm not so sure you should stay for this, Becky."

Tad winced as he unbuttoned the green plaid. "She's done some nursing, Pa."

"On Confederates," Jeroboam muttered.

"I sewed up a Union sergeant after the First Battle of Independence. He didn't complain about the results. But if one of you wants to do the sewing, go ahead."

Pa, who'd stitched his share of lacerations to equine legs, shook his head. Jeroboam gulped. Orr patted the doorjamb. "I'll go tend the horses."

Rebecca turned to Jeroboam. "Fetch water, please. Lots of it. Uncle Giff, I need soap — ah, there's the basin, never mind — but I could benefit from more light. Once Tad gets that shirt off, no one touches anything without clean hands."

"Yes, ma'am," they all said at once.

Where was Theodore? Tad had assumed he'd followed, but knowing him, a customer dropped in. Or he still loathed Tad too much to come.

Rebecca washed up at the basin while Pa helped Tad off with his shirt. When Pa tugged, the shirt stuck, making Tad gasp from the pain. But then the sting and ache was blessedly gone.

Rebecca perched on the side of the bed. "I'm sorry your shirt is ruined."

"Me, too. I kind of liked that one."

"So did I." Maybe it was his imagination, but her cheeks flushed. "Let's get this clean."

Tad's arm was going numb. "All I need is a bandage."

"You need more than that." Rebecca's bloodied hands moved from his side to swipe his arm and chest with a towel. Why was she so bloody? His arm must be numb, if he hadn't felt her ministering to his injuries. "You're right about it being a flesh wound. The bullet grazed your shoulder and should heal just fine, but what's this gash on your chest?"

Jeroboam returned with the bucket. "He fell off Solomon when he got shot, facedown on a rock."

Pa leaned to stuff toweling under Tad.

"Must've been some rock."

"That's enough." Tad's tone came out testy, but lying here bloodied and fussed over was not his idea of a pleasant afternoon. Pa's bedroom was cramped with people, and —

"Yow, that hurt."

"Sorry." Rebecca didn't look it. A tiny smile tugged at her lips. "The area must be cleaned, though."

Pa leaned against the headboard, making the bed jiggle. Tad winced from the motion, but Pa didn't seem to notice. "Tad was in the war, Becky. Did he tell you about it?"

Rebecca glanced up. "He didn't."

Tad grunted. "I don't count monitoring the Oregon Trail as being in the war, Pa."

"But that's just what President Lincoln needed from the men of Idaho Territory — safe communication routes between the east and west." Pa shifted his weight from the bed frame, making it jiggle again. Ouch. "You wore a Union uniform and served your country. You should be proud."

He was honored to have served, but he'd not endured what others had. Rebecca had seen far worse in Missouri and lost her brother Raymond, who'd undoubtedly protected more than a communication route — like companions.

161

He'd mustered out over a year ago, agreed to serve as deputy when Sheriff Adkins asked, and then the whole debacle with Dottie had started. Thinking about it made him tense up.

"Try to relax, Tad. And you fellows, no moving the bed." Rebecca spared glances for Pa and Jeroboam. "But stay close in case I need you to hold Tad down."

"I won't need holding down." But at the first pinch of the needle at his arm, he flinched. "Sorry. I won't move again."

"Give 'im a bullet to bite," Jeroboam offered.

"I've seen enough bullets today, thanks." Tad gritted his teeth.

"And needles, I expect," Rebecca teased under her breath. It didn't hamper her focus, however, and she made quick work of tending his arm and chest. Soon enough, Tad was swathed in soft bandages with his head on the pillow and the quilt tucked up to his neck.

He started to sit up. "I need a shirt."

"Why, pray tell? You aren't leaving this room." Rebecca dunked her bloodstained hands into the basin of clean water. Now that she wasn't sewing anymore, her hands started to shake.

Tad's eyes narrowed, watching those

162

hands. "I've got work to do."

"Not at the livery." Pa winked. "I've got him covered today, Becky."

"Thanks, Uncle Giff." Her tone was sweet and grateful, as if Pa had just bestowed her with a pound of candy, but her hands still tremored. She hid them behind a towel.

"And I'll cover your deputy duties today," Jeroboam said. "Speaking of, I'd best git over to the office and report to Orr."

Pa scooped an armload of soiled towels, and then he and Jeroboam left. Traitors, all of them. "I don't need to rest, you know. I'm fine."

"I'd say rest is exactly what you need."

Tad scooted to the edge of the bed. "It doesn't hurt so much anymore." The sting wasn't nearly as sharp as her glare.

"It will." Then she turned her back and plopped her nursing tools into Theodore's bucket. Her hands didn't seem to be shaking anymore, but he didn't have to be her real husband to notice the pinched set to her lips and the tension in her shoulders.

"I know my riding out must have brought back memories of your father. Stitching me up maybe reminded you of the war, too, since you probably haven't sewn up a gunshot wound since then." He started to stand, but his head got all cottony inside

163

and his vision dulled to gray, so he resumed his spot on the edge of the bed. "I'm sorry to bring all that up for you."

She spun back, her eyes shooting fire. "You think this is about my father? Or the war?"

Uh-oh. "I guess I was wrong, then. You just seem distraught. Is it because the Gang got away?" Had he failed her by not capturing the brigands who robbed her at gunpoint?

"I am not distraught about the Gang." Each syllable came out as sharp and icy as her glare. "You are more of a mule than Madge is, if you can't figure out why I'm upset."

Not her pa. Or the war. His shoulder was aching worse now and his mind was thick. He hadn't a clue what she could be upset about. She had Theodore and a stable future. A roof over her head. His pa wrapped around her little finger, and Tad, her soon-to-be cousin, trying to protect her. "If it's not because I failed you or this stirred up unpleasant memories, then what?"

"Failed?" She clutched the bucket to her chest like a shield. "You didn't fail me. Nor did you stir up old memories. You gave me new ones, awful ones. You rode off and I spent two days watching and worrying, and

when you finally did come back, you'd been shot off your horse. You could be dead right now."

"But I'm not."

Her eyes blazed, as if his protest made things worse. "I'm so angry at you, Thaddeus Percival Fordham. I almost can't bear it. No, there's no *almost* about it. I *can't* bear looking at you anymore, that's how angry I am. I'm going home, and you're going to stay in that bed until morning, and if you don't, I'll tell Uncle Giff to tie you down."

She slammed the bedroom door behind her.

Tad's jaw was still wide open as a fresh-caught trout's when the noise of her plowing out the front door echoed through the thin walls of the living quarters. He'd never been so shocked in his life — and it wasn't because of her display of temper, or even that she was angry at him for getting shot, because that made sense, considering what happened to her father.

She was worried about him. And not only that, but Rebecca Mary Rice remembered his middle name.

He leaned back against the pillow and started to laugh. Ouch. That hurt his chest. Just as well, since he had no business being happy that Rebecca worried about him or recalled his full name.

But he couldn't help smiling, which didn't hurt a lick, while he lay in the narrow bed.

CHAPTER NINE

Despite numerous scrubbings, Tad's blood was still under Rebecca's fingernails the next morning. She'd washed untold times, cleaned dishes, and rubbed bloodstains from the blue dress she wore yesterday when she stitched Tad up. Now that she'd finished breakfast and baking three dozen cookies, she stood at the sink, poking, scraping, and scouring before she dumped out the water, marched upstairs, and took a paring knife to her nails, cutting them to the quick.

There. Now all physical traces of yesterday were gone from her sight.

Too bad she couldn't say the same about the remaining traces that another person couldn't see: the memory of Tad, his shirt soaked in blood, his flesh ragged from the graze of a bullet. The way her stomach clenched all night, thinking of what might have happened if the bullet had been a few inches to the right, or if he'd fallen down a slope. Not to mention, embarrassment over chiding him.

Not that she didn't still feel justified for giving him what for, though. He should learn to think twice about risk and the effect his dangerous job had on people who cared about him, like his father. He wasn't as invincible as he probably thought he was. Knowing Tad, he'd probably disregard her instructions and already be working, busting his stitches.

She should check on those stitches and change the bandage. With a sigh, Rebecca donned her bonnet and scooped up the nursing bag she'd prepared last night, containing needle, thread, scissors, bandages, and balm.

"Mrs. Horner?"

"In the parlor." Mrs. Horner was curled up with a crochet hook and a skein of yellow yarn. "My niece in Nevada is in the family way. I thought I'd send a blanket for the little one."

"How thoughtful. She'll love it." The just-begun project didn't look like a blanket yet, but the yarn seemed fuzzy and soft. Rebecca smiled. "I'm heading to the livery to check Tad's wound —"

A firm rap sounded on the front door.

"Perhaps not yet."

Mrs. Horner offered a wheezy laugh before she fell into another coughing fit, poor thing. She tried to stand, but Rebecca waved her down and strode to the door.

The sight of the lean gentleman on the porch made her stomach swoop. Why would he be here, hat in hand, if he didn't have bad news? "Uncle Giff, is Tad worse?"

His brows shot up to his hairline. "No, Becky, he's fine."

The grip that had clutched her stomach all night loosened. Tad was hale. Whole. *Thank You, Jesus.* She stepped back. "Forgive my rudeness. Please, come in."

"Forgive me for worrying you. Say, is that cinnamon I smell?" Tad's father stepped into the parlor. "Hello, Jolene."

"Giff." Mrs. Horner bolted to her feet, dropping her duckling-yellow yarn and hook in her haste.

Uncle Giff bent to retrieve the bundle. "How's your cough?"

"Much better."

Not exactly. Mrs. Horner did seem better, but that cough still lingered and — oh. She and Uncle Giff grinned sheepishly at each other, their fingers lingering over the exchange of the yarn and hook.

Rebecca would give them a moment to

themselves. "Care for coffee and cookies?"

"I can't say no to good cooking and the company of two fine ladies." He sat beside Mrs. Horner, and Rebecca hurried to the kitchen to fix a plate and pour cups. She could hear their voices from the parlor as Mrs. Horner inquired about Tad. Rebecca couldn't help straining to hear.

"Wilkie stopped by. He says Tad's wound looks good and that Becky did a fine job with the stitches and the bandaging."

Fine praise indeed, from the barber. Rebecca chuckled. Now that she knew Tad fared well, everything felt lighter, from her spirits to her limbs. She filled the cream pitcher and added spoons to the tray.

"Wilkie's good enough at doctoring, when he's not drowning his sorrows." Mrs. Horner sighed. "My heart breaks for him."

"You and I know what that sort of loss feels like, don't we, Jolene?" Uncle Giff's tone was softer than Rebecca had heard it. "It's only been three years since your Herbert passed."

"But we never had any children, not like you. Losing them when they're small like that? And then your wife?" She tutted.

Tad had siblings? Rebecca chewed her lip.

It got quiet in the parlor, and Rebecca had been gone too long already. She carried the tray into the parlor.

"Thanks, dearie," Mrs. Horner said with a sigh. "I wish we could help Wilkie."

"Tad's tried getting him to join us when the preacher comes through every few months, but so far, he's refused." Uncle Giff took a cup of coffee. "In the meantime, I'm glad God brought you to Ruby City, Becky. We sure needed you yesterday."

They needed her? But she'd come to Ruby City for Theodore. No, that wasn't quite right. She'd wanted a family, since she didn't know where Johnny was or if he got her letters. She'd come to Idaho Territory for herself, so God could make *her* whole and full and warm.

Maybe God didn't bring her to Ruby City just for her sake. Maybe she could give something to this community, which was full of folks who'd seen troubles of their own.

Wilkie grieved a wife and baby. That mining family who'd come into the mercantile, the Evanses, knew lack. Ulysses flirted and teased to ease his loneliness. Mrs. Horner and Uncle Giff might be lonesome, too, although the way they were sneaking glances at each other indicated they might not be for much longer. Longbeard Pegg wasn't just lonely; he stayed apart from the others.

Cornelia might not be Rebecca's favorite person in town, but Rebecca couldn't know what ache she hid in her heart. It might not bother her that she wore too-large dresses, but she seemed to no longer wish to be viewed as a child. If Mrs. Horner was right, Cornelia experienced unrequited affection, which was sure to be painful.

Then, of course, there was Theodore and Tad, who'd let Dottie come between them months ago and hadn't spoken much since.

Rebecca couldn't fix a single one of those hurts, but she could be a friend to the members of her new community, remembering that each, like her, held hurts and griefs.

It was a small thing, but she knew just where to start. She stood, drawing Uncle Giff's and Mrs. Horner's surprised gazes. "Excuse me, but I have some errands to run."

She wasn't the least surprised that neither Uncle Giff nor Mrs. Horner seemed mournful at her departure.

Tad winced. Good thing he'd been grazed in the left shoulder, or he wouldn't have been able to work. Not that *this* was really working.

"What do you say, Lady? Lift." He gently pushed the sorrel mule's shoulder blade,

172

watching for the animal to respond by raising her hoof off the ground.

Lady's hoof elevated, an inch, maybe, but it was enough. Tad removed his hand from Lady's bony shoulder. "Good job, following instructions already."

"That's more than I can say for you."

He looked up. Rebecca strode into the livery with a basket on her arm, her mouth twisted. At least she wasn't as angry as she'd been yesterday. "You're supposed to be resting."

"I am." Tad patted Lady's broad neck.

"Doesn't look like it to me."

"This? It's easy. Even you can do it. Come here."

She hesitated, but after a moment, she set the basket on one of the workbenches and joined him. She stood close enough that her flower-soap scent filled his senses, a nice contrast to Lady's smell.

"So, who's this?" She patted Lady's side.

"One of the new mules Pa bought last week. He named her Lady."

"She's pretty, like Madge."

Only Rebecca would find a mule pretty. "She might be stronger, though. A mule kick's a powerful thing. They do it because they're scared, in pain, or remembering pain, and sometimes because they're just ornery, so we need to teach Lady not to kick us, for whatever reason, when we tend to her legs or she gets shoed. This is how we do that. Here, push on her shoulder blade."

Rebecca's hands pulled back from Lady. "I don't want to hurt her."

"It doesn't hurt. Here." He captured her small warm hand and returned it to Lady's back. He manipulated her hand over Lady's shoulder blade. "Feel the sharp bone? Now when we press it, look down and see if her hoof lifts off the ground."

"It did!" Rebecca swiveled to look back at him, grinning.

He removed their hands from Lady's back but didn't let hers go. "Now we do it two more times, so she gets used to the idea."

Once, twice. Lady lifted her hoof each time.

"Good job, Lady." Rebecca's encouraging tone was sweet in Tad's ears. Probably Lady's ears, too. "You're so smart."

A mule — pretty and smart. Tad snickered.

"What's so funny?" She spun in his arms, her shoulder knocking the cut on his chest. He grunted, and she gasped. "Oh, I'm sorry."

"I'm fine."

"You sound like a strangled cat. Sit down."

She pointed to the chair by the workbench where she'd left the basket.

"Wilkie changed my bandage already."

"I heard. Sit."

"Just a minute." If she hadn't come to check his bandages, why was she here? Before he could find out, he had to see to Lady, offering her a treat and then settling her in the paddock. When he returned, he peeked in Rebecca's wicker basket. "What's all this?"

"Willow bark tea for pain. Cookies for my apology."

"Apology?" He plopped onto the chair. "For what, Rebecca Mary?"

She turned red as the flowers on her calico dress. "Yelling at you. Getting angry. I had no right."

He'd been thinking the same phrase about himself. He had *no right* to think about Rebecca the way he did, first thing when he got up and last thing at night. No right to enjoy teaching her how to train Lady, with her close to his chest and his arm wrapped around her. No right to remember what it had been like to kiss her.

"I can handle you yelling at me." What he couldn't handle was the way her smile made his stomach flip.

God, take these feelings away. I beg You.

She unwrapped a dish towel, releasing the mouthwatering scent of cinnamon and sugar. "An offering. I promise I didn't put just enough poison in them that you'd get sick so you couldn't go out and get shot again."

"Never crossed my mind." The cookie melted in his mouth. Rebecca was an amazing cook, smart, pretty, and giving. Did Theodore know how blessed he was?

"You know, after what you just said about mules, I think I'm a lot like them. I lash out when I'm afraid or in pain or remembering pain."

"Or when you're just plain ornery." He snatched another cookie.

"That, too." She stared at her fingernails. "I want you and Theodore to be friends again."

The name was like a splash of cold water to his face. "That wasn't what I was expecting you to say."

"I know you two haven't gotten along since that fiasco with Dottie — yes, I know who she is. But now, I've made things worse between you."

"It's not you." Or Dottie, either. Little surprise Rebecca had heard about her. Ruby City wasn't that big of a town, and memories weren't that short. "I want to mend the

176

rift between Theodore and me, too. Although I have to admit, I really don't want to talk about Theodore right now."

"Why not?"

He reached behind her to pull a bill off the worktable and handed it to her. It was in Theodore's neat hand. Payment due for bandages, needle, thread, and other sundries. "Corny brought it over."

Rebecca grunted and shoved the bill into the basket. "I'll talk to him."

"Don't you dare. I pay my bills." His tone was light.

"That isn't the point." She helped herself to a cookie. "Me being married to you, after what happened with Dottie, has to stick in his craw. I don't want to hurt him like that."

Yet she brought Tad cookies and chatted with him in the barn, a contradiction — unless this was her way of saying good-bye to their relationship, whatever it was. Friends who accidentally married each other.

She was right to put distance between them, for Theodore's sake. And for their own. It did no one any good for Tad to like Rebecca more than as a cousin. "Apology and cookie accepted. See you at the annulment?" He said it with a smile, although the stirrings of panic chewed at his innards.

"I'm certain I'll see you every day, silly.

One of these days I'll remember to return your wedding ring."

The thought of putting it on someone else's finger gnawed at his gut. "No hurry. It's just an opal I dug out of the dirt."

Her brow quirked. "It's more than that, Tad. It's a symbol of your commitment, which doesn't belong with me."

He couldn't argue with her about that, or about her staying longer when she stood and brushed off the back of her skirt. He chose to smile his good-bye. "You're still mad at me about getting shot?"

"A little," she said with a tiny smile. "See you around, Tad. I have more errands to do."

"For Mrs. Horner?"

She shook her head. "You're not the only person in Ruby City who could use a cookie."

CHAPTER TEN

The basket knocked Rebecca's arm as she hastened up the street toward the mercantile. She still had a dozen cookies nestled in another dish towel, just enough to —

Make that eleven. She approached the stooped figure, coming around his side so she wouldn't startle him. He mumbled, so she cleared her throat. "Mr. Pegg?"

He didn't stop, so she quickened her step. "Mr. Pegg? Longbeard?"

There, that name made him turn. She didn't like using it, but it seemed to be the one he answered to, so she smiled. He didn't return the gesture, however. One eye squeezed shut, while the other squinted at her. She dipped her head. "I'm Rebecca Rice. Do you remember me?"

He didn't say anything, but his fingers clenched. No fork today.

"I have something for you." She stepped closer. He stank of perspiration and rot, like his teeth were blackening underneath that beard. Rebecca kept her smile in place and reached into the basket. "A cookie. Oatmeal and cinnamon."

"Why?" He didn't take it.

"We're neighbors. I baked them today, and I'd like you to have one."

Slowly, one dirty, gnarled hand reached out and snatched the cookie.

"Miz Rebecca, is that you?" The voice behind her pulled her gaze around.

"Ulysses? You know Mr. Pegg, don't you?" But Longbeard was already scurrying up the street, clinging to the shadows like a mouse. Sending up a prayer for him, she turned back to Ulysses and dug into her basket. "Would you care for a cookie?"

He propped his hands on his hips, pushed out his lower lip, and gave her a look of mock suspicion. "You don't want something in exchange, do you? Like more gemstones? Not as easy as you think. Ruby City didn't get its name because rubies line the streets. The soil's red, that's all."

"I don't want a ruby. I love my jasper." She held out one oatmeal cookie.

"Oh, then, sure." The snack was gone in an instant, and Ulysses smacked the crumbs from his lips. "You're a fine cook, ma'am. You sure you don't want to marry me?"

180

He was incorrigible. "One of these days some gal might take you seriously."

"Like who? You know anyone?" He looked around in an exaggerated display of pretend eagerness before bursting into laughter.

"I'd best be on my way. Have a good day, Ulysses." She mounted the steps to the mercantile.

"Bake gingersnaps next time," he called after her.

She waved and entered the mercantile. Not a single customer browsed, but at the sound of the bell, Cornelia's head ducked out from behind the gray curtain to the office.

"Mr. Fordham isn't here." Cornelia's voice was surly.

Rebecca would have to wait to give him his cookies, then. Much as she wanted to talk to Theodore, she'd been long awaiting a chance to speak to Cornelia in private. She lifted the basket. "I baked cookies. Care for one?"

"I'm busy." Cornelia disappeared behind the curtain.

Rebecca shut her eyes for the span of a deep breath before marching into the office. The curtain flapped behind her. "What are you doing? I'll help."

"Mr. Fordham entrusted a special shipment to me and me alone."

Spools in three sizes of red, white, and blue ribbons lay on the worktable. "Is this for Independence Day?"

Cornelia's chin lifted, wobbling the braids looped over her ears. "Mr. Fordham provides bunting to decorate the town, but he also sells rosettes. Mrs. Horner, my ma, and I make them, and he pays us half — a penny a piece."

"Is Independence Day a grand affair here?"

Cornelia's scowl melted, replaced by an eager grin. "Just before supper the brass band marches up the street. Mrs. Croft sells supper. When it's dark, there's dancing to fiddle music and then, real fireworks. Mr. Fordham ordered them already. I love the ones that blast into gold flowers and when they fade they sparkle like fireflies. Mr. Fordham told me he'd get those special."

"They sound pretty."

"They are. So's the dancing. Ladies with swirly skirts, twirling around the makeshift dance floor on the street —"

Cornelia's mouth clamped shut, as if she remembered she wasn't supposed to be talking to Rebecca, much less enjoying it.

Rebecca opened the basket and offered a

cookie. "What will you wear for the celebration?"

Cornelia held the treat, gesturing with it at her frock. It was brown calico, and while it wasn't too large, it was crafted for a woman of a different shape, like her mother, perhaps. Cornelia's dainty frame was well disguised. "This, I suppose."

"The color's good with your hair, but sometimes it's nice to have something new for a party. We have time to sew one, if you'd like. I'm not the best seamstress, but I manage. If your ma wouldn't mind, that is."

Cornelia's jaw dropped. "She's always saying we need to take her old things in for me, but we never have time, with me working and her busy with the young'uns."

So Cornelia did indeed wear her mother's castoffs. "How old are you?"

"Almost nineteen."

Definitely past time for her to own her own dress. "What color would you like?"

"I never picked fabric before."

Never? Rebecca had fixed on choosing from the bolts of pretty but serviceable calicos, but those wouldn't do anymore. "What about that bolt of blue striped satin we can't sell?"

Cornelia flinched. "That's too fancy."

"Not for a party. Besides, the blue will look lovely with your hair and complexion, and it's patriotic, too. It'll make quite an impression on the dance floor. I imagine there are plenty of young men who might ask for a reel or seek your company at the supper." Was Mrs. Horner right about Cornelia taking a shine to one?

Cornelia's shoulders slumped. "That won't happen."

"Why not?"

"Well, it might, but I don't care if anybody asks me to dance. The fellow I like best doesn't notice me like that."

So Mrs. Horner was right. Rebecca dusted crumbs from her hands. "He might be shy."

Cornelia shrugged. Rebecca gripped her hand and pulled her toward the mercantile. "Never mind him. Let's go look at that bolt. This dress is for you, not for anyone else. Just you."

"I wish I could. Not mind him, that is." Cornelia watched Rebecca slide the bolt from the shelf and lay it on the counter. The stripes of cobalt and paler blue shimmered.

"Sometimes it's hard to stop our feelings." Rebecca should know. Tad popped into her thoughts more than he should, and not because they still had an annulment on the horizon. But she would not think of him now. Or anymore. She wiped her hands together, even though she'd already brushed off the cookie crumbs. "We have to let God work and trust Him with the outcome."

"I haven't done that." Cornelia's fingers traced one cobalt stripe. "Why are you doing this for me? I'm the one who hid the receipts behind the candy jars."

"I know."

"Then why?"

"Mr. Fordham values you, Cornelia. You're important to him and the mercantile."

"I am?" Cornelia's eyes widened. "He said that?"

"He didn't need to." Rebecca unrolled the bolt. "I know it's not the same at the mercantile since I arrived, but I hope we can be friends. So, should we make you a dress?"

Cornelia's breath was shallow. "How will we pay for it?"

"Didn't Theodore say he was discounting the fabric? I bet we can pitch in together for the satin and notions. What are you thinking for the style?"

"A flounce, and tight wrist cuffs." Cornelia's words came out in a rush, as if she'd been holding back the vision of her dress for ages. "Nipped at the waist."

"Of course."

Rebecca and Cornelia talked cuts and yardage, and after a few minutes, Cornelia stopped and stared just behind Rebecca's ear. "How do you do your hair like that?"

"The curl? I wrap damp strands around my fingers and then pin them, so when they're dry —"

"I mean, half up, half down like that."

"I copied a picture in a magazine. It isn't hard. I'd love to show you how."

"Maybe on the Fourth of July, I could wear my hair like that." After Rebecca's nod, Cornelia mashed her lips together. "I'm sorry I hid the receipts. You deserved better than that."

"Let's start again." Rebecca held out her hand. "I'm Rebecca."

Cornelia laughed and shook it.

Ding-a-ding. Releasing hands, they turned to greet the customer entering the store. Rebecca's hand froze in midair. "Tad?"

He removed his hat, and his mouth turned up in a tentative smile. She'd all but told him good-bye. What was he doing here? She'd known she'd have to see him around town, of course, but it hadn't been an hour since she left him at the livery. Her knees jellied, along with her resolve to distance

186

herself from him.

God, help me stay strong and ignore this ridiculous pull toward him.

"I brought my bill," he said, holding out the paper he'd shown her. At the same time, Theodore pushed aside the curtain from the office with a jaunty, "I'm back." He must have come in through the mercantile's back door.

Rebecca stood between them, her heart galloping in her throat while they all looked at her.

At last she managed to smile. "Cornelia, will you assist Tad with his bill? I'll help you with the ribbons in the back, Theodore."

She turned and joined Theodore, who looked surprised but happy. Good. Now everyone knew. She was the sort of woman who kept her promises.

She's promised to Theodore. Now let her be. But three weeks on, Tad couldn't. Time seemed to have stopped in the mercantile when Rebecca left him with Corny to pay his bill.

Life moved on, of course. Jeroboam Jones lurked at the county offices, offering his services and indicating he'd prefer a career in law enforcement to wood hauling. Longbeard lurked in the shadows, but Tad kept

187

inviting him to church or a meal at Mrs. Croft's — which he refused. Likewise, Wilkie declined to attend church, preferring to hole up in his barbershop with his pain. Mrs. Horner's cough was better, and Ulysses kept asking every woman in town to marry him. Nothing new there.

The Gang of Four wasn't active, though, which was a welcome relief after three months of onslaught. And with Sheriff Adkins's return from patrol, Tad had more time to help at the livery and assist in the new occupation of moving businesses, walls and all, to Silver City on mule-drawn sledges. Already, the street reminded him of a gap-toothed smile, with buildings uprooted and hauled away. A year from now, would anything be left in Ruby City?

Tad ached at the thought, but he ached about plenty of things as June progressed. The calendar page would turn to July later this week, which meant Judge Harris would be back. Tad and Rebecca would get their annulment.

The mistaken marriage would be undone. It was best. Still, Tad's gut clenched whenever he saw Rebecca, in the street or when she poked in to ask how his wound was healing. He wished his feelings for her healed at the same rate as his shoulder. Even now, he couldn't help watching her while he was supposed to be listening to the reading from the Psalms. It wasn't because he couldn't hear, because Orr read, and he had the loudest voice in town.

Worship services were held Sunday mornings behind the livery because it had a flat green spot perfect for the benches and chairs they used for seating. Since the preacher wasn't here often, townsfolk read scripture, shared sermons from books, offered testimonies, and sang hymns. As much as Tad wanted a church in town, he would probably someday look back with great fondness on these services, held in the cathedral of nature.

Although the June morning was already warm, Rebecca wore the blue dress with the undersleeves she wore when they married. While the ensemble appeared heavy and hot, she looked just as pretty as she had the day they swapped I-dos.

Don't go thinking about that again. Tad had to look down, and when the service ended, he jumped in to help return the seats to Mrs. Croft's. His shoulder and chest were fine, if he didn't lift his arm over his head.

Rebecca glared at him, like she wanted to scold him for exerting himself, but she didn't. He wished she would. Anything to be close to her.

Three weeks of cousinly distance hadn't eased the ache in his gut, even though he knew it was best. He'd gone into the mercantile three weeks ago with the excuse of paying that bill Theodore sent to him, but in truth, he'd wanted to see Rebecca again, to make sure this was what she wanted.

She'd made it clear that she did. She chose Theodore. It wasn't like he had another option for her. For one tiny second, he thought of offering her himself, but he was a deputy and had dreams that wouldn't fit into her tidy world.

It was high time he started to live his life, too.

Rather than picnic with the other church-goers, he saddled Solomon and rode up the paths until he reached a crest. He slid off the saddle and hiked onward until he could look down on a view of the flat emerald sea of bunch grass and white sage below.

More than a week ago, he'd volunteered to patrol for the sheriff, requesting to take a detour along the way. He'd followed directions to a parcel of grassland below near a creek, and he'd stood on its sage-scented soil, listening to the black-throated sparrows and praying. And he'd come to a decision.

Pa wouldn't like it. Tad might not succeed,

either. He was taking a risk, and he'd be alone in his venture, but he was ready to set down roots near the community he loved. Tomorrow he would file papers, and then he'd see about purchasing cattle.

He was going out of the livery business and starting a ranch.

CHAPTER ELEVEN

Late on Thursday afternoon, Rebecca hurried to Mrs. Horner's to serve supper, blowing on her fingers. They ached from a productive afternoon of sewing at Cornelia's house. Theodore had given them the fabric for Cornelia's dress, generous man that he was, and for the past three weeks after supper each evening at the boardinghouse, Rebecca had ventured to Cornelia's to measure, cut, and stitch the dress. At last, the dress was almost finished.

Many of those evenings, Theodore was at the Cook family table when she arrived, having enjoyed a supper. Rebecca joined in for dessert, squeezing into the table. Theodore had been correct: Ingrid Cook had a way in the kitchen. She was a short, portly woman with faded red hair and a pleasant smile, and she and her husband, Ebenezer, bantered with such affection it was impossible for Rebecca not to be jealous of their marriage. Their home was chaotic, with seven children, but it was wonderful to be there amid the noise and fun.

It was pleasant to spend time with Theodore on those evenings, too, but Rebecca couldn't help wishing they could spend time alone on occasion, courting. True, he escorted her home on those evenings, and he sat with her at church and worked with her at the mercantile, but his polite, restrained demeanor wasn't precisely that of a courting swain with his sweetheart.

Well, they weren't engaged. For now. But shouldn't he want to know her better?

Rebecca cringed. How ungrateful she was. She was warm and fed. She even had a new friend now, too, in Cornelia, who showed interest in Rebecca's nursing skills, because she was always patching up one of her younger brothers or sisters.

Rebecca hadn't patched anyone up of late, however, nor had she examined Tad's wound again. She sighed, preparing to turn onto the main street of town. Just thinking about Tad made her insides whirl like a cyclone, probably from guilt, because she should not be thinking of him at all. At worship services Sunday, she'd seen how he looked at her, like he missed her. Well, she missed him, too, but they were to be cousins-in-law and no more. Once the annulment happened, her stomach would settle and things would be as they should be. Nice and quiet —

The street was not the least bit quiet. Townsfolk hunkered in groups in the street, including a handful gathered around one of the saloons, peering in the grimy windows. A few townsmen, including Ulysses and Tad, hauled shouting men she didn't recognize into the county offices.

Her heart stopped beating.

Jeroboam burst out of the barbershop, his eyes wide. She marched across the street. "Jeroboam? What's happened?"

"It's Bowe."

Wasn't Bowe banished from town for holding her hostage and striking Tad?

Jeroboam doffed his hat. "There was a brawl. He got hit and his head's bleedin' somethin' awful and he won't wake up. I went for Wilkie, but he's not in a state to do any doctorin'. Not a surprise, seeing as it's his wife's birthday."

Oh dear. "Where is Bowe?"

Jeroboam pointed. Rebecca gulped.

The saloon. Well, there was nothing for it.

She stomped past the gathering of folks into the saloon. The odors of unwashed bodies and liquor hit her at the same time that her vision darkened, adjusting to the dimmer light.

Blinking, she made her way toward the figure on the floor. Jeroboam hadn't exaggerated. Blood matted Bowe's dark hair and pooled around his head. She sank to her haunches, and her fingers crawled around his skull. The wound was jagged and riddled with glass shards, indicating he'd been struck with a bottle, but it could be sewn shut. She glanced up. "I need more light, hot water, and my nursing bag from Mrs. Horner's."

"I'll fetch the bag." Jeroboam dashed out.

The scruffy barkeep appeared at her elbow with a lamp, but crouching like this wouldn't do. "Is there a table long enough to lay him on?"

"The bar," the barkeep said. "But I don't want nobody dyin' on it. Bad for business."

And a brawl wasn't? Rebecca rose and followed the fellows who hoisted Bowe atop the bar. He was too wide, but they'd hold him down if he stirred. "If you have a clean towel to put under his head, that would be a help, Mr. . . . What's your name?"

"Modine, Miss Rice." The barkeep shoved a damp-looking rag under Bowe's head. It would have to do. "Not surprised you don't know me, but ever'one in town knows you and your matrimonial troubles."

Rebecca choked. Thankfully, Jeroboam rushed in, holding out her bag. "Mrs. Horner says she's on her way with linens."

"Good." But her gaze wasn't on him or the bag. Tad followed Jeroboam inside, the badge pinned to his plaid vest winking in the dim. She nodded at him, cool and cousin-like, but her heart pounded against her rib cage.

He moved beside her, smelling of wood and wind. "The Anderson brothers are locked up. Orr's keeping an eye on them since the sheriff's on patrol. How can I help?"

"Would you hold the light? I need to clean the wound."

Before she finished speaking, Jeroboam bit the cork out of a bottle. "Cleaning? Whiskey works."

A sharp smell permeated Rebecca's senses. "Water will do —"

"Hey, you didn't pay for that." Modine yanked on the bottle. In an instant, the contents sloshed out, splashing Rebecca and running down the counter.

Rebecca didn't have time to mop herself, not the way Bowe's blood was flowing onto that soggy towel. While Modine and Jeroboam bickered about the whiskey, she removed her tweezers from the bag. She had to remove glass fragments before she stitched.

When she shifted position to improve her vantage, Tad lifted the lamp and held it so she could easier see. "Is that a piece, there?"

"Good eye, thanks. It isn't easy to spy dark glass in wet brown hair." She plucked it out and then splayed her fingers through Bowe's thick curls, feeling for any more glass shards.

Light spilled over the bar, indicating the door opened again. Mrs. Horner, probably. Rebecca could use those linens to replace the soggy, glass-strewn rag under Bowe's head.

"What are you doing, Rebecca?"

Theodore's sharp voice dragged her gaze up. With the light behind him, Rebecca couldn't make out his expression, but there was no mistaking his horrified tone.

"Bowe's got a gash behind his ear that needs tending." She found her scissors and cut a swatch of hair as close to the scalp as she could. Pity Wilkie wasn't sober enough to shave the area.

Theodore moved to her elbow. "But Rebecca, you know who this is and where you are. Someone else can do this."

Like who? "Wilkie's passed out cold. Tad

197

and Uncle Giff have tended mules, but that's not quite the same as a head wound." Rebecca squinted, threading the needle.

Ulysses tapped her shoulder. "I could try. I got experience stitching soles back on my shoes."

"I think Rebecca can handle it." Tad's gaze was on Theodore, however, not Ulysses.

Theodore took Rebecca's arm, forestalling her from further motion. "You're running your fingers through his hair."

"Searching for glass. Theodore, can we discuss this later?"

His hazel eyes flashed black as jet.

The door swung open again. Mrs. Horner, just in time. Rebecca issued instructions, and Tad lifted Bowe's head while Mrs. Horner swapped out the blood-and-whiskey soaked rag for a clean towel. Rebecca set to work. "Tad, hold the light here, please."

Tad complied. A few seconds later, the door swung again, but this time, Rebecca knew without looking that no one had entered the saloon. Theodore had left it.

It was close to suppertime when Tad stepped out the back door of the county office. He'd left Jeroboam inside, standing guard so Tad could clean up and eat before a long night ahead. The office cot was never comfortable, but the way Bowe Brown and the Anderson brothers carried on, fighting about who was to blame for the brawl, Tad guessed none of them would get much rest tonight.

At least Bowe was awake, locked in one cell while the Anderson brothers occupied the other. It seemed Bowe had accused them all of cheating at cards, and he'd been right. They all claimed to have hit him with their fists, but none would admit to striking him with a whiskey bottle.

A crowd still milled on the street out front, so Tad had chosen to take the back route behind the businesses so he wouldn't have to chat on his way to the livery. All he wanted was supper and a change of clothes.

The back door to the mercantile was left open to the breeze. Theodore hadn't been happy at the saloon, so Tad wouldn't poke in to say hello. He wouldn't even look at the open door. He'd just walk past and hopefully Theodore wouldn't even see him.

A conversation carried out, stopping him short before he reached the door, however.

"It's uncouth, you combing a man's hair with your fingers." Theodore's unmistakable voice was clipped.

Tad should just turn and go back the other way, but his feet wouldn't move. It seemed he lost the good sense God gave him where Rebecca was concerned.

"I was removing shards of glass from his scalp, and I assure you, I did not enjoy touching his bloody, whiskey-soaked hair." Tad could imagine her face: parted lips, eyes wide with surprise at Theodore's comment.

"That's another thing." Theodore's voice rose. "The whiskey. You reek of it. A lady like you, making yourself at home in a saloon —"

"I didn't make myself at home, and if I stink, it's because Jeroboam Jones spilled alcohol on everything. Which bothers you most, that I stepped foot in a saloon, or that I sewed up a fellow like Bowe Brown? Because I don't think the Lord is upset that I tended a man who didn't deserve it. That's what grace is. Who would I be if I don't extend some myself?"

Tad inched back so he could round the bank and take the front way to the livery. Much as he wanted to burst into the storeroom and defend Rebecca, she didn't seem to need it. *Nor is it your place. They're to be married, after all. Couples need to work out their troubles and misunderstandings from time to time.*

What had his mother said about her squabbles with Pa? Better to let some steam out of the kettle than to get burned when things boil over.

Still, Theodore's judgmental attitude stuck in Tad's craw. Rebecca had taken charge and helped Bowe, despite her discomfort with her surroundings. She'd shown fortitude, and he couldn't help but admire it.

"Don't you care about what folks think of you, Rebecca?" Theodore's shout reached Tad's retreating ears, making him stop again. "Your reputation's already questionable, seeing how you're married to my cousin instead of me. Sleeping in his room at the boardinghouse. Now you smell like a saloon after *touching* that — jackanapes. People'll think you're —"

Vision swimming gray, Tad turned on his heel and stomped into the storeroom before whatever vile word on Theodore's tongue spewed out. "Watch your tongue, Theodore."

Theodore spun, his face purpling. "Eavesdropping, Tad? That's low, even for you."

"You heard all that?" Rebecca's hands went to her mouth.

"The door's wide open." And she had nothing to be embarrassed about. Theodore was the one who'd gone too far, starting to insult her like that.

Theodore barked a phony laugh. "You

can't let me alone, can you?"

Rebecca groaned. "This isn't about Tad, Theodore. So Tad, maybe you should leave."

Tad shook his head. "Rebecca's got a reputation, all right, Theodore. As a kind woman who helps folks in need. She did the right thing, and she wasn't the only lady to do so. Even Mrs. Horner came into Modine's and pitched in."

Theodore scowled. "Jolene Horner is a widow woman, not an unmarried gal. Besides, this is none of your business."

"Enough." Rebecca's hands rose in front of her. "We're all tired and agitated, and we should wait to speak until we're all more ourselves."

Herself, as she was, was just fine, but Theodore was too muleheaded to see it. Tad bit back the words, though. She was right. Tempers were high and he'd say something he'd regret.

"I'm going to the livery."

"And I'll go back to Mrs. Horner's and change out of this dress." Rebecca lifted her arm as if to sniff her sleeve.

"Um, you might want to wait on that, Rebecca." Corny's face peeked between the curtain separating the storeroom from the mercantile, her face flush. Clearly, she'd heard everything, too.

The way they'd been talking, Tad had assumed the mercantile was closed. Maybe they had closed it and Corny's appearance was a surprise, because Rebecca paled and Theodore turned a darker shade of violet.

Tad kicked himself for raising his voice earlier, but he seemed to be the only one who had one left, since Rebecca and Theodore said nothing. "Corny, this isn't the best time —"

"I'm sorry, Rebecca." Corny beckoned with her hand, eyes wide. "There's another man out here who says he's got a claim on you."

CHAPTER TWELVE

All the blood that heated Rebecca's cheeks drained to her feet in a rush, leaving her tingly limbed and light-headed. A man in the mercantile, claiming her as his . . . what? "I beg your pardon?"

She'd thought Cornelia was past her tricks. After all the hours sewing, the evenings growing together as friends, now this?

Theodore didn't spare her a glance when he pushed past her to Cornelia. "Who is he?"

"Never seen him before, but I came back for some more thread and he followed me in, saying he's here for *his* Rebecca. That makes three menfolk with some sort of claim on her."

Theodore's jaw clenched. Tad covered his eyes with his hand.

Enough. "No one has a claim on me, and I don't have three menfolk." Rebecca pushed through the curtain.

A lean man held one of Theodore's prized coffee grinders. A hat disguised his hair, but his shoulders were broad and his arms long under an unfamiliar patched brown coat. Who did he think he was, telling Cornelia she was *his*? Her hands fisted on her hips. "Can I help you, sir?"

"I sure hope so." He set down the grinder, turned, and stretched out his arms.

She squealed and ran into them. "Johnny!"

Her brother spun her in circles until she was dizzy. He stank of dirt and sweat, but she didn't care. She stank, too. She kissed his stubble-rough cheeks.

"See?" Cornelia's tone was icy. "She does have three menfolk."

"Four, if you count Ulysses," Tad said. His arm extended to Johnny. "Welcome, Mr. Rice. We've heard plenty about you. I know it means a lot to Rebecca to have you here."

With one arm still around her, Johnny pumped Tad's hand. "I can tell from that smile that you're the happy fellow who married my sister. Nice to meet you, Theodore."

Tad's grin faltered. Rebecca slipped from Johnny's hold and reached for Theodore's stiff arm. "Johnny, this is Theodore. My fiancé."

Corny stepped forward. "I'm Cornelia

Cook, and that's Tad, her husband."

"Long story." Tad actually looked sheepish, but that was preferable to Theodore's glower.

Maybe she should change the subject. "Didn't you get my letter about what happened? But — you couldn't have. I just mailed it a few weeks ago."

Johnny tugged off his hat. His dishwaterblond curls were in need of a good washing. "I don't know about that letter, but I decided to come the minute I received your note about your intention to move to Ruby City. It was time for me to make a change, and truth be told, I missed my sister so I thought I'd drop in for a visit. Or longer. Seems like there was some important information I missed from that second letter, though." He looked from Tad to Theodore.

Rebecca offered a hasty, passionless explanation, hoping to spare everyone's feelings by sticking to the barest of facts. Theodore didn't need any more guilt over not meeting the stagecoach in time, Tad already felt bad enough, and she certainly didn't want to dwell on how taken she'd been by Tad that she married him on sight and still got jittery when she remembered their kiss.

She might be able to undo the mistake of their marriage, but she could never undo

206

that kiss.

Johnny's laugh drew every eye, so thankfully, no one saw her blush. He swiped his tearing eyes. "I've never heard something so unbelievable in all my days."

"Nobody has," Cornelia agreed.

"It'll be over soon enough." Theodore moved behind the counter. After his vehement response to her being in the saloon and stitching up Bowe, Rebecca couldn't help wondering if he referred to her annulment when he said things would be "over soon" or if he meant he was done with her altogether.

It was difficult to diagnose the emotions swirling in her stomach.

"Where are you staying, Johnny?" Tad changed the subject, bless him.

"I don't rightly know. I'd planned to bunk with Rebecca and her husband, but er, I'm not sure about that."

"There's no spare room upstairs, anyway." Theodore didn't look up. What about the small rooms he'd mentioned for children? At her stare, he met her gaze, and then looked down again. "They're full of furniture and wares I haven't sold."

Rebecca's mind whirled. Would Mrs. Horner allow Johnny to sleep on the horsehair sofa? "I'm at Mrs. Horner's boardinghouse until things get straightened out. Maybe she'll have an idea."

"Tell you what." Tad clapped Johnny's shoulder. "If you don't mind sleeping in a barn, there's plenty of room in the hayloft at the livery."

"I've slept worse places."

"Just come on down when you're ready. Now if you'll excuse me, I'd best ask your stagecoach driver if he's heard anything new about the Gang." Tad doffed his hat and exited out the front.

"Thank you kindly." Johnny turned back to Rebecca. "Gang?"

Theodore shook his head. "A group of four robbers troubling the area."

Trouble seemed a mite too mild a word. "They shot Tad and pointed guns at me."

Johnny gaped. "They held you at gunpoint? Aw, sis."

"It was all in that letter you missed. Come on, let's go to the livery and get some supper."

Theodore's brows rose, but she didn't invite him to join them. It wasn't as if Theodore offered her brother any hospitality — not a bed or a basin, or even a cup of water. Besides, it might be best if they both cooled down from their argument.

As they moved toward the door, a slender

figure slipped into the mercantile. The miner's wife, with the two malnourished girls at her side, offered a shy smile. "Oh, you're still open. I'm so glad."

Rebecca hadn't seen her since the day they'd met, when she'd offered the woman credit. Today, twin spots of peach bloomed in her cheeks. Rebecca patted Johnny's arm, her age-old way to tell him to wait a moment. She couldn't leave yet, considering Theodore's feelings toward the miners and credit. "How can I help you, Mrs. Evans?"

"It's Miss. Eloise Evans. These are Pauline and Wilma." She nudged the girls, and they dipped their heads in greeting. "Their pa, Donald, is my brother."

The moment she announced her single state, Johnny doffed his hat and grinned. "I'm Johnny Rice, Rebecca's brother. Nice to meet you."

What was this? Raymond had been the flirt in the family, not Johnny, but it seemed things had changed. Johnny was almost as bad as Ulysses.

"Come to settle your bill, Miss Evans?" Theodore cut to the quick.

"I have." She approached the counter, released the girls' hands, and pulled a nickel from her bag. "I'd also like to purchase additional beans and rice, please."

Cornelia's mouth soured. "No more credit."

Theodore stared at Rebecca. "It's fine, Corny. We're happy to serve Miss Evans."

In that moment, Rebecca's heart softened. He was willing to work with Miss Evans for Rebecca's sake, if not Miss Evans's, but that was a start. Small thing though this might be, Theodore was making an effort to co-operate with Rebecca, maybe even to please her, after their argument.

She was still angry, still hurt, and still hoped he didn't mean those things he said about her combing Bowe's hair. His gesture was a hopeful sign for their future, though.

Miss Evans lifted her purse. "No need for credit. I can pay cash."

"Very well. What sort of beans?" Theodore led her to the foodstuffs. "We just got in a shipment of navy and lima. . . ."

She should offer him a gesture, too. "We'll be at Mrs. Croft's at six, Theodore, if you'd care to join us. Now, Johnny, we really must visit Uncle Giff and get you settled."

"You have an uncle now? Do tell." With a final doff of his dirty hat to the room at large, and a smile for Miss Evans in particular, Johnny escorted Rebecca out the door.

Ulysses slumped on the bench outside the mercantile but rose to full attention at the sight of them. His features wrinkled in an exaggerated display of vexation. "So you won't marry me because you've already got a man too many, but you'll take up with this young feller? Is it my age? You can be honest, now."

"Ulysses, I assure you, your age has naught to do with it. And you should know, I'm keeping this fellow, no matter what anyone says."

"Serious now?" The teasing spark in Ulysses's eyes cooled.

"Of course I am." She ignored Johnny's questioning look.

Ulysses sputtered for words for a minute before pointing at the mercantile. "Now, missy, that's just — do your husbands know about him?"

This was so much fun, being the one to tease Ulysses for a change, that she didn't bother to correct him about her multiple so-called husbands. "They most certainly do. He's my brother Johnny."

Ulysses blinked. Then he gripped Johnny's right hand and pumped it so hard Rebecca feared her brother's shoulder would pop from its socket. "Welcome to Ruby City, sir."

She leaned into Johnny. "Ulysses Scruggs was one of my first friends."

"How do you do, Mr. Scruggs." Johnny's smile combined confusion and amusement.

"Mr. Scruggs was my pa. Call me Ulysses." Then he eyed Rebecca. "You've still got the smell of the saloon about you, if you don't mind me saying so."

"Not at all." She waved farewell and led Johnny away.

"You were in the saloon?"

"Yep. My dress is soaked in whiskey, too. I stink."

Johnny eyed her as if she'd grown wings. "You sure have changed, Rebecca."

"Of course I have." She'd been on her own since he left when she was sixteen and Raymond enlisted. They hadn't seen one another in six long years.

Then she caught sight of Tad in front of the Idaho Hotel, talking to Mr. Kaplan beside the stagecoach. For better or for worse, coming to Ruby City had changed her beyond the differences that came from six years of life.

Not that she wanted to dwell on why that was, because if she did, she spent far more time thinking about Tad than Theodore, to her shame.

What gal wouldn't be changed by marrying the wrong cousin?

CHAPTER THIRTEEN

Tad shook Kaplan's gloved hand. "I'll let you be on your way then, Kap, so you can get to Silver City by dusk. Glad to hear you haven't had any trouble lately."

"I'm takin' precautions, but the Gang's activity seems to have lessened up since you got shot, sorry though I am that it happened." Kaplan climbed back to his perch atop the stagecoach. "Are you healing up?"

"Good as new." Tad rotated his shoulder to demonstrate.

"I heard you had a pretty nurse." Kaplan cackled at his own joke. "I still can't believe she wasn't your missus. Craziest thing I ever heard told."

"You and everybody else, Kap." Tad patted the side of the empty stagecoach. "Godspeed to you."

Kaplan saluted. "Take care, Deputy."

Tad backed away from the cloud of dust kicked up by the stage, but before he could make his way back to the livery, his name was called from the hotel porch.

"Deputy, I've got troubles here." The hook-nosed hotel owner's hands fisted on his hips. "One of my guests said he'd pay me in gold, but even I know pyrite when I see it. He fled like a coward when I insisted on real coin."

Tad followed him into the hotel. "Let me get a description from you."

Tad left the hotel ten minutes later with notes directing him to look for a man of medium height with brown hair, a scruffy beard, and brown clothes. He sounded like half the residents of Owyhee County, but Tad made inquiries at a few establishments, anyway.

At the bank, he overheard a beef broker announcing his intent to sell half a herd of cattle. Tad pulled him aside. He'd just filed a claim on the valley land today. Was it possible he could fill it with stock soon, too?

The livery was his last stop. Pa was alone in the stable office, tallying figures. He looked up and grinned. "Howdy, Son. I just met your brother-in-law."

Tad let the reference roll off his back like water from his Boss hat. After everything with Theodore today, Tad couldn't muster the wherewithal to either protest or join in the laugh. "You don't mind if Johnny stays, do you?"

"He's kin." Pa tucked the pencil behind his ear. "Becky said she fixed up Bowe Brown in the saloon. What's he doing back?"

"Making trouble. I'm afraid I can't just escort him out of town this time."

"Theodore causing trouble, too? Oh, don't give me that look. Becky didn't come out and say Theodore was upset, but I've known that boy for twenty-six years. I love him, but any excuse he can find to get mad at you, he'll take."

Tad leaned against the desk. "I want to make things better between us, but it keeps getting worse."

"It doesn't help that you don't think he and Becky would suit."

Tad didn't deny it. "It's not my place to say so, Pa."

"You're right. Your place is rubbing down the mules that got rented out today." He chuckled and retrieved the pencil from his ear.

"Soon." Tad related the story of his hunt for the man who skipped out on his hotel bill. "I should tell you, I'll be having supper with a hotel guest, that beef broker. Know him?"

"Comes through every so often, yeah. Why?"

"Because he knows someone looking to sell off half their herd of cattle. And I want to buy it."

"We aren't in the business of cows, Son. Ponies and mules, yes, because we're bound to expand in Silver City."

"I won't be moving to Silver City." He took a deep breath and looked at his father, willing him to meet his gaze. "I want to ranch."

Pa looked up then, smiling an indulgent smile. "In Ruby City? There'd be grass in summer, but the winters are too cold."

"That's why I'll settle in one of the creek valleys below for winter."

Pa's smile fell. "That's ridiculous."

"I'm looking ahead, toward the future, when the mines have no more to give."

"We aren't miners."

"But we depend on them and we live like they do, never settling anywhere. We could run a livery in any town, somewhere with some permanence, but we don't. We pack up and follow the gold or silver. I don't want to start over anymore."

"But that's exactly what you're doing, starting something foolhardy miles away from the only family you've got left."

True, they'd only had each other — and Theodore — these past few years since Theodore's pa, Uncle Stanley, died. Before that, they'd clung to one another after the losses of Tad's and Theodore's mothers. Tad had been too young to remember much of his baby sisters dying from the measles, but since he was small, it was just him and Pa. They'd never been apart.

But Tad wouldn't be far from Pa, and despite the fact that he was starting something new, it would hopefully be the last job change he made. That was one of the reasons he sought a wife and proposed to Rebekah Rhys. He wanted a home, a haven. A family of his own. And she'd wanted those things, too.

Just not with him, as it turned out.

"I filed a claim this morning. I was thinking of building a cabin near the creek up here, so I can keep an eye on the herd while it grazes up here in the summer. But I've got plans for a homestead down on the claim. This is something I've wanted to do for a long time. Setting down roots and living in a real home with bedrooms and a river rock hearth and a garden. You could come with me. Put down the pencil and let's talk."

"I don't want to talk, unless you're going

to tell me you're not serious. Ranching." Pa spat the word like he had a stray piece of straw in his mouth. "You need to clear your head. Go on after that Gang of Four and reconsider your priorities."

Pa pushed back his chair, yanked open the office door, and disappeared into the barn. Tad stood there a minute. He respected his father, loved him, but right now, he was bound to say something he'd regret if he followed him. He wanted his pa's blessing but wouldn't get it here. Not today.

Tad rubbed his face with both hands. What a day. The saloon brawl, then Theodore's tantrum, then Pa . . . the only bright spot in the day was watching Rebecca use her nursing skills. Well, that and meeting Johnny. His presence had made Rebecca glow, like a candle burned behind her eyes.

"Uncle Giff?" Rebecca's cheery voice called from the livery door. She kept speaking, but it was hard to make out anything beyond, "This is Madge. Isn't she pretty?"

He ambled out to meet Rebecca. Johnny's face shone, and his hair was damp from the bathhouse. Rebecca had changed into that blue dress of hers, the one that matched her eyes, and twin spots of color brightened her cheeks. "I'm introducing Johnny to Madge."

"She's a mule, sis."

"She's a dear. And that over there is Lady. I helped teach her to lift her foot."

"Did you, now?" Johnny quirked a brow at Tad.

Pa reappeared from the stalls, refusing to look at Tad. "Welcome back, you two."

"Thanks for letting me bunk in the loft." Johnny set down his travel bag. "I'd like to earn my keep, so let me know what needs doing. I'm pretty handy."

"Speaking of earning one's keep, I'd told Mrs. Horner I'd be back soon to clear up supper dishes. You both will join us for supper at Mrs. Croft's, won't you? I invited Theodore, too."

Her glance at Tad was apologetic. He understood why she included Theodore — she was marrying the fellow, after all — but he didn't much cotton to spending an evening with Theodore.

"My treat," Johnny announced.

Pa rubbed his stomach. "I've been hungry for some of her pot roast."

Pot roast that would cost a lot less if the cattle was local. Tad shoved away the acerbic remark on his tongue. He was tired, true, but what man didn't crave his pa's support and blessing instead of his disapproval?

"Tad's too busy." Pa waved his hand in dismissal, as if telling Tad to go.

Rebecca sent Tad a querying look, but Tad shook his head.

The livery door scraped open, and Tad turned to help the customer, but it was Orr, his lips compressed in a contrite smile.

"How-do, folks. Got some news you all might be interested in. Judge Harris fell from his horse outside of Silver City this morning and broke his leg."

Rebecca winced. "How painful. Poor man."

Tad strode closer. Judge Harris had headed home earlier than expected.

"The doc told him to lay flat for a spell before he rushed up the mountain to tend some fellers down with a rash and stomach troubles." Orr's gaze flitted between Tad and Rebecca, and his shaggy brows rose knowingly. "I think it'll be a while before Judge Harris returns to Ruby City, if you ken my meaning."

Pa rubbed the back of his neck. "No business at the courthouse for a while yet. Bowe Brown and his sparring partners will have to sit in jail a while longer."

Tad couldn't keep his gaze from Rebecca. "That, and no annulment."

She blushed bright as a berry.

Theodore would be apoplectic. But what did Rebecca think? Despite everything that happened today, Tad felt . . . happy.

More time. For what, he wasn't sure. But he felt as if he'd been pardoned from a heavy sentence.

Rebecca looked at the straw at her feet. "Maybe we should go to him."

"What?" Tad couldn't have heard her mutter correctly.

She lifted her head but couldn't quite reach his gaze. "To get the annulment. If he can't come here, maybe we should go to Silver City."

"A courtroom in the sickroom," Johnny joked, but Pa didn't even laugh. Then Johnny's brows furrowed.

Tad didn't move. Didn't even want to breathe. It seemed like nobody wanted anything he wanted. He'd fought Pa over the cattle, Theodore over Rebecca, and he was tired of fighting.

"Fine." The word burst out before Tad could pinch it back. Everyone looked at him, surprise on their faces. But why should they be shocked? Hadn't this annulment been planned for nigh on a month now? "Let's leave in the morning and take the wagon in case the judge wants to return home with us. Invite Theodore to come."

"Are — are you sure?" Rebecca's eyes were bright.

He nodded. "Now if you'll all excuse me, I'd like to inquire about buying some cattle. Have a good supper."

"Cattle?" Rebecca's question followed him out the door.

CHAPTER FOURTEEN

After supper, Rebecca stood outside the restaurant and kissed Johnny's fresh-shaven cheek. "I'll see you in the morning. Be good to Uncle Giff, now."

"He won't hear a peep out of me after I hit the hay — literally, because I'm bunking in the loft."

Uncle Giff nodded at Theodore. "You'll see her home safely?"

"Yes, sir." Theodore offered his arm to Rebecca. "To the boardinghouse?"

She took it and they walked in silence. Rebecca's mind journeyed from Johnny sleeping in the hayloft to Uncle Giff's little house behind the livery, apparently too small for Tad, too. He'd have a rough night sleeping on the cot, if the prisoners were difficult. His deputy duties kept him plenty busy. Now he'd have to lose a day of work to take her to Silver City for the annulment —

"I don't blame you for not wanting to talk to me."

Rebecca blinked. How silly she'd been to let her mind wander when she was alone with Theodore. "There's a lot on my mind, I suppose." She halted her steps. "I didn't like arguing with you, Theodore."

"Me, neither." He turned and faced her but looked everywhere but her face. "It's just hard sometimes, our situation."

She licked her lips. "I couldn't let Bowe bleed out, Theodore, no matter what he's done or where he was. And if Mr. Wilkie is the only other person in town who knows how to bind a wound, what else can I do? I'm sorry it embarrassed you, though."

"Seeing you in the saloon shocked me, I won't lie. But I shouldn't have shamed you like that, and I accept why you did it. Healing folks is part of you, even if it's still a little difficult for me. I didn't know that about you."

It was part of her, wasn't it? She hadn't hesitated today. "There's an awful lot about a person that can't fit into a stack of letters, isn't there?"

He chuckled. "I'm amazed I filled up a stack of letters to you. My life is boring as mush."

"Hardly."

They looked into each other's eyes for a half minute. Would he kiss her? He hadn't so much as taken her hand, because she was married to Tad — oh, now that she'd thought of him, it was difficult to stop. He was the only person she'd ever kissed, and her lips tingled just remembering it.

But Tad had no business here, between her and Theodore — who still didn't bend his head to kiss her.

Instead, he pivoted away from her and offered his arm again.

Maybe he was thinking of Tad, too, or at least her temporary marriage. Or maybe her breath smelled like her trout supper.

She kept her head down, just in case. "Thank you for being willing to help Miss Evans earlier."

"I did it for you."

"I know." Even though it would have been nice if he'd done it to be compassionate to a hungry family instead. "Johnny seemed to like her."

"I'll get to work cleaning out a room for him. He should be with family, especially once we're married."

"Thank you." She owed Theodore so much. He'd provided for her, as he promised in his letters. More than she could ever repay.

There was no good night kiss on Mrs. Horner's porch. "Good night, Theodore."

"Sleep well, Rebecca." Theodore doffed his hat and left before she was in the door.

She went upstairs with the realization that she and Theodore hadn't discussed the visit to Judge Harris tomorrow.

Sleep eluded her, and eventually, the cold fingers of a gray dawn touched her room. She rose, dressed in a clean white shirtwaist and her red calico skirt, and pinned her hair into a tidy knot. She gathered a calico bonnet, her paisley shawl, and checked her appearance in the mirror on the dresser. Two little glimmers sparkled in the lamplight: Ulysses's jasper and Tad's opal ring.

She had yet to return it to him, but if ever there was a day to do it, this was it. Her holey skirt pockets were fine places to carry handkerchiefs but not valuables, and it didn't seem appropriate to let it roll around in her beaded bag. The safest place for it was on her finger, so she slipped it on for the first time in a month and headed downstairs.

If anyone noticed the opal ring during breakfast, no one said a word. She'd told Mrs. Horner about the judge's accident last night. "We should be home by supper, I expect."

"Safe travels, dearie. I . . . hope everything goes just as it should today."

A quick, easy annulment. Rebecca nodded. "Thank you, ma'am."

Mrs. Horner's eyes creased when she said good-bye, a look Johnny also bore when she walked into the livery. He hitched Madge to the wagon, along with another mule named Sheila. The wagon was already stocked with blankets for the judge's journey home. Had Johnny done that, or had Tad?

"Are you earning your keep?" She cast him a teasing look and then greeted the mules. She wasn't as well acquainted with Sheila as she was with Madge, but both mules nuzzled her arms with their broad noses.

"I sure am, and I appreciate the opportunity. I don't cotton to mining anymore, so Gifford offered me a temporary job until Tad and the sheriff find that Gang of Four."

The thought of Tad pursuing the Gang made her breakfast roil in her stomach. But enough of that. She had a safe life ahead of her, and now Johnny was here, too. Things looked bright.

Johnny ambled to her side. "Gifford and Tad are out and about, so it's just you and me here, sis. I've got to tell you, you don't look happy."

"I didn't sleep well, is all." She rolled her eyes.

"Neither did I. That hayloft isn't as comfortable as Gifford claims, but that's not what I meant. Why are you doing this?"

"The annulment has been the plan since the moment Tad and I realized our mistake. He had a commitment, and I had mine."

"I mean the marrying part. Why did you come out here to marry a fellow, sight unseen?"

So many reasons, all twisted together. "Survival."

Johnny's brow furrowed. "You were fine in Missouri."

"No I wasn't." Her hand slipped from Madge's gray coat. "You were gone; Raymond was gone; Ma and Pa were long, long gone; and I was lonely and hungry and aching to be part of a family again, to have someone care about me and who I could care about. Where I'd be loved again."

He gaped, wordless. Then he blinked. "You're right."

Remorse flooded to her fingertips, not for what she'd said but how she'd said it. "I shouldn't have been so blunt. I didn't mean to hurt you."

"I didn't mean to hurt you when I left, either, but I did." He kicked the straw underfoot with his toe. "I was seventeen and figured you'd be just fine with Raymond to watch over you. He didn't have much choice but to leave you when the war came, I suppose, but I should've come back. You were only sixteen."

"If you had come back in '61, you would've enlisted and fought, too." She reached for his hand. "Nothing would have changed."

"Rebecca —"

"Don't feel badly, Johnny. Hurting your feelings was not my intention when I told you."

"I know, and I understand why you came here now. But I'm not sure why you're going through with it. You and Theodore don't seem happy."

Johnny might be her brother, but in many ways, he didn't know her anymore. "You mean well, but this life Theodore offered me, that I accepted, is the life I always wanted. I will marry Theodore and that's final."

"Here you go: my testimony that the marital mix-up was entirely accidental, unintentional, and immediately regretted." Orr stood from his spot at his desk and handed Tad a folded sheet of paper. "For good measure, I added that I'll be certain of the bride and groom's full names before I officiate any more weddings."

"Wise." Tad shoved the letter into his coat pocket without looking at it. "Although you'd think the bride and groom would've taken care of introducing themselves just fine."

Orr thumped Tad's arm. "It'll be over soon."

That's what Tad kept telling himself, and someday he'd look back on this crazy month and get a good laugh at the ridiculousness of it all. Today, though, it didn't feel right, like a bone had broken and wasn't setting the way it should. It would heal but it would never be the same again.

Tad tapped his desk, where Jeroboam Jones made himself comfortable, crossing one ankle over the opposite knee. "Thanks for keeping an eye on things. The sheriff's supposed to be back today, but I'll rest easier knowing there's someone keeping an eye on our *guests.*"

The bickering of Bowe Brown and the Andersons carried into the office from the jail cells.

"No problem, Deputy." Jeroboam's chest puffed out. "Happy to help while you take care of business with the missus."

It was a joke, but he couldn't rouse a smidgen of humor when he left the office. Yesterday, when Rebecca asked if they could go to Silver City and get the judge, he'd succumbed to the anger he'd been doing his best to control. He'd fought against Theodore, hating his disapproval of Rebecca nursing Bowe. Then he'd fought with Pa about the ranch. The lack of his father's blessing aggrieved him to the bone, but he'd fought against the pain and anger.

When Rebecca asked if they could go to Silver City today for the annulment, though, the ability to control his anger snuffed out. He couldn't fight it anymore.

He had no business being angry. This annulment had been planned since the moment Rebecca learned he was a deputy. Tad knew where things stood. He didn't want to hurt Theodore or Rebecca. And yet — he didn't want to do this today. He'd rather sit in the county office, processing a pile of paperwork and drinking stale coffee while listening to Bowe and the Andersons argue.

It didn't even help that he'd started to settle his ranching plans. After speaking to the broker and inquiring with a few fellows who were familiar with the stock, he'd withdrawn his savings from Bilson at the bank and purchased the available herd.

231

Tad turned into the livery, where Johnny checked the wagon hitch. Rebecca, bright in her white blouse and red skirt, had arrived, ready for her annulment. Theodore stood at her side. Tad's teeth clenched, even though Theodore's presence was expected. If Tad were in his cousin's fancy catalog-bought shoes, he'd want to ensure the annulment went as planned, too.

Theodore fed Madge a chunk of something from his hand, revealing a glimpse of the boy who'd been raised in the livery business. It was easy to miss that fellow most days, hidden as he was beneath the fancy clothes and shopkeeper's apron, but at that moment, Tad missed his cousin and the way things used to be, when they'd been like brothers.

From now on, he'd do his best to recall *that* Theodore when he was tempted to lose patience. Still, Theodore's dandified tie and coat lacked something for the journey. "You might want to wear a hat to Silver City. Looks to be a warm one today."

Theodore brushed off his hands, and flakes of orange fell to the livery floor. Ah, Madge and Sheila had enjoyed carrots, then. "I'm expecting the fireworks and a shipment of crystal today. Corny won't be able to handle them herself, so I'll be staying here."

Whoever delivered the shipment could leave it in the storeroom, couldn't they? Tad had just seen the old Theodore, but he was gone again, replaced by this stiff stranger who was more concerned with his mercantile than anyone or anything. Maybe Tad was wrong, but it sure seemed Theodore didn't want to close the mercantile and miss out on the opportunity to make money, even for something this important.

Then again, that was what appealed to Rebecca, wasn't it? Theodore's ability to provide for her?

Johnny took Rebecca's elbow. "Should I go along to Silver City with you two?"

Tad peeked at her, but her eyes were on her brother. "Not on your first day of work. It's only a mile. We'll be back soon."

"Is it proper?" Johnny's loud whisper almost echoed in the livery.

Tad almost answered that he was legally her husband, a very proper escort, but Rebecca laughed. "I imagine we'll cross other travelers along the way, and the judge will be with us on the way back."

"Travel safely, then." Theodore waved and was gone before Johnny helped Rebecca onto the wagon seat.

Tad climbed aboard and doffed his hat to

Johnny, who waved despite his furrowed brow. With a few words to the mules, they set off to put an official end to their blunder of a marriage.

Lord, help me to keep my mouth shut and get to Silver City.

Because once he opened his mouth, he'd burn a bridge between him and Theodore that could never be rebuilt.

CHAPTER FIFTEEN

The mile-long ride to Silver City wouldn't take long, but Rebecca couldn't sit still on the hard wagon seat. She fidgeted with the torn cuticle of her thumb, loosened her bonnet strings, and then shifted position. Riding off to seek an annulment so she could marry her husband's cousin would undoubtedly prove to be the most awkward event of her life, and Tad wasn't making the experience any easier. He bent forward, elbows on his knees while his hands held the reins, in a posture that communicated he didn't want to talk.

Well, she wanted to, to show they could still be friendly cousins. "Pretty day, isn't it?"

"Mm-hm."

"The clouds are like cotton batting. I'm glad it's not like my first day in town, when it rained buckets. Remember that?"

He looked at her then. "I don't think I'll

ever forget it."

That rainy day was their wedding day. *Fine thing to talk about on the way to dissolve our marriage — which isn't a marriage, so quit feeling so guilty about it.* She chewed her lip. *Think of something else to say, quick.*

"So what did your father mean last night about the cattle?"

"I purchased some."

"Cows, for the livery?"

"Nope." He urged the mules to the right. "I'm starting a new venture. I filed a claim in a creek valley some miles distant and I'm going to start a ranch."

Shock pried her mouth open. Leave his father and a successful business for a risk that might leave him with nothing? Then again, it was none of her affair. He was to be her cousin.

Tad glanced at her, at long last. "Are you going to tell me I'm a fool, like Pa?"

She found her tongue. "Not if this is what you want."

"I'm tired of moving. I like Ruby City, and I can have land both places, and tending cattle seems the best way to settle somewhere permanent." He looked away. "So when's the wedding?"

"We haven't discussed it." She swiped her damp palms on her red skirt. How long did

236

an annulment take, anyway? She'd assumed she and Tad could show up in court, plead their case to the judge, allow him a good laugh at their expense, and be done with it.

That may have been naive of her. This could take months, but maybe that was a good thing. Now, she and Theodore would have time to plan a real wedding like she'd always secretly dreamed about, surrounded by friends and family.

Although she hadn't minded the lack of friends or family at her wedding to Tad —

She swatted away the dangerous thought like Madge's tail batting a horsefly. "Can Johnny remain with you and Uncle Giff awhile longer? I hate to ask, because I don't want my brother to be a burden on you."

"Johnny's practically kin. He's no burden, and he shouldn't be considered one to Theodore, either."

His swipe at Theodore's lack of hospitality stung. "Theodore and I talked last night. Once we're w—wed, Johnny will stay with us."

The rugged road — what there was of one — pitched downward. The mules skittered down a rocky incline and the wagon slid forward. Tad yanked on the reins with his left hand while his right arm flung out in front of Rebecca, bracing her on the seat.

When the wagon stilled, he looked down at where his forearm hovered over her. He snatched his arm back. "Sorry."

"You kept me from tumbling from the wagon, silly. Thank you."

Instead of answering, he jerked the brake and hopped down from the wagon. He bent to check the animals' legs, backsides, and ears. He sure was thorough. He did everything but examine the mules' teeth.

"Are they hurt?" If not, they needed to move along.

"Doesn't look like it." He climbed beside her on the seat and released the brake, making that "let's go" click of his tongue for the mules. "Come on, gals."

Sheila lifted her feet, but Madge refused to twitch so much as an ear. Tad clicked his tongue again, Sheila moved forward, but Madge didn't budge.

Rebecca's eyes narrowed. "What is it?"

"I don't know. Madge is being stubborn."

A tiny smile tugged at her lips. "She is a mule, after all."

Tad snickered, a good sign that they might still be friends after their annulment — and their tense words moments ago. She might have complicated feelings where he was concerned, but the truth was, she didn't want to lose Tad altogether.

The thought of it made her queasy.

He reset the break, descended again, and crossed to Madge's side. "You don't often live up to the reputation of your kind, but today you're as muleheaded as they come."

Rebecca sat back against the tiny wagon seat. "Why'd we bring mules instead of horses, if they can be unreasonable?"

"They're more sure-footed on climbs. They can see where their hind feet are going. If they see something questionable or dangerous, they won't step into it. Unlike people."

Was he referring to her? Or maybe she was battling her own will and heard every word as condemnation. But marrying Theodore wasn't questionable or dangerous. It was safe and smart.

Still, her ankles wobbled when she slid from the wagon and inched to Madge's side. "Come on, Madgie. The ground is flatter up here, see?" She ambled up to where the road straightened out and beckoned with her hands.

"She's not a dog, Rebecca. She won't come if you call her like that."

"She might. She's smart, aren't you, Madgie?" *Come on, Madge. We've got places to be.* "We'll buy some nice oats in Silver City for you."

"Rebecca, that's pointless."

Her patience snapped. "What's pointless is you petting her instead of urging her in this direction."

He threw up his hands. "Fine. I'll stop soothing my animal so we can get your precious annulment." He clambered back into the seat and released the brake.

Sheila tugged, but Madge stood still. So did Rebecca, who was rooted, hands on hips, in the middle of the so-called road. "Precious? What's that supposed to mean?"

"Nothing."

Her eyes narrowed. "Why'd you use a barbed word like that? This annulment isn't precious. It's necessary, and you're hardly urging the mules on —"

"I'm trying." Tad puffed out an exasperated breath. "I don't know why you — never mind."

"Why I what?" *Look at me, Tad.*

He didn't. His gaze stayed fixed ahead.

Her hands fisted. "Say it."

He didn't, so she threw her hands in the air. "I know you're angry you're missing work for this when it's my fault for not speaking up when I heard Mr. Orr call you *Tad* and I thought he said *Ted.*"

"Missing work is the least of my worries, and this isn't your fault. I called you *Reese,*

240

and when you said *Rice,* I thought R-h-y-s must be pronounced different and I didn't say a word, either. Our wedding was an accident."

"And Theodore's the one paying the highest price for it."

"He said that?" Tad's entire manner changed. He yanked on the brake — as if Madge was going anywhere — and hurried down to her.

He hadn't been this close to her since their wedding, and his proximity brought her back to that day. Just as she had during their wedding, she could now see the green flecks in his eyes and the dew of sweat at his temples. Her gaze fell to his lips. Her hand lifted, as if moving on its own volition to land over his heart, just an inch or so lower than his deputy badge —

Her hand jerked back and covered her mouth. What had they been talking about? Oh, yes, Theodore. "He didn't say anything, but how could this not be hard on him? Especially after what happened with Dottie," she said from behind her hand.

"But Dottie isn't your fault. Neither is our mistaken marriage. He shouldn't make you feel guilty for something beyond your control."

"He's not. I just do." She forced her gaze

241

away before she did something stupid again, like almost touch his chest.

"You care about him and his feelings."

"Of course I do."

"But you don't love him."

Her head jerked up. "What?"

"You don't love Theodore." Each word was clear as the crystal Theodore sold in the store, and just as costly.

She swallowed. Hard. "Love is an action. A choice."

"You can choose to put him first and work for his good, sure, and that's love, but you know what kind of love I mean. That pull like a magnet's inside him and you're drawn to him and you can't think about anything but being with him."

She couldn't lie. "No, not yet."

"You never will. It's been a month, and he hasn't even courted you properly. No walks or suppers or evenings in Mrs. Horner's parlor —"

"How would you know that?"

"Everyone knows."

How humiliating, that all of Ruby City noted Theodore's lack of attention. Her chin lifted. "He's had no need to court me. I already said yes."

"Has he even kissed you?"

"He's too honorable a gentleman to do

that when I'm officially married to you, not that it's any of your business."

His brows rose, as if he would kiss her if he planned on marrying her. Heat coursed up her neck, and thankfully, he looked away. "Marrying him is a mistake. You don't love each other."

She might love Theodore someday. She'd pray for it, and she had decades to try to make it happen.

Except *that* sort of love, the magnetic pull Tad described, didn't come from years of effort. And oh — How dare Tad stand there and judge her, anyway?

"Did you love Rebekah Rhys?" Her arrow hit its mark, and his face hardened. "For a man who answered an advertisement for a bride, you seem to have forgotten how this works. Marriages are founded on compatibility and respect, not kisses —"

"You aren't compatible with Theodore. And I'm not so sure you respect each other the way you want to." His eyes were softer than his tone. "The way he treated you when you stitched up Bowe's head?"

Tad's observation pierced the part of her that was already tender from Theodore's actions, but Theodore was to be her husband. They'd started to mend their rift, and she needed to make sure she didn't harm it further. "Theodore's protective after what Bowe did at the restaurant, that's all. Bowe did hold me captive for a spell."

"But you helped him anyway. It was brave and selfless and beautiful."

Theodore had called it uncouth, and his judgment had made her feel unseemly, like her hands were dirty from more than Bowe's sticky blood and the alcohol Jeroboam poured over the wound.

"Theodore's disapproval doesn't mean I should break my commitment to him."

"Your desire to stay true to your commitment is something I admire, but you aren't married to him yet."

No, she was married to Tad, but that wouldn't last more than the afternoon, if Madge ever picked up her feet. "Love like you're talking about is a luxury I can't afford. So is taking a risk like you are, starting a ranch, when you could have more stability with your pa."

A muscle worked in his jaw. "We aren't talking about me. This is about you."

"You don't understand what it's like to be hungry and alone. I spent the last six years afraid. Pa died; Johnny went to California; our other brother Raymond enlisted and died; and I had no one and no means."

"I can't imagine."

Rebecca shut her eyes, because looking at Tad weakened her resolve. "After emancipation, I was hired as a maid in Independence. Little pay, but room and board. I thought working for a woman would be safe, but it wasn't."

"You said the house served as a hospital for a spell. The war must've been close."

"There were two battles in Independence, but I don't mean the war. She — my employer, Mrs. MacGruder — rationed my food, saying it was on account of the shortages, but I shopped for us, so I knew better. She withheld food from me to toy with me, or punish me. I was so hungry, and I slept on the floor in the wet attic."

"That's barbaric."

"When her son visited, he'd corner me in the pantry or in the courtyard where I did laundry. His mother never saw, and he didn't touch me, until one time." She opened her eyes. "I slapped him. Hard."

Tad's eyes were no longer soft. Fury turned them almost black. "Did he stop after that?"

"Yes, but he made my life even more miserable, lying about me to his mother. She denied me meals and insisted my work was so shoddy I needed to stay up all night scrubbing things. I fell asleep making her bed once, and she had her son whip me. I'm sure you're wondering why I didn't leave."

His jaw clenched. "You had nowhere else to go."

"And I was afraid Johnny wouldn't be able to find me again, a foolish hope, because I knew he'd never come home. But then the lower floor of the house was commandeered for a hospital, and Mrs. MacGruder had no choice but to let me nurse. I fainted the first day, and the doctors fed me from their rations, so I was eating better than I had in months. Considering how food shortages affected us in the South, that says something." She laughed a little.

"You were abused and mistreated, Rebecca."

"But I still shouldn't have — Tad, before the army came, after I was whipped, I stole Mrs. MacGruder's food."

"You were entitled to square meals, Rebecca."

Her head shook violently. "I snuck in the pantry and I ate a whole loaf of bread and a tin of peaches, and I lied the next morning and told her the bread had gone moldy and the peaches had been eaten the week before. I was so filled with shame, I vowed I would never again be in a position where I would be tempted to steal and lie like that."

Tad's arms folded. "So marrying Theodore will protect you from stealing again?"

"From being hungry. From resorting to — that."

"I can't imagine what you went through. But only God's strength will keep you from stumbling. Theodore can't do that for you."

The admonition nipped at her conscience. She'd thought herself above certain sins, but the truth was, she was capable of anything. "Theodore is God's provision, a way out, and a future. I can't expect you to understand. You're a man, so you can ride off or stay put. You have family."

"So do you, now. You have a home here." His hand rested on hers.

"With Theodore." She spoke through gritted teeth.

"With all of us. Mrs. Horner. Pa. Johnny. Me." His gaze fixed on her lips. "There was something between us on our wedding day, Rebecca. We were both promised to other people —"

"I still am." She would not discuss any attraction she may hold for him. And if he felt it for her, too — no, she couldn't even think of it. "I chose Theodore, on our wedding day and three weeks ago when I left you in the mercantile, and again yesterday when I asked for this annulment."

"Don't choose him today, Rebecca."

He was looking at her with such tenderness that the marrow melted inside her bones. He cared for her — it was in his eyes and in everything he'd done for her good since her arrival. But that magnetism he spoke of — that she felt for him — would someday dissolve like candy floss. It was pretty and sweet, but it never lasted. It wasn't enough to base a marriage on.

The foundation she chose was commitment, a solid home, something she would never have if she allowed herself to love a lawman. She could never live worrying about her husband every day he was on duty.

And yet — she was so, so tempted to fall in love with Tad. It would be easy.

"I have to marry Theodore." The words squeezed out, past her near-to-bursting heart clogging her throat.

Ka-whack. Rebecca jumped as the report of a rifle reverberated off the mountains. Tad gripped her shoulders and pushed her under the wagon.

Would there be another shot? Who'd done it? A hunter, or, oh mercy, it could be the Gang of Four again. Rebecca curled her knees into her chest.

At that moment, Madge decided to move. The wagon lurched with Rebecca still underneath.

CHAPTER SIXTEEN

Her heart thundering in her ears, Rebecca cried out in alarm.

"The wagon's braked," Tad hollered. "Stay put."

She scrambled to her hands and knees anyway. "Where are you going?"

"To make sure it's safe for us to get out of here." His footsteps disappeared from her view as he dashed up the ragged road around the curve.

If it was the Gang, he'd be outnumbered. Rebecca crawled out from the wagon and chased after him. A ridiculous thing to do, considering she couldn't protect him if she tried.

I can't do anything, Lord, except cause trouble wherever I go.

She ran around the hilly curve, almost colliding with Tad where he'd come to a stop. She skidded on the gravel. "What's happened?"

He didn't need to answer, because she saw it then. A woman slumped on the side of the road, writing in the dirt. Blood darkened the back of her pale green dress.

Rebecca rushed to her side. It didn't take a skilled nurse to determine the woman had been shot in the back, clear through, but the wound was high enough that nothing vital should have been affected. "Can you speak?"

"It hurts," the woman wailed.

"I know. I'm sorry." Rebecca tugged off her shawl, wadded it, and shoved it against the wound to staunch the flow.

"Ow!" The woman curled up, her face obscured by a curtain of near-black hair.

"Who did this to you?" Tad's words were for the woman, but his gaze scanned the area, searching for threats.

"They took my horse."

"Was it four men?" Tad eyed the road now. Nothing else had been left behind, except an upended brocade valise that didn't appear to have been touched. That wasn't like the Gang of Four to leave luggage unopened, but then again, they'd never shot anyone until one fired on Tad.

"Yes." The answer came out through gritted teeth.

So it wasn't some rogue assailant. Rebecca's pulse skittered at the knowledge that the men who'd robbed her and shot Tad were so close.

Tad's fingers alighted on Rebecca's shoulder. "What can I do?"

She shook off the fear that nipped at her neck. "Get the wagon."

He hurried back the way they'd come. *God, You told Balaam's donkey what to do. Urge Madge to move, please.*

In the meantime, Rebecca checked the woman for other injuries. She'd finished examining the lady's slender torso and legs — an inspection best conducted before Tad's return, for modesty's sake — and was about to check her arms when the familiar sound of wheels on gravel carried from around the bend. *Thank You, Lord.*

"Madge must've listened to you." Tad pulled the brake and leapt from the wagon.

Madge tossed her head, as if in acknowledgment, but Sheila just blinked.

Tad crouched to his haunches. "I'm sorry, ma'am, but I can't think of a way to get you into the wagon without hurting you, so I'll be quick."

She grunted her assent, and his arms slid under her. She screamed, arching her back and twisting toward them. Her hair slid away from her face. She was young and

252

exceedingly pretty, with a pert nose, full lips, and lush lashes. She was also in terrible pain. That was probably why Tad didn't lift her.

"Go ahead, Tad," Rebecca encouraged. He didn't want to hurt the woman, but he had to in order to help her. "Smooth and steady."

He didn't seem to hear her. His lips were parted and his eyes were wide.

"What is it?" Rebecca bent over him. "Is it your shoulder? It must hurt you to lift her."

"Dottie?" The name came out in a strangled whisper. "Is it really you?"

After all this time, Dottie was back. How Tad had missed her when she left ten months ago, wondered where she'd gone, prayed for her.

It hadn't taken long to recognize she'd never been the woman he cared for, though, and he'd healed. He wouldn't have sought to marry Rebekah Rhys if he hadn't. Then he'd met Rebecca, and his world turned inside out and upside down.

Or so he'd thought, because now he didn't know what was going on inside him, except that his throat felt like he was strangling from the inside.

253

"Howdy, Tad." Her bloodless lips cracked a strained attempt at a smile.

The red of Rebecca's skirt brushed his leg as she squatted beside him. "You mean, your — Dottie?"

"Yes." And she was bleeding in his arms while he gaped like a fool. He hoisted her from the ground and carried her to the wagon. Good thing they'd brought blankets so the judge's ride home would be more comfortable. Nevertheless, Dottie cried out when he gently lowered her to the wagon bed.

She'd been shot and left for dead on the road. No matter what had happened between them in the past, the idea that someone had done this to her made his stomach revolt.

Rebecca hauled the valise and shoved it over the side of the wagon, where it landed beside Dottie. "I presume this is yours."

"Yes, ma'am." Dottie winced as the wagon bed jiggled but looked up at Tad. "Is this your wife?"

If she only knew. "This is Rebecca."

"And I'm going to take care of you." If Rebecca was bothered by Dottie's identity as the woman he and Theodore had fought over, she hid it well behind a mask of efficiency as she settled Dottie into a more comfortable position. "The Silver City doctor is up at the mines, so we'll return to Ruby City, but your wound needs compression now. The wagon bed can do that from below you, but can you press down on the front?"

Dottie nodded, but Tad touched Rebecca's shoulder. "You do it while I drive."

"Go find Sheriff Adkins in Silver City." She tried to smile. "I can manage Madge and Sheila. It's not the first time I've handled a wagon. Maybe the second time, but it'll be fine. Go on."

He should. It was his duty as deputy to pursue justice, and the Gang had literally been in this spot mere minutes ago. Unfortunately, he was alone and without transport, so Rebecca was right. He needed men and mounts, and Silver City was closer than home.

Yet he hesitated. "I'm sorry, Rebecca." About leaving her, facing the Gang again, having Dottie thrust on her. But not about challenging her.

"Be safe, Tad." She clambered into the wagon, her eyes soft. Then she released the brake and flicked the reins. "Come on, Madge, Sheila."

Madge obeyed before Sheila did — this time. The wagon lurched as it made the awkward turn around, and while Rebecca looked uncomfortable with the reins, she proved capable.

He couldn't watch them go farther. He started his footrace to Silver City, his thoughts a jumble, his prayers more groans than words.

One thing was for certain. After today, nothing would be the same again for anyone he cared about.

CHAPTER SEVENTEEN

Murmuring prayers for Tad, Dottie, and the mules' feet to move a little quicker, Rebecca drove as fast as she dared back to Ruby City. The street was blessedly empty, so she was able to navigate straight to the barbershop, pulling the wagon to a jerky but thorough stop. "Mr. Wilkie!"

"What's the hollerin' about? Where's the deputy?" Ulysses jogged to the side of the wagon and assisted her down. Then he peered in the wagon bed. "Why, you ain't the judge."

Dottie groaned.

Rebecca flung open the barbershop door. Wilkie stood over a barbering chair, a straight razor in one hand and Jeroboam's lathered chin in the other. At least he was sober. "Wait on the bench if you want a trim."

"I don't want a — I need your help."

He took the razor to Jeroboam's face. "I

ain't a doctor."

"Neither am I, but the two of us are the only people in town with a measure of experience with a needle, and Dottie Smalls has been shot clean through."

She expected him to argue, but with brisk clarity, he dropped the razor and grabbed a leather bag. "Dottie Smalls, you say?"

"Tad and I found her on the road to Silver City." She followed Mr. Wilkie outside.

"On the way to your dee-vorce?" Jeroboam stood and toweled shaving cream from his half-shaved face.

"It's not a div— Jeroboam, help Mr. Wilkie carry Dottie inside, please."

Wilkie eyed her. "First we ought to know where we're taking her."

"Not here?"

"I sleep on a cot behind the shop. I don't have room for patients."

Where did they take injured folks before she arrived? And why was everyone looking at her as if she held all the answers? She squared her shoulders. "The Idaho Hotel."

"Full up." Ulysses inclined his head down the street. "I say the livery. Dottie can lie down in a clean stall, until you figure out what to do with her."

At least Uncle Giff would be a help and support. Rebecca nodded.

Jeroboam leapt into the wagon and drove it the short distance to the livery. Uncle Giff stood outside with the animals in the paddock, as did Johnny, with Cornelia's father, Eb Cook, on the other side of the fencing. "Becky? What're you doing back? Where's Tad?"

"He ran on to Silver City to fetch the sheriff and a posse." She pointed to the back of the wagon. "We found Dottie Smalls in the road. She's been shot by the Gang of Four. We have nowhere else to take her, Uncle Giff."

"Say no more. Take her to my room." He led the way while Johnny lifted Dottie from the wagon.

Rebecca followed into the livery, through a door by the office into a small but tidy kitchen, past a parlor with two chairs and a short sofa, into the small bedchamber where she'd stitched up Tad three weeks ago. Johnny set Dottie on the bed, and Wilkie began to cut away the back of Dottie's dress. Rebecca tugged the bloodstained fabric away and he probed the wound, front and back, with Dottie moaning on her side. "Yep, bullet went clean through."

He always seemed surprised when Rebecca was correct. She dunked a washrag in the basin and squeezed out the water with too much force.

Suddenly, Uncle Giff's room was crowded with men: Eb Cook, Jeroboam, and Ulysses. Eb thumped Rebecca's shoulder. "I'll tell Orr. He'll want to grab a few men to meet up with the deputy."

Jeroboam lifted a finger. "I'll go, too. I'll make sure the deputy don't get shot again, ma'am."

"Who'll watch the jail if you and Mr. Orr are both on posse?" Rebecca looked up from washing the wound.

"I will," Ulysses volunteered. "How hard can it be, takin' a nap and makin' sure nobody escapes? They're locked in. Say, there's a free supper for me, when Mrs. Croft brings food to the felons, isn't there? I sure hope it's a meat loaf sandwich."

Johnny patted her back as he passed to the door. "I'll go, too."

"No." The word ripped from Rebecca's throat. He knew what it was like when Pa —

"Don't worry. I'll be careful." Johnny kissed her forehead and dashed off, leaving her with a bloody rag in one hand while the other reached for him.

"Before I make myself comfortable at the jail, I'll tell Theodore the news," Ulysses said, raising his eyebrows. "This might not go over well, Dottie Smalls bein' here and you returnin' without the judge, and all."

Theodore was the least of Rebecca's worries right now. Johnny, Tad — facing those armed villains . . . the thought made her skin go cold and her stomach go sour.

"Everybody out, now," Wilkie ordered, but someone else pushed inside. Cornelia panted from exertion, her hand on the too-large neck of her cast-off pink gingham dress.

"I saw you at Wilkie's from the window, and somebody said it's Dottie and she'd been shot." She waited for Rebecca's nod, and her eyes went round. "What can I do to help?"

"Do you faint at blood?" Mr. Wilkie's brow rose.

"Where do you think that chicken dinner my mother fed you last Sunday came from?" Cornelia's arms folded. "If you don't need help, just say so, but Rebecca's taught me a few things, and I'm offering my hands to you."

Mr. Wilkie shrugged. "Suit yourself."

Smiling, Rebecca handed her the washrag. Cornelia was not the same person she was a month ago when Rebecca arrived. Offering to help, putting others first, why, she'd grown up, indeed. "You can cleanse the area so I can help Mr. Wilkie. Gently, now."

Cornelia nodded and set to work.

"It hurts," Dottie wailed.

"It should," Mr. Wilkie agreed. "We'll fix you up, though."

They'd give it a good try, at least. Rebecca had never sewed an artery or vein. Had Mr. Wilkie?

While he washed his hands, she began unpacking his bag — bottles, bandages, and a complement of instruments. It appeared that he had a full medical kit, but the tools meant nothing if Mr. Wilkie didn't know how to use them properly. This town needed a real doctor. Maybe she should have driven the wagon to Silver City, instead, in hopes that the doctor was back from the mines, but she'd have been afraid to take that chance. At least here, she had Mr. Wilkie, if he was as competent as folks said he was.

"Hurry," Dottie begged.

Mr. Wilkie offered a bottle to Rebecca. "Ever use chloroform?"

"I've seen it, but no, I never used it personally."

He formed a cone out of a square of cotton. "Hold it over her mouth and nose, like this, and add a drop when I say so, but don't breathe it, you hear?"

"I have no desire to swoon on you, Mr. Wilkie."

He smirked. "Then let's begin. Go ahead. One drop."

Rebecca took a deep breath, held it, and willed her hands not to shake when she removed the stopper. Gently, she tipped the bottle over the cotton cone.

Had it worked? Rebecca let out her breath, and then Dottie's eyes fluttered closed. Mr. Wilkie nodded. "Miss Rice, stand ready with the sponge. Gifford, you out there?"

Uncle Giff popped his head back in the door. "Right here."

"I need you and Corny to get lamps and stand here and here" — he indicated. Before they returned, he set to work on Dottie's back. Rebecca watched his work and dropped the chloroform into the cotton cone at regular intervals, while Uncle Giff and Corny held still, keeping the lamps steady. In their illumination, she could watch his precise motions, his nimble hands, his tidy stitches.

Rebecca glanced up at him. "You've handled gunshot wounds before. The war?"

He tied off a stitch. "Hundreds of boys in a field hospital in Virginia. Not what I'd expected when I went into medical school, of course."

Medical school? "If you're a doctor, why do you keep telling folks you're not?"

"I'm a barber, but I can't ignore folks who need a tooth pulled now and again, can I?"

"You ignored Mrs. Horner's cough," she said before she could stop herself.

"I kept an eye out, even if she never knew it." He looked up to wink at her. "Don't let Dottie wake up, now."

"Of course." She added another drop of the chloroform.

They all fell silent while Mr. Wilkie — *Doctor* Wilkie — worked. Rebecca used the time between drops of chloroform to pray for Dottie, Johnny, and for Tad, too — oh, that their last conversation hadn't been an argument. *Lord, keep them safe. Guide them, so this ordeal would end.*

She couldn't lose her brother out on a posse. Nor could she bear losing Tad, even if she was supposed to marry Theodore.

Her hands fisted, and the opal ring bit into her palm like a bite.

She flinched. She'd forgotten she was still wearing Tad's ring.

The other members of the posse kept watch while Tad dismounted and splayed his fingers beside the horseshoe tracks. Most of the men the sheriff recruited from Silver City were strangers to him, but his friends from Ruby City like Orr and Jeroboam had

264

met them at the spot of the accident and joined the search, making their numbers a full dozen men ready to bring the Gang of Four to justice.

He hadn't been happy to see Johnny and his eager grin, though. The fellow had a good seat and sharp eye, but Rebecca must be beside herself with her brother out on a posse like the one that claimed their pa.

God help her, and help me find what we need.

They'd followed the Gang's tracks off the road from the site of Dottie's shooting, but the Gang had gotten smart and ridden through brush, hiding most of their tracks. Tad had managed to find enough to follow, however, leading them on a crazy, twisted path.

One of the Silver City men shifted in his saddle. "You sure he's the best tracker you got?"

"He's the best in Owyhee County, unless you're making that claim." Sheriff Adkins, a man of middle years with a sun-weathered face and a black mustache, dismounted and crouched beside Tad.

"I am not a gifted tracker, and you know it." Tad kept his voice down.

"You're better than him, or he wouldn't still be on his horse." The sheriff gestured with his thumb. "Single file riders always got something to hide."

"That's what I'm thinking, too. The tracks are fresh, and it's impossible to guess their number, although one shoe is broken, and then there are these prints, drifting off to the side now and again." Tad gestured at a stray track of a horseshoe. "It could be Dottie's horse, tethered on a lead."

"That's why you're my deputy." Sheriff Adkins clapped Tad's shoulder and rose. "Fellas, I'm confident we're on their heels."

Someone cheered, but Tad wouldn't rejoice until the Gang was behind bars in the Ruby City jail. Tad mounted the horse he'd borrowed from the Silver City livery, a fine gelding, but not as responsive as Solomon.

Jeroboam rode up beside him. "You think they've got a hideout in an abandoned mine?"

Tad nodded. "It'd be a good, quiet spot where most folks wouldn't look."

"They're in for a surprise when we catch up to them." One of the Silver City fellows trotted ahead of Tad, almost obscuring the Gang's tracks. "Armed robbery, shootin' an officer of the law, and now horse thievin' and attempted murder of an innocent gal? Plenty of folks wouldn't hesitate to shoot first, ask questions later."

"That won't be us." Tad lifted his voice. "We'll bring them in for trial so they can account for all of the hurts they've caused."

Rebecca's face loomed in the forefront of his thoughts. She deserved justice for what the Gang had done to her. Taking her things. Trying to touch her. Tad's molars ground together. If she hadn't had that paper knife handy —

"Get a gander at that cloud." Johnny's voice made Tad twist in the saddle.

It was a dark beast of a thing, threatening a storm. If it came this way, they might have to turn back. He kept his gaze on the tracks, harder to make out now that the soil turned rockier. While he focused, his brain turned over the day's events. Finding Dottie was a shock, but the greater jolt to his system came when he stood close enough to kiss Rebecca, wanting to, seeing in her eyes that she wasn't indifferent to him in the least.

And then she'd gone and chosen Theodore.

Not that she'd had a reason not to. To her the only other alternative to marrying his cousin was starvation and banishment from Ruby City. Didn't she understand how many people cared for her?

Tad certainly did, although his feelings were complicated by an attraction that wouldn't go anywhere. There were too many problems between them, aside from Theodore. She didn't want a man like him, for one. Not only was he a deputy, but he was also taking a risk and starting a ranch, and Rebecca wasn't much on anything that wasn't guaranteed. Like Theodore.

Johnny trotted up alongside, careful not to ride ahead of Tad. His sheriff father had taught him well. "I've been thinking, Deputy."

About Rebecca and what she must be enduring right now with them out on a posse? Or was he concerned with his sister's honor? Tad had married her less than an hour after seeing her face, after all. It seemed like the sort of thing a brother might take umbrage with.

He was ready. "It's Tad."

Johnny nodded. "She had baggage with her, right?"

Tad blinked before he realized this wasn't about Rebecca at all. "Dottie? Yes, a valise."

"What was she doing out here by herself on a horse? A gal with luggage like that should've taken the stage."

Or caught a ride on a cargo wagon. "I've been thinking about that, too."

"Another thing doesn't make sense." Johnny's tone drew Tad's gaze around. "Why'd the Gang shoot Dottie in the back? You think they wanted the horse that badly?"

"Seems we're thinking the same thoughts today." Shooting a woman in the back while she fled was extreme, even for the Gang. Something wasn't right here.

The hairs on his arms rose. Then thunder rolled across the sky, east to west, reverberating through his bones. Beneath him, the blood gelding shifted, uncomfortable.

"Storm's comin' this way," Jeroboam hollered. Surely even the Gang could hear him.

The first drops pelted his Stetson Boss in soft pats, but then the skies parted and a torrent of rain doused the land and turned the earth to muck.

"Time to turn back," Sheriff Adkins urged.

Tad waved them off. His eye fixed on one of the broken horseshoe tracks in the dirt. They were so close —

"Come on, Deputy." Jeroboam trotted up, splattering mud. "Them womenfolk o' yours will be worrying even more about you now that we've got ourselves a gully washer."

"I don't have womenfolk," Tad protested. Not Rebecca and certainly not Dottie. What he did have was a heap of trouble. Tad didn't look up from the broken horseshoe print. It filled with water and then disappeared as a rivulet of rainwater washed it away.

Reluctantly, Tad turned the horse around. It was time to go home, empty-handed, empty-hearted.

Chapter Eighteen

After a long afternoon watching a sleeping Dottie, Rebecca returned to the boarding-house to change clothes and to return Tad's opal ring to the dresser, where it winked at her alongside Ulysses's jasper. She scooped up spools of patriotic ribbon, needle and thread, so she could work on rosettes for Theodore to sell on Independence Day, packing them alongside a few toiletries in the wrapping paper she'd saved from her first night in Ruby City, when Theodore gave her the hairbrush and tooth powder to replace what had been stolen from her.

Mrs. Horner waited at the foot of the stairs. "I'll be along after supper to spend the night with you. Don't protest, dearie. It's not proper for you to sleep at a man's house, no matter that he's your father-in-law and he'll be bunking in the hayloft."

"That's ridiculous. I'm tending a patient."

"People will judge and talk, though. They

always do." Mrs. Horner glanced at Rebecca's tiny bundle. "Can I bring anything else for you?"

Rebecca's shoulders slumped in fatigue. "Just pray for the posse. The last time Tad went out, he got himself shot."

"First of all, Tad didn't get himself shot. The Gang did that. Second, seeking justice is his job, and he did what he had to do. Third, he's healed. Why are you so angry with him?"

"I'm not." But she was upset, and there was no use denying it. "I'm worried, is all. My pa was a sheriff. It's not a safe life, and there's nothing more important than safety."

"Isn't there?" Mrs. Horner led Rebecca to the door. "Well, if bein' safe is what you want, you did right choosing Theodore."

Rebecca's jaw dropped. "There's nothing wrong with security."

"O' course not, and you owe people like Tad your gratitude for keeping you that way."

As if her own pa hadn't given his life for the cause of justice? The hair on Rebecca's nape rose like hackles. "I am thankful. I know what sorts of sacrifices folks like him make."

Mrs. Horner's eyes were frustratingly kind. "But you're forgetting that there's feel-

272

ing protected behind a bolted door, and then there's the peace that doesn't depend on locks or the law. It comes from love and trust." She patted Rebecca's shoulder. "See you in a few hours."

Rebecca probably looked like Longbeard, mumbling to herself all the way to the livery, but she was too angry to care. She understood the difference between security and peace. It was none of Mrs. Horner's business what she valued or whether or not she loved Theodore. It wasn't Tad's concern either, though he questioned her today and sent her thoughts jumbling and her pulse out of rhythm.

She'd chosen Theodore before she met him. Obstacle after obstacle prevented them from marrying, but soon those would be gone and she'd have the life she needed.

After a brief word with Uncle Giff, she returned to his bedroom, where he'd moved one of the comfortable parlor chairs in for Mrs. Horner. Rebecca resumed her place in the hard-back chair at the still-sleeping Dottie's side, determined to recover from Mrs. Horner's words before her landlady arrived to keep her company. She prayed and took up a length of ribbon to stitch one of Theodore's rosettes.

She had finished two when a shadow fell

over the bed. Mrs. Horner had come much earlier than she'd said. Rebecca looked up, but it was Theodore who lingered in the threshold.

His hands stuffed into his pockets, making him look younger and more vulnerable than she'd ever seen him. Had he looked more like that when Dottie broke his heart?

Rebecca rose and offered him the chair. "Come in."

"It really is her." Theodore lowered himself into the chair, staring at Dottie without revealing any of the emotions that must be churning beneath. "How is she?"

"She should recover well. Wilkie said — did you know he's a certified medical doctor?" When Theodore didn't respond, Rebecca gestured at Dottie's bandaged hands and wrists. "Well, aside from the gunshot wound, she has some scrapes. Cornelia did a fine job tending them."

"It was kind of Corny to help." Theodore's gaze still didn't leave Dottie. What did he think about? Did his heart still leap in his chest at the sight of her pretty face?

Rebecca turned away to tidy the bandages spread on Uncle Giff's bureau, giving herself time to think. Theodore and Tad had both loved Dottie. Maybe they both still did. What if Theodore didn't want to marry

Rebecca anymore, now that Dottie was back?

A booming crack made her jump. Another gunshot? No, it was just thunder, rolling long and loud. The first *pat-pitters* of rain-drops hit the roof. The posse was still out in this weather. Maybe they were close enough to Silver City or one of the other mining towns to take shelter. She shouldn't expect any word on Johnny or Tad for a while, but she prayed for them while Theodore kept his silent vigil at Dottie's side.

Theodore sat back in his chair, adding the creak of wood to the noise of the rain. "Why do you suppose the Gang shot her?"

In the back, of all places. She must have made those cowards angry. Rebecca could relate to that. "Maybe she refused to give them her horse and tried to outrun them. Maybe Tad's right, and they're getting bolder and meaner. Whatever the reason, now they've shot two people."

"Attempted murder is a serious charge."

Theodore's words sent shivers down her arms. Sometimes when she thought of her encounter with the Gang, she wanted to find them again and kick them in the shins. Other times, she wanted to hide, like she did now. She shivered and pulled her thick gray shawl tighter around her shoulders.

"You're worried, aren't you?" Theodore's eyes glimmered in the dim of the lamplight. "Not about Dottie, but the posse."

"People I care about, including my brother, are out there, and I'm trying not to worry, but it's hard to trust they'll be well when my pa wasn't."

"How insensitive of me. I wasn't thinking." Theodore rubbed his brow. "I've been a brute, Rebecca, and I'm sorry about that."

"It's not been an easy few days for any of us."

"True, and things may get stranger, now that Dottie's back. Try not to worry about Johnny, though. The sheriff and others from Silver City will outnumber the Gang, and Tad knows what he's doing. He won't do anything that would put Johnny in danger. You can trust him."

It was the first time she'd heard Theodore compliment Tad. "It sounds trite, but trusting anyone, including God, isn't easy for me tonight. I'm making the choice, minute by minute, to depend on God to take care of our men."

"You can trust me to be honest with you. I'm not perfect, Rebecca, but I wouldn't lie to you, even to comfort you."

Nodding, Rebecca stepped closer. Theodore rose from the chair, and for a moment, she thought he might hug her. Instead, he extended his arm to the chair back, offering her the seat.

"You're spending the night here?"

"Mrs. Horner will keep me company, and Cornelia will spell us in the morning. I hope you don't mind her helping here instead of at the mercantile."

"Of course not." The ghost of a smile played about Theodore's lips. "She's a giving person, isn't she? I never noticed until recently how hard she works at the store and at home, with all of those siblings."

"She's a gem."

"Guess what?" Theodore crossed to the doorway. "The fireworks didn't come today, after all, but I sold several pieces of the crystal in the front window."

"Really?"

"At last, eh? Less for you to dust."

She smiled. This was the closest they'd ever come to bantering. "You'll order more."

"I suppose I will."

"I don't know what a miner wants with crystal, anyway."

"Neither do I, but if they buy, I'll order more. Miners can be spontaneous when they've struck it rich. Which reminds me, I was thinking, if the county seat moves to Silver City like folks are saying, more min-

277

ers will go, so the mercantile should move, too."

Disappointment pinched Rebecca's stomach. She'd only been in Ruby City a month, and she'd come to view it as home.

A home was the people, more than the place, though, wasn't it? She swallowed down her doubts, lest Theodore think she was unsupportive. "You know business far better than I do, Theodore."

"The shops in Silver City can withstand the competition. The Cooks are eager to make the move, Wilkie said he'd probably go, and Uncle Gifford wants to move the livery so he and Tad will have more business."

Rebecca probably shouldn't share Tad's news, but Theodore would be her husband. He should hear things from her first, shouldn't he? "Actually, Tad isn't going to Silver City. I'm not sure how he'll serve as deputy, but he's going to try his hand at ranching."

"Really?" Theodore looked confused then happy at the prospect of Tad being out of their lives. He continued to talk about Silver City until Mrs. Horner arrived. Theodore took his leave, Mrs. Horner settled into the padded chair, and Rebecca shifted against the hardback one. Once both ladies curled in thick quilts, Rebecca dimmed the lamp.

She let her eyes shut and listened to the rain, praying for the posse and for Dottie, too. And Theodore, of course, last but not least.

Their conversation had been pleasant. A step in the right direction, even if it didn't plunge to the depths of vulnerability she'd felt when they first discussed her father's death.

Not once, however, had they mentioned the fact that the annulment hadn't happened today, and when Theodore mentioned moving to Silver City, he'd only talked about the mercantile. Not the people involved, not them as a pair.

Rebecca's eyes opened again and didn't shut for a long while.

It was probably near dawn, but the night was still dark and wet when Tad lit a lone lamp, illuminating the livery in a pale glow. He hung his soggy coat and hat on hooks, and then dried, fed, and stabled his borrowed mount. Johnny did the same with his horse before he climbed the ladder into the hayloft.

"Oh, your pa's up here." His whisper from above was a mite too loud.

But if Pa slept in the livery, Dottie must

be in the house. Tad would go inside and check, but first he wanted to get Johnny settled. "You won't get much rest up there once dawn breaks and Pa opens shop. Want to bunk on a bedroll on the parlor floor?"

"Nah, thanks." Johnny's voice carried down from the loft. "I could sleep standing up."

They would have slept under the stars if not for this storm, so each member of the posse had headed for their respective homes. Nothing sounded better than a change of clothes and a soft mattress, and even the narrow, lumpy cot at the jail sounded appealing.

"Good night, then." Once Johnny was out of sight, Tad doused the lamp and slipped into the house. A faint glow emanated from Pa's bedchamber. Tad's wet boots made sucking sounds as he crossed the wood floor.

Dottie lay on her side, her dark hair splayed over Pa's pillow. A lumpy figure with light brown hair curled into the padded chair — Mrs. Horner? That left Rebecca in the hard-back chair, wrapped in a quilt, sleeping upright, propping her head on her fist.

He wouldn't wake them. He took a step backward. *Squelch.* Rebecca's eyes flung open, as if she hadn't been fully asleep. Seeing him, she sighed in obvious relief. "You're back."

"All of us." He tipped his head in the direction of the livery. "Johnny's in the hayloft."

"So's your pa." She smiled. "Did you find the Gang?"

He shook his head and dropped to the floor. "The rain washed away their tracks. How's Dottie?"

"She's been fitful from pain but is resting well now. I'm sure you have a lot to talk to her about, but I'm not sure tomorrow will be the best time for anything serious —"

"We need to know details about the Gang, Rebecca."

"I meant about her, and you, and Theodore."

That? "I don't care a lick about dredging up the past."

"Don't you want to know where she's been? Or why she came back?"

Tad could just make out the top of Dottie's head from his spot on the floor. He gazed at the dark curls, searching his gut and his brain for a reaction. He'd had plenty of time tonight to think about her, but he'd spent more time thinking of Rebecca.

"I'm curious, but the minute she left, I decided I didn't want to be with someone who baited folks against each other, someone who was one person with me and someone else with another."

"Then why did you and Theodore fight?"

"Theodore blamed me for pushing Dottie away, and I got tired of defending myself. Although it seems to me, neither of us drove Dottie anywhere. Ralph White didn't force her to run off with him." He thought a minute. "You know, I'm curious about one thing related to her leaving town. What happened to Ralph? Did she say?"

"Not a word." She plucked at the quilt.

He could fall asleep right here, wet clothes, sitting upright against Pa's dresser, but the sounds of stirring carried from the kitchen. Pa must've awoken when Johnny stumbled into the hayloft. Tad should rise and greet his father, but he didn't have the strength to move yet. "I know you must have been afraid when Johnny rode off."

"I was, for both of you. I've spent all night entrusting you into God's care, ripping you back from His arms so I could worry about you some more, and then repeating the process." She smiled, but her eyes were sad. "You know how I am. Scared to death."

He did know. It was what drove her to want to marry Theodore, that and the commitment she made to him, sight unseen. It was no small thing.

But neither was the fact that she was still making a mistake.

Mrs. Horner stirred. Tad stood, and Mrs. Horner rubbed her eyes. "Is Dottie worse?"

"No, ma'am," he said. "Sorry if we woke you."

Pa's grinning face peered in the doorway. "Welcome home, Tad. Catch the Gang?"

"Not in this weather."

"Another time. Go get changed, and I'll get something hot on the stove for you."

"I should start breakfast at the boarding-house, if you don't need me, Rebecca." Mrs. Horner stood and folded her quilt into a precise rectangle.

Rebecca was insisting she was fine when Tad slipped out. After rubbing down his wet hair with a horse blanket and changing into a set of dry clothes he stored in the livery office, Tad padded through the kitchen door in his stocking feet. Rebecca and Pa cradled mugs of coffee in their hands, and Theodore stood at the head of the table, presiding over a tray of toast and eggs.

When had he arrived? It must have been when Tad was toweling off his hair, because he hadn't heard a thing.

Theodore acknowledged him with a nod of his head before turning to Rebecca. "It's from Mrs. Croft's. I figured you'd all be tired."

"How thoughtful." Rebecca cast him a grateful smile.

Breakfast on a rainy morning after a difficult night. It was the sort of thing a fiancé would do for his ladylove. If Rebecca was determined to stay with Theodore, at least he was starting to treat her better.

Tad would have to be content with that. Maybe Rebecca was right and love would grow with Theodore. Tad sat at the table and forced a smile. "That's right kind of you, Theodore. Join us."

Theodore did, sitting by Rebecca. It was the first time Theodore had sat at this table in months. "Any news with the Gang?"

Tad spooned up a portion of the steaming eggs. "Rain washed away their tracks, but we'll head out again once things dry out. I have to take that horse back to the livery in Silver City, so I suppose I'll do that when the sheriff and I form another posse."

Rebecca stiffened, but Pa bent over the table. "What's the livery there like? Are they up to a little competition from Fordham and Son?"

Pa knew full well that Tad intended to ranch. Why was he ignoring that? Tad just nodded, glad he had a hunk of toast in his mouth that prevented him from speaking.

A soft knock sounded on the door. Rebecca hopped up to admit Corny Cook. "Good morning."

"I can stay until noon, unless Mr. Fordham needs me — oh, hello Mr. Fordham. I didn't see you there." Corny's cheeks went as red as her hair.

"Howdy," Pa said, since three men in the room went by Mr. Fordham, but it was obvious Corny's words were for Theodore.

Hmm. Tad chewed, smiling.

Theodore swallowed a swig of coffee. "Take your time, Corny. It's good of you to sit with Dottie."

Rebecca offered a tired smile and gestured to Corny. "Dottie's still asleep. I expect Dr. Wilkie will be here soon to check on her."

"What should I do in the meantime?" Corny's voice trailed as Rebecca led her back to Pa's room.

Pa rubbed his belly and stood. "I'd best feed the stock."

Theodore rose. "And I should open the mercantile."

"Before you go" — Tad set down his mug — "I'm sorry we never made it to Judge Harris."

"It's not your fault." Theodore didn't meet his gaze, but at least he didn't issue recriminations. "You had to help Dottie."

"Thanks for understanding."

Tad sat at the table for a while after his cousin left. He should clear the dishes and find somewhere to sleep after a long, draining, confusing day.

Maybe one good thing had come out of the night, though, if his relationship with Theodore was beginning to heal.

CHAPTER NINETEEN

Rebecca returned to the boardinghouse and marched to the kitchen, prepared to scrub the breakfast dishes. She found Mrs. Horner wiping a serving bowl with a dish towel.

She rushed forward, her stomach lurching with guilt, and reached for the towel and bowl. "Oh, that's my job. I took too long with Cornelia."

"Don't be a goose, dearie. You were up all night."

"So were you."

"I'm embarrassed to say that I wasn't." Mrs. Horner laughed, and to Rebecca's relief, the traces of wheeziness were gone. She might be a trifle uncomfortable with her landlady, after what she'd said last night about Rebecca choosing the wrong sort of security, but her anger diminished sometime during the night while the two of them worked together when Dottie was violently sick.

"I remember well you holding back Dottie's hair."

"And I fell right back to sleep afterward. I don't remember another thing all night long. That chair was mighty comfortable."

More so than the oak chair, for certain. Rebecca's backside still ached.

Nevertheless, she had committed to assist Mrs. Horner in exchange for her room, and Rebecca didn't want to be thrown out on the street. "I promised to help with breakfast and supper. I need to keep up my end of the bargain, and I'll be sure to find someone to sit with Dottie while I get supper going here."

"Never you mind about supper. I'm capable of cooking."

"But —"

"Dearie, I'm cooking supper, I'm cleaning it up, and you are free to do what you wish until whatever time Cornelia needs you back at the livery."

She was about to protest when she thought of her comfortable bed upstairs. "Maybe you're right."

"Go on and do something fun while I launder the sheets." Mrs. Horner grasped the dish towel and shooed Rebecca out the door with it.

Fun? Nothing sounded more fun than a

nap, but if the sheets were to be laundered, she couldn't argue. Rebecca plodded back outside with a *thank you.* She could have gone to the creek, but her feet traversed by memory and took her to the mercantile, where Theodore set her to work scooping nuts into small muslin pouches tied off with red ribbon for tomorrow's Independence Day festivities while he decorated the porch with red, white, and blue garland.

An hour later, he strolled past her. "Those look festive."

"I think they're a wonderful idea. Sometimes, a person works up an appetite dancing the night away. And a thirst."

Theodore snapped his fingers. "Excellent strategy. Mrs. Croft will have lemonade on hand, but I could offer an alternative. There are a few jugs of pressed apple cider in the back."

Rebecca smiled at Theodore's enthusiasm. His hazel-brown eyes twinkled, and he started to hum "Yankee Doodle" when he passed through the gray curtain to the storeroom. He'd seemed so pensive last night, but he'd brought breakfast this morning, which had been a gracious gesture. If Dottie's return bothered him much today, it didn't show.

It was starting to bother Rebecca more

and more, however. Fatigue could make a mind go places it shouldn't, and questions rose that she couldn't construct answers to, no matter how hard she tried.

Rebecca finished scooping nut meats, tidied the scraps, and set the basket on the shelf behind the counter. Then she poked her head behind the curtain. "It's close to noon, so I'm off to the livery."

He looked up from his inventory. "I'll see you tomorrow, then, but I don't expect you or Corny to work with me. Just enjoy the festivities."

"That's kind, but I don't mind helping you." Her place was by his side, if this was to be her mercantile, too.

"You'll be pulled away to dance, anyway."

She hadn't given the matter a thought. "I won't be dancing."

"I'm sure Ulysses won't take no for an answer." Theodore chuckled.

Rebecca shook her head, waved good-bye, and strode to the livery. While she'd packaged nuts at Theodore's, the street had been transformed for tomorrow's Independence Day celebration. For several nights over the past few weeks, Rebecca had stitched on Cornelia's party dress while Cornelia, Mrs. Horner, and Mrs. Cook fashioned garland of red, white, and blue flags. They hung off the businesses now in a festive display. She smiled as she walked.

A flag fluttered over the barbershop door when it opened, and Dr. Wilkie paused in the threshold. She hurried toward him as he turned the OPEN sign over so it read CLOSED. "Dr. Wilkie?"

"I'm closed for dinner." He gestured to the sign. "No haircuts."

"I don't need a haircut."

"Well, I can't fathom why else you'd seek me out. I'm the barber. That's what I do."

He was surly, but at least he didn't reek of alcohol. "That's not all you are, and you know it. Dottie had a rough night." She explained Dottie's retching.

"Chloroform can leave a person nauseated. It passed, didn't it?"

"Yes, but she's groggy. I admit I'm anxious for her to be well enough to tell the sheriff and Tad about her run-in with the Gang."

"So am I." Dr. Wilkie leaned against the doorjamb. "I met the Gang myself."

"You did?"

"Right before you came. I quit doctoring after the war, except for the usual things a barber does like splint broken bones and pull teeth, but real doctoring, well, I hadn't touched a person with that intent since my wife — anyway, that particular day, I heard

Longbeard was laid flat by illness. The Silver City doctor was away, so I thought I'd make an exception to my decision to stop doctoring. I headed up the mountain and offered him some care. Guess who I met up with on the way back?" He grinned.

"While you were on a mission of mercy? That's awful."

"Nothing for 'em to take but my stethoscope. Maybe they thought they could sell it, since I didn't have any coin on me."

"I had very few coins, but they took those anyway." She shook her head. "I'm sorry about your stethoscope. Those are expensive."

"I don't need one if I ain't doctoring." He wiggled his brows.

"It's a pity, you know. People here need a doctor."

"There's one in Silver City, where everyone's going soon."

"People need you. They trust you."

"You sound like your husband. Sorry, I mean your mistaken husband." Wilkie tipped his chin behind her, and she turned. Tad stood on a ladder, hanging bunting off the county office. She turned back to Wilkie, who was stepping back into his barbershop. "He's wrong, though. He's the one in town folks trust."

And with that, he shut the door in her face.

But she wasn't looking at Dr. Wilkie anymore, anyway. She watched Tad. Dr. Wilkie was right. She trusted Tad, too.

Which is why she marched over to tell him something.

Tad yawned, rubbed the sleep from his eyes, and stretched to hang the end of the garland on the hook Orr had hammered under the roofline last year. The roofline pitched in such a way that he couldn't place the ladder directly underneath the hook. Orr, who was taller than Tad, had not had an issue reaching the hook, but Tad sure did.

A basket of red, white, and blue gewgaws and streamers sat at the foot of the ladder, decorations for the Independence Day celebration tomorrow. Nothing remained of last night's rainstorm but a heavy stickiness in the air, leaving him sweating and tempted to douse himself in a horse trough, but tomorrow was the Fourth of July and the decorations wouldn't wait. He could get a drink when he finished embellishing the town.

It had taken half an hour to decorate all the buildings on the street, except for two. Theodore had already taken care of his property, hanging garland on the mercantile porch above a painted sign reading: 1776–1866. GET YOUR ROSETTES HERE.

That left the county office to festoon, which Tad left for last because it was the hardest to do. He stretched farther. One more inch —

"You're going to break your neck."

He strained, at last fastening the garland of red, white, and blue pennants to the hook. There. Now it was safe to look down, although he didn't need to peek to know who stood below him. "My neck's fine, Rebecca. It's my arm I'm worried about."

Her fingers were tight on the ladder, holding it still, her knuckles white as bone. "Your shoulder hasn't healed yet? Have you told Dr. Wilkie?"

"Not that arm." He waved his right one, the one that had reached to hang the bunting. "This one's about to fall off from all this decorating you gals are making me do."

"We aren't making you do anything. You volunteered." Her eyes rolled. "I don't feel sorry for you anymore."

"Why not?" He descended the ladder, glad they were able to have a lighthearted discussion after the heaviness of the past twenty-four hours.

"Because I've made so many ribbon rosettes for Theodore my eyes have crossed. I poked my thumb with the needle, see?"

She held it up, showing him a red mark on her thumb. The temptation to kiss it and make it better coursed through him, but he shook it off and gestured up at the office's roofline. "How's my handiwork?"

"I think Cornelia and Mrs. Horner cut those pennants and stitched the bunting, so it's not really your handiwork, is it? But oh, you mean the *hanging* of it." Her playful grin was wide. "Nice."

Her nonchalant tone made him bark a laugh. "Nice? That's all you can say after I almost lost my arm beautifying this town?"

"Is that what happened? We'd best get your arm in a sling, then."

Her teasing smile was the most beautiful thing he'd ever seen. Prettier than the sunrise over the mountains, prettier than the willows bending over the creek bed, prettier than the spring flowers he'd plucked for her wedding bouquet. Pretty as it was, the time was coming soon when he wouldn't see it anymore. They'd get the annulment, she'd marry Theodore, and Tad would watch them leave for Silver City. So he took this moment and captured it in his memory: the freckles dotting her nose, the pale hue of her eyes, the delicate pink of her upturned lips.

Theodore was a blessed man.

"Tad?" From the change in Rebecca's tone, it was clear she had something serious to discuss. The annulment, probably. A quick glance assured him she no longer wore his opal ring.

"No trip to Silver City today. Maybe not until the Gang of Four is behind bars. I suspect I'll be out on posse quite soon."

"Oh, of course." Her fingers fidgeted against her green dress. "But that wasn't what I wanted to discuss with you. It's Dottie."

"Is she worse?"

"I've been at the mercantile, but I expect I'd have heard something if she'd taken a turn. No, I've been thinking about what happened to her. Doesn't it seem odd that she was shot in the back and left for dead? Why would the Gang do that? If they wanted her horse, they could've caught up to her easily enough. Or fired a warning shot."

Tad rested against the ladder. "I've wondered the same thing. I talked about it with Johnny, too, but we don't have a good answer."

Rebecca fussed with the needle pokes on

her thumb. "Maybe they wanted her dead because she saw their faces. She could identify them."

Tad's stance widened so he could stand at her height, the better to see her eyes. "Did she say anything to give you that impression?"

"She didn't say much at all." Rebecca wouldn't look at him.

A current of unease rippled under Tad's skin. "Did she say something else, then? Something to cause trouble between you and Theodore? Or say that I — because I don't have any feelings for her anymore, and neither does Theodore."

"No, she didn't and I — I'm not worried about that." Her head tipped down, though.

"What's bothering you?" He gently lifted her chin with his thumb and forefinger.

She didn't meet his gaze. "I'll breathe easier when this is all done, that's all. She could have more information about the Gang than any of their previous victims. They're dangerous, Tad."

"I know you're worried because that kid in the Gang saw your name on the envelopes, but they won't hurt you. I promise."

Her lips parted, but Tad's eye caught on the movement of a man just beyond her bonnet. Theodore exited his mercantile,

297

broom in hand, and started to sweep the porch. Tad dropped his hand before Theodore could look up. What a foolish thing, touching Rebecca like that, whether or not Theodore or anyone else could see.

God had provided Tad the desire to ranch, he was certain of it. It would keep him a fair distance from Rebecca and Theodore, and he'd heal from whatever he felt for Rebecca. He mounted the ladder, gripping another stream of red, white, and blue bunting. "I'd better get back to work."

"So should I. Dottie might wake up, and in the meantime, these rosettes won't sew themselves. Why so many menfolk want large ones for their lapels, I can't fathom." She held her hands out so her forefingers and thumbs made a circle the size of a saucer.

"That's a lot of ribbon." Tad stretched and hung the bunting.

"Theodore will charge extra for the large ones." Rebecca held the lank end of the streamer while he moved the ladder to hang the opposite end.

"Who wants one that big, anyway?"

"The assayer, for one."

Ah. "That's because he plays tuba in the brass band. They like to show off their patriotic spirit."

"You'll come soon to question her?"

He wanted to tease that Dottie often slept the day away before she left, but Rebecca's face was grave. "I assure you, the sheriff or I will check in soon."

"Thank you." Rebecca turned to walk toward the livery. Tad waved at his cousin, who, thankfully, waved back.

Tad's heart dropped to his toes, though. Rebecca's questions about Dottie were valid and troubling.

He'd do his best to find the answers to them, for Dottie's sake, for the town's, and for Rebecca's. She wasn't his real wife; she was Theodore's concern, but he'd do whatever he could to set her mind at ease.

It was the very least he could do for her, and it might be the last thing, too, before they parted ways.

CHAPTER TWENTY

Rebecca hurried to the livery, passing the patriotic bunting bedecking the paddock. She waved to Johnny and Uncle Giff then let herself into the house through the livery. Cornelia met her in the parlor.

"She didn't really wake up. All I did was stitch rosettes and stare at her. I forgot how pretty she is. No wonder Theodo — Mr. Fordham liked her so much."

She's not spindly as a bird or speckled as an egg like me, that's for certain. But neither she nor Cornelia should be comparing themselves to another female. She smiled at her friend. "Beauty on the outside isn't the same as beauty on the inside. You have both, though."

"You think I'm pretty?"

"I sure do, with that gorgeous red hair and your bright eyes."

Cornelia grinned, but then her hands flew to her cheeks. "Before I forget, my mother came by. She said she'd sit with Dottie tonight."

Why? Rebecca shook her head. "There's no need."

"She told me she'd do it so you and I can finish my dress, but that's not the real reason. Mrs. Horner called on her and said that caring for Dottie shouldn't fall on you alone, just because you've done nursing before, and she said you didn't sleep more than two winks last night and she's worried about you." Cornelia's words came fast, and Rebecca had a difficult time following who said what, but it didn't matter, because Mrs. Horner was worried about her.

Even though she'd had harsh words for Rebecca about Theodore, she was worried. She cared. "I'm fine. I'll tell her so."

"But she's not the only one who's noticed how hard you work for her, and Theodore, and stitching up folks. My ma agreed with her, and so did Eloise Evans, that miner's sister your brother's sweet on, so we're all going to take turns sitting with Dottie. That's five of us to carry the load."

Rebecca's lips parted, and not in shock over Johnny cottoning to Eloise. No one had ever thought of her like that before, at least, not that she remembered. Her heart swelled and tears stung her eyes. This must be what it was like to be part of a community.

"I can take my turn with Dottie tonight, though."

"You took your turn last night, and you're crying, you're so tired. A full night's sleep will do you good, once we're finished with the dress, of course." Cornelia giggled.

It didn't sit right, though, letting other folks sit with Dottie. A sense of dread loomed over Rebecca's shoulders. Mercy, she must be exhausted, to harbor thoughts like that. It was probably no more than anxiety to hear Dottie's story about the Gang, but she must be patient. "Thanks, Cornelia."

"I was teasing about you helping me with the dress tonight. You don't have to. Unless you want to." Cornelia offered a tiny smile.

Rebecca couldn't let her down. "I want to. I will be there at seven. If your hair is damp, I'll help set it in pin curls, too."

"Thank you!" Cornelia embraced her. Rebecca froze at first, still shocked by the change in their relationship, but then she returned the embrace as hard as she could.

Tad scanned the main street, examining his bunting-hanging skills. Not too shabby, if he said so himself. Which he did, since no one other than Rebecca had said so much as boo about it while he perched on that ladder.

"Deputy! Tad!"

He turned, brushing off his hands. Johnny stood in the center of the street in front of the livery, waving his hat. He ran toward him.

"She's awake," Johnny yelled. "Rebecca wants you to come quick."

Tad clapped Johnny's shoulder as he passed him into the barn. In a moment he was in Pa's room. Rebecca held Dottie's shoulder, pinning her to the bed with obvious effort, although her voice was soft. "You'll open the wound, Dottie. Try to lie still."

"But it hurts!"

Johnny had followed him, and Tad cast him a quick glance. "Get Wilkie." Then he was at Dottie's other side. "Try to breathe, Dottie. Let Rebecca care for you."

"Tad?" Her voice changed and her body went limp. "It hurts so much, Tad."

He knew firsthand what a bullet felt like, although he'd only been grazed. "I'm sure Wilkie has something for the pain."

Now that Dottie wasn't fighting anymore, Rebecca doused a rag in the basin and patted Dottie's head with the wet cloth. She murmured comforting words, like the nurse she was. Or like a mother. At that moment, he missed Ma, and he missed the family he thought he'd be having with Rebekah. Rebecca's gentle sounds soothed him, and for a moment, he was lost in the tenor of her voice.

Then Dottie cried out. "It hurts so."

Tad snapped out of his stupor. He felt ineffective in the sickroom, but he could do something as the deputy. "We'll find those responsible, Dottie, and you might be able to help. Is there anything you can tell us about the Gang?"

"Tad," Rebecca murmured. "I'm eager, but now might not be the best time."

"Once Wilkie gets here, she won't be awake for long." He leaned closer to Dottie, hovering over her ear. "Did you see or hear anything that can help us?"

"They're robbing a bank," she shouted, enunciating and scornful, as if she'd been accused.

Rebecca stood up. "They don't rob banks."

"Which bank?" Tad squatted by the bed. "Did you hear them say?"

Dottie sobbed, flailing.

Wilkie stomped into the bedroom, shoving Tad aside with a none-too-gentle push. He poked and prodded, nodded, and administered a dose from a dark bottle.

Dottie's sobs subsided, and soon she was sound asleep. Rebecca plopped into the oak chair, exhaustion lining her features. "I didn't see infection, did you?"

Wilkie grunted. "No. The pain's always worse the second or third day."

"The way she was screaming . . ." Rebecca's voice trailed off.

"Dottie Smalls was always dramatic. I was shocked she didn't join an acting troupe." Wilkie pointed at the bottle. "Laudanum tonic. Give it to her for the rest of the day and night. She needs rest. I ain't a doctor anymore, so don't fetch me unless she develops a fever."

Rebecca's laugh was mirthless when Wilkie strode out. "That man puzzles me."

"This whole thing puzzles me." Tad rubbed his jaw. "I'd better fetch Sheriff Adkins. If the Gang is going to be robbing a bank, we need to warn Bilson and the other banks in the area."

Rebecca's hands clutched at her waist. "But she was delirious with pain. The Gang doesn't rob banks."

"What if they start, and we didn't do anything?" He wanted to touch her, but it wouldn't be right. He'd forgotten himself and touched her chin on the street, and he'd learned his lesson. He needed to keep his distance from her.

"I know. Stay safe."

"It's not a posse, Rebecca."

"I know," she repeated, her jaw clenching.

He stood there too long, far longer than was appropriate considering he was her accidental husband, far longer than he should have considering a bank might or might not be robbed sometime soon. At last he expelled a sigh.

"It will be well, Rebecca." God willing. He prayed it to be so and sought out Sheriff Adkins.

For four hours, Rebecca stitched rosettes for tomorrow's festivities and stared at Dottie. At last, Dottie stirred, but she didn't cry out in pain as she moved. That was a start.

Rebecca rose and touched Dottie's forehead. Cool.

"I'm thirsty."

"Let's remedy that, then." Rebecca gently assisted Dottie to a propped position that was half on her back, half on her side, so she could eat and drink while keeping pressure off her wound. Dottie winced during the adjustment, but when they were finished, she took a sip of the water Rebecca lifted to her lips.

"Did Granddaddy come by while I was asleep?" Before Rebecca could answer, Dottie sighed. "Never mind. He'd be here if he was alive."

"I'm sorry." It was no small thing to lose the man who raised you. Still, Dottie had abandoned her grandfather without a word, along with Tad and Theodore and everyone else in Ruby City, leaving them all to wonder why and where she'd gone.

Rebecca didn't approve, but in truth, she'd taken people for granted, too. Like Theodore. *Make me more grateful for the husband You gave me, Lord.*

"There's broth in the kitchen. Should we try it?"

Dottie scowled. "I hate broth."

Well, Rebecca had learned from the soldiers she'd tended that sometimes folks in pain just weren't hungry. "You're still in your shift. Do you have a nightgown?"

"That'd feel good. I'm filthy."

Rebecca found the nightgown at the bottom of the valise: fine linen, trimmed in pale blue ribbon and exquisite lace. It was far nicer than anything Rebecca had ever owned. Wherever Dottie had been the past few months, she'd had the means to afford a pretty wardrobe. Rebecca's fingers trailed the delicate gown while her brain filled with questions, but where Dottie had been or why she returned to Ruby City weren't Rebecca's business. Neither were the contents of Dottie's bag, but it was interesting that Dottie's hairbrush looked just like the one the Gang had stolen from Rebecca.

Same brand of tooth powder, too, which Theodore didn't carry. Maybe someone in Silver City did. Is that where Dottie had purchased the fancy pink dress, ruffled and flounced? And were these trousers? Dottie hadn't mentioned the man she ran away with, Ralph White, but it was safe to assume she'd married him. These must be his trousers, but he was a slender man, indeed, to fit into these.

"Are you coming?" Dottie's complaint startled Rebecca, but the woman was in pain. No wonder her words were terse.

"Let's sponge the dirt off, first." Rebecca made quick work of washing Dottie's face, arms, and legs, avoiding her torso and bandaged hands. Then she held up the nightgown. "I should remove those bandages on your arms so we can get this on easier."

With gentle fingers, she unfastened the bandage on Dottie's left arm. Cornelia had done a good job binding it.

"Do you know who I am?" Dottie's voice was laced with curiosity, despite whatever pain she must be experiencing.

"Yes." Rebecca unwound the cloth.

"And you're tending me, even though you're married to Tad?"

Rebecca didn't look up from examining the scratches on Dottie's arm. Dottie's wound must still throb, but it sure seemed she had enough strength to attempt to stoke jealousy in Rebecca. She wouldn't succumb, however. She continued to examine the scratches, judged them negligible, and got to work on the other arm. "The truth is, I'm intended to marry Theodore."

"Oh." Something like recognition flashed in Dottie's eyes.

Someone else could reveal the whole sordid story of the marital mix-up, but Rebecca didn't want to discuss it. She'd be lying if she didn't admit a pinch of jealousy toward Dottie, even if both Tad and Theodore claimed she held no hold over their hearts. *God, forgive me and give me nothing but compassion for this woman.* She tugged off the bandage.

A pink slash of a scar, weeks older than the other scratches, marred the top of Dottie's forearm, midway between her elbow to her wrist. Rebecca bent closer.

"What's this?"

Dottie glanced at it. "Must've happened yesterday."

The healed gash had to be over a month old, and it was too neat to have been inflicted from a fall. It was the work of a blade — not a scalpel, either. It was larger, as if it came from something like her paper knife, the one she'd used to defend herself against the Gang of Four.

Rebecca jumped to her feet. The robber she'd stabbed wasn't a boy. It was a woman.

"You're in the Gang of Four."

Chapter Twenty-One

Dottie's eyes narrowed for a fraction of a second before she burst into phony-sounding laughter. "What nonsense."

"I remember your eyes now, how you seemed to recognize my name on the envelopes of the letters you pawed through, but it wasn't my name you knew. It was Theodore's. And I'll never forget when that horrible man reached for me and I slashed you instead."

The laugh died in an instant, replaced by a look of pure disdain. "That scrape doesn't prove a thing."

Rebecca stood tall. "That's my hairbrush in your bag, and my tooth powder, too. I imagine you stole the very nightgown you're wearing. It's rather expensive for — what have you and Ralph White been doing for employment?"

When Dottie didn't answer, Rebecca tossed the washrag atop the tray with a splat. She'd prayed to forgive the Gang for taking her things. She hadn't been as successful in forgiving them for hurting Tad. "You *shot Tad.*"

The scornful look transformed into one of panic. "That wasn't me. I would never — I didn't even want to rob people, but Ralph made me. He's my husband, and I had to."

"You didn't seem unwilling to me, nicking my toiletries and rifling through my correspondence."

"We just took what we needed to get by."

Mrs. Horner's stolen lace didn't fall into that category, and neither did Dr. Wilkie's stethoscope. Not to mention that the Gang seemed to rob some folks just to torment them, yanking Ulysses's tooth out of his mouth and taking things of no value beyond the owner's sentimental attachment, like Longbeard's fur collar and Bowe Brown's photograph. "I don't believe you."

Dottie winced. "Once they shot Tad I knew I had to leave them."

Rebecca's toe tapped. "He was wounded weeks ago."

"I had to bide my time until I thought I could get away, and when I did, they came after me and tried to kill me to keep me quiet." Dottie's chin trembled, like she was fighting back tears. "You don't understand what it's like to be so hungry you'll do anything to survive."

Now that, Rebecca understood. She understood desperation and the temptation to sin so well, her stomach clenched at the memory of the night she'd stolen the food from her employer's pantry.

She also understood grace, and how one day while she shopped for her employer at a mercantile much like Theodore's, her gaze had landed on the matrimonial magazine. She'd borrowed a pencil and paper scrap to copy the address inside, and she'd sent in her advertisement.

When Theodore replied, it had seemed God answered her prayers and provided her the way out.

Rebecca's eyes shut. From what she'd heard of Dottie, the woman was a skilled manipulator, so she sent a prayer heavenward that she wasn't falling prey to it now. No matter how well she related to Dottie's tale of desperation, she would do well to stay on her guard.

But the truth was, while she liked to think she wouldn't rob anyone, she didn't know for sure what she'd do if she'd been in Dottie's shoes. Walking in her own worn-out half boots had been challenging enough, and she'd stumbled plenty.

Her breath released in a long sigh. "I can't imagine what you've been through, and when you finally broke free, they tried to kill you. Thankfully, your testimony and directions to wherever the Gang's been hiding the past four months will —"

"Oh no. I'm not saying a word beyond what I already did about the bank."

"The Gang tried to murder you. Why protect them?"

"I'm protecting myself." Dottie pushed up onto her elbows, as if ready to bolt from the bed, but then she winced and cried out. "It hurts so."

While Dottie surely meant the pain from her injury, Rebecca couldn't help thinking about the wound in Dottie's heart. What would it be like to have a husband who made you steal and then shot you? Or if not him, one of his so-called friends? "I know you're scared, but Tad will make sure you're safe."

"He won't need to, because all I'll tell him is that the Gang wears bandannas over their mouths. I didn't see anything, and I don't know who shot me." The weepy look vanished and the answer came easily, with confidence, as if Dottie was a skilled liar. If she'd sweet-talked Tad and Theodore with such conviction, it was no wonder they each

314

believed they were the only man in her life. "But that isn't true."

Dottie's face transformed again, her jaw setting and her eyes narrowing. "If you open your mouth and tell him I'm in the Gang, I'll say you're a jealous liar, making up tales because you think he and Theodore still want me."

Rebecca flinched at the harshness of Dottie's tone and the venom in her glare. "Is that so, when there's proof aplenty that you're guilty?"

Her eyes rolled. "Why are you so mean, telling on me?"

She made it sound like they were schoolgirls and she'd copied someone's spelling test. "You were part of a Gang that robbed people, shot a lawman, and tried to murder you."

Dottie's expression changed yet again as her chin trembled and her eyes grew wide and pleading. "You can't tell. I'll hang."

Rebecca's stomach lurched from the back-and-forth of Dottie's behavior. Vulnerable one minute, threatening the next. She was a manipulator, no dispute. But she was also in tremendous pain, and she'd been shot in the back, a betrayal Rebecca could never understand. She chose her words with care. "I don't know much about the law, but I'm pretty sure if you cooperate with the law and come clean, your assistance will be taken into consideration by the judge. The Gang forced you and shot you. If you're right about the bank robbery —"

"I didn't lie about that."

"Then where is it? Which bank?"

"I don't know. They were just starting to plan it." Dottie leaned back, wincing. "If you're going to snitch anyway, I might as well speak for myself. It looks better to the judge, right?"

Rebecca wasn't a lawyer. She didn't know Idaho regulations, but she knew one thing: "It's the right thing to do."

"Then you have to let me do it so I won't hang."

"Agreed." Tad would be back in a few hours, and this would be done.

"I hurt so bad." Her breathing hitched and her fingers clenched at the quilt.

A glance at the clock confirmed that the laudanum was wearing off. "Time for another dose." She measured it out and spoon-fed it to Dottie. "By tomorrow, you won't need the medicine, I hope. You'll still hurt, but it will be much more tolerable."

"Tomorrow's the Fourth of July, isn't it?" Dottie's voice was wistful as she twisted her head into the pillow. "Do you suppose I can hear the goings-on from the jail? They had a grand celebration when I was last here."

Rebecca glanced at the pile of rosettes she'd left here this morning. "They still do, I think."

"Oh, good." Dottie sounded sleepy. "The fireworks were something to see."

There would be fireworks of a different kind altogether, too, when Ruby City learned one of their own was a member of the Gang of Four.

Rebecca wanted to tell someone about Dottie. Every time Uncle Giff or Johnny poked their heads in the door, she wanted to confide the heavy burden of Dottie's confession.

But she'd given her word that Dottie could be the one to tell, for her own sake. A few hours longer would make no difference. Neither Tad nor the sheriff was in town yet, and no one else had authority to arrest Dottie, nor did they have a place to confine her, with the jail full. Except maybe that closet where Tad slept.

Besides, Dottie was sound asleep, her soft snores punctuating the air along with the ticks of the clock.

An outer door opened, and Uncle Giff's voice carried from the kitchen. Was Tad back? Rebecca set aside the last rosette she'd been stitching and hurried out, but it was Ingrid Cook who stood with Uncle Giff and Johnny in the kitchen, bearing a smile and a basket.

Johnny assisted in emptying the basket, releasing the delicious aroma of fried chicken. "Sure is kind of you to bring supper, ma'am."

"Sure is kind of you to open your home to Dottie." Mrs. Cook set out bowls of potato salad and biscuits.

"I don't mind the hayloft, and I'll stay there until we find a place for Dottie." Uncle Giff pulled plates from the cupboard.

Mrs. Cook sighed. "Not sure where that will be, with the boardinghouse and hotel full, and she has no people in town now that her granddaddy passed."

Rebecca knew just where to put Dottie. That closet in the jail.

"Thanks for bringing supper, ma'am, but no need to stay the night. I'm happy to." She should be here when Tad returns.

"You deserve a night off, Becky." Uncle Giff scooped forks from the drawer. "Besides, you promised to help Corny with her dress."

"I can come back after that —"

Mrs. Cook's hand propped on her ample

318

hip. "It's been decided. You've worked too hard, and not a single one of us is going to let you do it. No arguments."

But — Rebecca swallowed back the words forming in her throat. She'd promised to allow Dottie to confess. She couldn't blame her, because she'd want to be the one to admit to her crimes and clear her conscience. Still, it didn't sit right, letting Mrs. Cook sit up when she didn't know she was nursing a criminal. Should Rebecca tell?

Her stomach twisted, almost in hunger, reminding her at once with sharp swiftness what it had been like in Missouri to be so hungry she stole from Mrs. MacGruder. So hungry she knew she might do it again, even though she hated it and begged God to take away the temptation.

Rebecca hesitated, praying for guidance. Then her shoulders slumped. Dottie had been desperate, too, so Rebecca would give her one last chance.

But she wouldn't leave her loved ones without warning. "When Tad gets home, tell him Dottie has more information for him. It's important."

"She's supposed to saw logs all night with that tonic," Uncle Giff reminded her. "Doctor's orders."

So she wouldn't be awake to tell Tad,

anyway. Nor could she flee, had she a mind to. Still —

"Dottie needs a word with him between doses, though. Tell him it's important. Please."

"We will, sis." Johnny's eyes rolled. "Have some of this fine-looking grub before you leave."

Rebecca's stomach was hollow, and she never passed on a meal, but tonight, she wasn't hungry. "I'd best help Cornelia now. I'll be back at dawn."

"Get some sleep," Uncle Giff called. "You look like you could use it."

Maybe she could, but she probably wouldn't get any rest for worrying until things were settled with Dottie.

CHAPTER TWENTY-TWO

Rebecca half expected Tad to call after she finished at Cornelia's, but he didn't. Had he heard Dottie's confession? Maybe he had, and just hadn't come to see Rebecca. He was busy, of course, with a posse to form, and it wasn't like he owed her anything.

She spent a restless night wondering and wishing he'd come, though.

The moment a pale stream of golden light peeked under her window shade, Rebecca rose and dressed in her dress the hue of a robin's egg — not a patriotic shade of blue, perhaps, but it would have to do — and paused at the dresser to twist her hair into a braided bun, allowing four tendrils of pin-curled hair to hang down her back. Her hairpins made *plinking* sounds as she scooped them from the glass dish beside Ulysses's jasper and Tad's opal. She should return the ring today, but now didn't seem the best time. With a final pat, she hurried to the kitchen. The scent of brewing coffee wafted through the kitchen, and Mrs. Horner had an empty cup ready at her elbow while she cracked eggs into a speckled bowl.

"Morning." Mrs. Horner's tone was never chipper in the mornings until she'd sipped down that first mug of coffee.

"I'll set the table, but if you don't mind, I'd like to run to the livery before breakfast."

"Mrs. Cook's watching Dottie so you don't have to, remember? Eloise Evans and I will sit up tonight after the festivities. It's all arranged."

"That's not it." She counted forks for the table. "I said I'd be back at dawn."

Mrs. Horner glanced up from the eggs. "You're as pale as a snake's underbelly. I'd hoped you'd rest better in your own bed. Well, go on, then. I can set the table. Take some coffee cake with you for the Fordham fellas. Be sure to tell Gifford happy Independence Day."

"You can tell him yourself later today." Rebecca cut a hunk of cake, wrapped it into a clean dish towel, and kissed her landlady's cheek.

She'd waited all night for word. *Please, God, let Tad have made it home safely.*

■ ■ ■ ■

Pat-a-pat.

Tad recognized Rebecca's knock. It was brief without being tentative. It was also timely, since she'd told Pa she'd be here early and Mrs. Cook had left half an hour ago to tend her family. Besides, few folks knocked on the door between the livery and the kitchen. Who else would drop in to visit Johnny while he mucked stalls before calling at the house?

Tad dropped the chunks of bread he'd just cut into a bowl, brushed off his hands, and opened the door.

Rebecca stared up at him, her eyes shadowed with fatigue. She was pretty as ever, though, and her blue dress was the perfect choice for the Fourth of July, a flawless canvas for the rosette she'd later pin to her collar for the town's festivities. He was dressed for services and the party, too, in a clean white shirt and his Sunday shoes. His hair was still damp from his morning ablutions, making his collar stick to the back of his neck. "Good morning, Rebecca. Come in."

"Thank you. I brought cake." Her flowery scent filled his senses as she handed him a bundled dish towel and ducked into the kitchen.

Pa looked up from frying eggs. "You're late, Becky. I expected you at dawn."

Her lips twitched. "I am late, but I hope not too much so."

"Dottie's fine since Mrs. Cook left." Tad poured a pitcher of warm milk over the bread chunks in the bowl for Dottie's milksops. Nasty, slimy stuff, in his opinion, but just the thing for a body in recovery, according to Pa. "I came here last night after visiting the banks, and Johnny was waiting for me, half asleep at the kitchen table. He said you wanted me to talk to Dottie."

"Did you?"

"Sure did. She was awake, and she kept saying she was sorry." That was all Rebecca needed to hear, anyway. There had been an embarrassing, garbled speech about never forgetting Tad despite marrying Ralph White that made Mrs. Cook roll her eyes and Tad wish he could bolt from the room. "She hurt bad, so Mrs. Cook gave her more tonic."

"But she didn't say anything about the Gang?"

"I asked her, and she said she didn't see their faces. Same as you."

Rebecca's mouth opened, but another

knock sounded at the kitchen door. Pa turned around. "Come and join the party, whoever you are."

Theodore stepped in, his eyes wary. "Johnny said I could just go on in, but I thought I should knock."

"What can we do for you, Theodore?" Tad tried to keep his gaze on his cousin, but he couldn't help watching Rebecca, whose mouth set in that grim line that told the world she was angry. What had happened?

"I saw Rebecca hurry up the street." Theodore glanced between them. "Is everything well?"

Rebecca hoisted the tray of sops. "I'm glad you're here. We were just about to speak to Dottie."

"What's wrong?" Theodore gave voice to Tad's question.

"I promised to let her tell you." Rebecca strode into Pa's bedroom.

Dottie rested against the pillow, her hair in disarray. Her eyes widened at seeing them, but then she winced. "I'm so glad you're here. My wound's aching somethin' fierce."

Theodore tutted. "Is it time for more tonic?"

"No." Rebecca plunked down the tray. "It's time for you to tell these gentlemen something."

"Well, yes." Dottie ducked her head then looked up at them through her thick lashes in a way that made her look young and vulnerable. "Tad, Theodore, I'm sorry I played you false. The truth is, I couldn't pick between you fellas, so I married Ralph. Forgive me?"

Rebecca rolled her eyes.

Theodore rubbed the back of his neck. "Sure, Dottie."

"I forgave you a long time ago." But there was no way Tad believed she ran off with Ralph White because she couldn't decide between the Fordham boys. Tad leaned against the wall and crossed his ankles. "That's not what this is about, is it?"

"No," Rebecca barked.

"Of course it is. You need to understand why I was coming back to Ruby City." Dottie glared at Rebecca then turned a softer gaze on Tad. "Ralph wasn't who I thought he was. He had a wild streak a mile wide."

Ralph had been just like Bowe Brown: brash, good-looking, with a thirst for trouble that landed him in front of the sheriff more than once. "My mule Madge has better manners than Ralph. What were you expecting?"

326

"Don't be jealous, Tad." Dottie offered a coquettish smile. Wasn't she supposed to be in great pain? How did she manage to look downright flirtatious?

"I don't much care who you married, or when or why or how. Was Ralph with you when you got shot?"

"You could say that."

Rebecca sucked in a breath. "Tell them now, Dottie, or I will."

Dottie's chin trembled. "Theodore, you won't hate me, will you? You've always had the sweetest heart. That's why Rebecca's marrying you, you know. You wouldn't hate me, with that heart of yours."

He stepped closer to the bed. "Of course not —"

"Enough." Tad pushed off from the wall. "What's going on, Dottie?"

She started plucking the yarn ties on her quilt. "Rebecca says the judge will be lenient if I cooperate, which I will do to the best of my ability. You'll protect me when the time comes, won't you, Tad? Because you won't find the Gang without me."

"Why not?"

"I know where their hideout is." Her fingers stilled.

A shroud of dread settled over his shoulders. "How do you know that?"

Her gaze dropped to his boots. "Ralph is part of the Gang of Four."

Theodore sputtered like a dying wick. "But they shot you."

"I know." Dottie sniffled, her chin trembling again. "Ralph would've helped me, but they heard Tad coming and had to run. I'm sure he's worried sick."

What sort of bizarre marriage did Dottie and Ralph have? Tad shook his head. "Ralph would've helped you. Does that mean he didn't shoot you?"

"I'm sure he didn't. But I can't say who did."

"But you can say plenty more." Rebecca shook her head. "Who else is in the Gang, for instance."

"Skeet Smucker and Flick Dougherty." Now that she'd started, the speed of her words picked up, and there was no trace of tears in her eyes. "Flick's the one that made eyes at you, Rebecca. He thought you were real pretty, despite your being thin as a stick, and that's why he tried to — oh, sorry."

Tad's hand fisted, as if Flick Dougherty were in the room ready for a smack to the jaw. *God, help me.*

Rebecca had gone white. "So it was Flick I saw in town."

Tad forced his fingers to relax and to

behave like the officer of the law that he was. "So Flick, Skeet, and Ralph. Who else?"

"I couldn't get away." She batted her eyes, not answering. "Ask Rebecca. She knows what it's like to be stuck in a bad situation you can't get out of no matter how bad you want to."

Theodore's head jerked around. "What is that supposed to mean?"

Rebecca sputtered while Dottie laughed. "Not you, Theodore. I meant in her past. She didn't tell me about it, but I can tell. It's called intuition. I read about it in a gazette."

Rebecca's jaw clenched. "My intuition tells me you'd better start talking, and not about me, Dottie. We're talking about you."

Dottie stuck out her tongue at Rebecca.

What had Tad ever seen in this woman beyond her pretty face? Then he recalled how she was neglected by her grandfather, teetering on the edge of the sorts of choices a person can make when she's lonely, and he'd thought he could help her. He wasn't sure now if she'd ever wanted help, but he thanked the good Lord that He'd never had Dottie in mind as Tad's wife. "Where's the hideout? Who is the fourth man?"

She pouted. "I don't want to say."

Rebecca hung her head in disbelief, and

Tad brushed past her toward Dottie. "They shot you. You deserve justice."

Dottie covered her eyes with her arm. "I lied. It wasn't Ralph. I was just mad at him, so I said it to get him into trouble. I don't know who's in the Gang. They set upon me and took my horse. I was comin' to visit my granddaddy, that's all. I don't know anything —"

Rebecca shoved past him to gently but firmly take hold of the arm Dottie used to shield her eyes. Dottie shrieked in protest, and Theodore burst forward. "Rebecca, stop this, you're hurting her. I never thought you capable of violence like this —"

"I'm not hurting her. Look." Rebecca pointed to a pink scar on Dottie's forearm. "I told you the Gang had a boy in it. I stabbed him with my paper knife."

"It's from a rock," Dottie whined, but Theodore fell back.

"You're the fourth man." Tad stared up at the ceiling.

"Her valise contains evidence. Trousers and my hairbrush." Rebecca dropped Dottie's arm.

"Why didn't you tell us?" Theodore's question wasn't for Dottie, but Rebecca. "You knew this when, last night?"

"She asked me to allow her to confess, so

330

the judge will be lenient —"

"You should have told us." A muscle worked in Theodore's cheek. "I didn't think you were like Dottie, keeping secrets from me."

"Theodore." Rebecca gaped.

Tad held up a hand. "Don't take it out on her, Theodore. She didn't withhold it from you as much as she granted Dottie the chance to demonstrate remorse. It has nothing to do with you."

"All of this concerns me." But he glared at Rebecca. "This is like ten months ago, all over again."

It was nothing like ten months ago. "Rebecca never asked to be dropped into the middle of the mess between you, me, and Dottie, and she's done what she could to help each of us. Even Dottie, allowing her to speak for herself."

Theodore mussed his perfect hair. Rebecca chewed her lip. They had some talking to do — all three of them — but now wasn't the time. Tad tipped his head toward the door. "Why don't you go on and get ready for worship? Send the sheriff over first, though, please, and I think it would be best if neither of you told anyone about Dottie just yet. I don't want anyone in town hearing the news and coming here with

331

vengeance on their minds."

Waving his hand in halfhearted dismissal, Theodore turned on his heel and left. Rebecca watched him go, sighed, and then followed. As she passed Tad, her fingers landed on his arm. The contact was brief, but her touch set his skin on fire. "Thank you."

He was still rubbing the spot on his arm when the kitchen door shut behind her. Tad pulled Pa's chair around to face Dottie, took a seat, and bent to rest his elbows on his knees. The milksops would be stone cold by the time they got to them this morning.

"So, Dottie, care to tell me why they really shot you in the back?"

CHAPTER TWENTY-THREE

Why did the Gang shoot Dottie in the back? To keep her from informing on them, of course, but in the back, right in front of her husband? All through the worship service in the flat space behind the livery, Rebecca's mind struggled to focus on the word from Galatians on freedom. She lent her voice to the others in their makeshift outdoor chapel as they sang hymns of praise and thanksgiving, but her gaze kept flitting to the livery.

Neither Tad nor the sheriff emerged to join worship, and Rebecca's curiosity burned holes through her best intentions to give the matter over to the Lord.

When she wasn't thinking of Dottie, though, her thoughts wandered to Theodore, who lurked in the back. Once the service was finished, he didn't attend the picnic by the creek.

Tad had been kind to defend her this morning, but his heart might harbor disappointment that his words didn't convey. He might be just as frustrated by her choice to allow Dottie to turn herself in as Theodore was. And he was absolutely disappointed. Even when the day progressed and then, toward supper, he avoided her, setting up a table of rosettes, nuts, and other treats near the end of the parade route. She busied herself, too, helping Mrs. Horner spread red-checkered tablecloths over the plank tables set up at one end of the street, her gaze flitting between the mercantile and the county offices.

So far, no one seemed to know about Dottie. Tad had asked her to stay quiet, probably until Dottie was secure behind bars, but it felt odd not to discuss it with anyone, especially Mrs. Horner.

"Where's Corny?" Her landlady glanced up. "I thought she would help us. She's been wonderful, pitching in lately."

"I expect she's at home, putting the finishing touches on her party dress." Rebecca couldn't help but smile.

"I thought she'd wear it to services this morning."

"Oh no. She wanted to save the dress and her hairstyle for this evening. It's as you said a few weeks ago. Cornelia has grown up, and she'd like to make an entrance."

"For a young man?"

"For herself." But maybe the fellow Cornelia admired would appreciate it, too.

"I haven't made an entrance since I got married twenty years ago."

"Residents of Ruby City!"

They looked up at the booming voice. Mr. Orr wove through the people gathered on the street and climbed the steps of the county offices. He waved his arms, flapping his blue frock coat. An enormous red, white, and blue rosette pinned high on his lapel tickled the underside of his chin. "Come one and all, small and great."

"Some folks *always* make an entrance." Rebecca laughed.

"I'm glad the biggest rosette sold. That one Orr's got on has to be a three-center, and that's a penny and a half for me. Come on. We're finished here, anyway."

Rebecca took her landlady's arm, and they ambled to the shady side of the street. Uncle Giff, dressed in his finest striped shirt and smelling like bay rum, joined them.

Rebecca peered around him. "Are Tad and the sheriff still with Dottie?"

"Not since noon. Dottie's asleep, but Johnny's keeping an eye on things so Tad could run out. He said something about Dottie knowing where the hideout is, so a posse will set out at first light." He rocked on his heels. "The sheriff sure relies on him. He won't be able to do without him in Silver City if he follows through with that ranching idea."

The comment set Rebecca's teeth on edge. It was no light thing for Tad to go out after the Gang again, and Uncle Giff repeatedly seemed to ignore Tad's desire to turn to ranching.

Before she could reply, Mr. Orr waved his arms again. "It is my honor and privilege to read a copy of the Declaration of Independence to you fine citizens."

The gathered crowd hushed.

The words were ninety years old but still as powerful as the day they'd been put to paper. Life, liberty, and the pursuit of happiness — the words swirled in Rebecca's thoughts and touched her heart. Freedom came at a steep price, and her forefathers had made tremendous sacrifices during the Revolution.

Her greatest freedom, however, came from God's sacrifice for her. Did it bother Him that she made mistake after mistake, taking His provisions for granted?

After the final words of the Declaration faded, her head turned toward the mercantile. Theodore smiled at Eloise Evans, who bent to pin rosettes to her nieces' collars.

She joined him. "Theodore?"

He came around the table to meet her. "You don't need to help, Rebecca. You'll miss the parade."

Sure enough, the first notes of "Yankee Doodle" carried from the far end of the street. "I can see them fine from here. Besides, I don't yet have a rosette."

He stepped behind the table and offered the basket. "Take your pick. Even one of the large ones. You, Mrs. Horner, and Corny worked hard on these."

"Small's fine." She chose one with more red than blue and pinned it to her bodice. They stood watching the band march toward them, and Rebecca expected them to stop at the end of the road — a short parade, indeed. Instead, the eight men with gleaming brass instruments turned off the road and marched through the rows of tents and back again in an improvised route. Eloise Evans's nieces chased after the band, playing pretend trumpets and lifting their knees high in the air in imitation. It was sweet and delightful, but standing here with Theodore, her heart ached.

"I didn't really come over here for a rosette, Theodore. I couldn't go any longer with you angry at me."

He sighed. "I was shocked, but I shouldn't have blamed you. Tad was right. I'm sorry for accusing you."

"Thank you, but I'm not sure I was right. I did what I thought was best, for Dottie's sake, but the way it unfolded, well, I'm sorry, too."

He nodded but didn't say anything more, leaving her a moment to think. They'd both apologized, but something still felt hollow between them. Despite his apology, it seemed like he tended to think the worst about her when conflict arose, attributing her motives to malice. Was it because she had proved herself untrustworthy to him, or because he bore the scars Dottie inflicted? Or was there something else about their relationship that needed to be examined?

The band finished, and the sun began its steady descent in the west, leaving a pink glow to the sky.

"Supper!" Mrs. Croft rang a triangle bell. "Brisket and corn bread."

"Will you join me?" She tipped her head at Theodore.

He shook his head. "I don't want to leave the wares unattended."

"Then I'll join you. Wait here."

He held up his hands as if to tell her no, but she moved to the food line, took two plates, and returned to Theodore's little table. He wasn't alone when she returned, however. Tad stood beside him, a smile on his lips but fatigue lining his eyes.

"Here." She offered both men plates. "Eat while they're hot."

"Thanks." Tad took his plate but set it down. "First I must buy one of these rosettes. I don't feel totally dressed without one."

He was dressed impeccably, rosette or not, in his white shirt, plaid vest, and string tie. Still, she offered the basket. "Two pennies, Deputy."

"Two?" he teased. "Are there rubies in them?" He scooped a rosette without looking and pinned it with haphazard swiftness to his vest.

"It's not a deputy badge, Tad. It's a rosette."

"What's wrong with it?"

"It's too low on your chest, and you pinned it sideways, so it's floppy." She pointed, because it wouldn't do to adjust the rosette herself. She glanced at Theodore.

Tad feigned exasperation. "It doesn't matter how you pin it. Maybe the rosette is floppy."

"Our rosettes are not floppy."

He grinned and refastened the pin. "How do I look?"

Handsome, but she couldn't say that. "Better."

"How's Dottie?" Theodore set down his plate. Rebecca startled, amazed that she'd worked so hard to keep her focus off of Dottie and the whole Gang mess all day, but thirty seconds with Tad, and the matter had flown right out of her head.

"Less pain, and once she got started talking, she didn't stop," Tad said. "She said the hideout's an abandoned mine shaft, like we thought. She left because she'd had enough of living there. Flick Dougherty is probably the one who shot her because she took his horse and the contents of his wallet when she left."

Shuddering, Rebecca imagined the scene. "Wouldn't Ralph be angry about Flick shooting his wife?"

"I'd imagine so, even if she had left him, but I take it she's done this before to get his attention." Tad's gaze scanned the gathering. "If Ralph hasn't retaliated against Flick by now, I'd be surprised."

"And there's the third fellow, Skeet." Rebecca chewed her lip. "Do you know him?"

Tad shook his head. "Not well, but he struck me as being more of a follower, so I expect he's along for the ride."

Theodore scraped the last of his supper from his plate. "And Dottie's behind bars?"

"That's what I've been up to most of the day." Tad tipped his head back to the county offices. "Sheriff Adkins and I have been fashioning a temporary cell for Dottie in that room with the cot, so she'll be separated from Bowe and the Andersons. The sheriff is finishing it up right now."

Theodore's eyebrows lowered. "Dottie's tied up, though, right?"

"Wilkie says there's no need to restrain her, because of her injuries, but to be safe, Jeroboam's sitting with her." Tad looked askew at Rebecca. "Where's your dinner?"

"Oh, I'll get it now."

"You eat this one. If you haven't had your supper before the dancing starts, you might never eat. Ulysses has plans for you."

Sure enough, the first strains of a fiddle pierced the evening air, and even though it was still plenty light, Uncle Giff and Johnny lit the lanterns and lamps on the tables and crates surrounding the dancing area.

Rebecca hesitated to pick up her fork. "Maybe I should sit with Dottie."

"From what I heard, it's not your night," he teased. "It'll be my night, actually. She's a prisoner. I'll rest in the office. But try not to worry about Dottie anymore. She's done enough harm in your life. Don't let her ruin your Independence Day, too." Tad sauntered toward the food line.

"Sorry." Theodore glanced at his empty plate. "I should have let you eat mine."

It seemed they were always saying sorry to one another. "It's fine, Theodore." She took a bite of the tender brisket. Delicious. "I —"

Theodore's eyes went wide. Rebecca turned.

Donned in her new dress of rich cobalt blue, Cornelia passed the dancing area, the bell of her skirt swaying with her steps. The tailored bodice accentuated her dainty figure, set off to perfection by the blue-on-blue striped ruffles they'd finished sewing last night. Cornelia had done well with her hair, too, pinning some of the curls atop her head and allowing a few strands to dance over her shoulders in bronze display. She created an impression of a young woman, no schoolgirl, who was ready to start her own life.

Rebecca turned back to Theodore. "Doesn't she look lovely?"

"That's Corny?"

Who else would it be? "Do you recognize the fabric? We had so much fun. I should tell her how pretty she looks. Do you mind if I go?"

He shook his head, still goggling.

She dashed toward Cornelia, who held out her hands. "Did I do it right? Is it pretty?"

Rebecca clutched Cornelia's hands. "You're gorgeous every day, no matter what you wear or how you style your hair, but yes, you look splendid."

Ulysses leapt behind Cornelia, a rosette pinned to one greasy suspender and his wide grin revealing the gaps in his teeth. "Happy Independence Day, ladies."

"And to you, Ulysses." Cornelia grinned.

"The dancin' is startin' up. Would either of you two do me the honor?"

"I should love to, but I haven't eaten supper." Cornelia's head tipped to the side.

"That'll give me time to dance with Miz Rebecca." He gripped Rebecca's hand and tugged.

"I haven't really eaten, either." But they were already in line for the reel, men on one side, ladies on the other. The fiddles struck up a familiar old tune, "The Girl I Left Behind Me," and Ulysses whirled her around.

It was like trying to dance with popcorn as it bounced in a hot pan, lots of hopping and uncertainty about where she would land, but it was fun. When he bowed like a knight of old at the song's end, she curtsied. "Thank you, sir." She meant it.

She was still smiling while she returned to Theodore's table and finished her plate. Two girls bought more rosettes for their hair, and once they were gone, Rebecca tipped her head at the dance floor. "Come and dance?"

"Me? I'm not much of a dancer."

"None of us are." Except maybe Uncle Giff and Mrs. Horner, who moved smoothly through the figures of another dance. Rounding out their set was Johnny and one of the little Evans girls, Eloise with the other, and Cornelia's parents.

"I can't leave the table, but it looks like you have another partner already."

She turned. Mr. Orr bowed. "A dance, ma'am?"

"I'd be honored." She placed her hand in his large one.

After dancing with the justice of the peace, Rebecca danced with Ulysses twice more, and then Uncle Giff, Johnny, a few fellows she didn't know, and both Evans girls before Ulysses collected her again. She spun on his arm until she was dizzy, and when she twirled to a halt, she caught Tad's laughing eyes glowing in the lamplight. Ulysses saw, too, and beckoned him over as the strains of a waltz began. "Your turn, Deputy."

"Thanks, but I shouldn't. I got shot in the shoulder a while back, you know." It was a flimsy excuse, but Rebecca appreciated it. Dancing with her husband-who-wasn't-her-husband wasn't the best idea.

"Well, she can't dance with her fiancé." Ulysses pointed. "He's already on the floor."

Rebecca twisted. Cornelia had somehow convinced Theodore to leave his wares and dance. Good for her. His posture was stiff as a marionette's as they stepped back and forth in one-two-three time while other couples twirled around them. Cornelia didn't seem to mind their lack of movement, laughing with him over their missteps.

"Mrs. Horner ain't got no partner." Ulysses rubbed his hands together and hurried off, leaving Rebecca standing alone with Tad.

Tad peeked down, his eyes almost black in the lamplight. "You don't mind?"

"Not dancing, you mean?"

"Theodore with Cornelia."

"I don't mind either one," she answered in all truthfulness. "My toes are sore, and I'm glad he's enjoying himself."

This was perfect, this moment, with the breeze cooling her hot cheeks and lifting her hair from her nape, standing where she could see all the people she cared about enjoying the festivities. Johnny and Eloise Evans stood off to the side, drinking lemonade. Uncle Giff laughed with some menfolk. The Evans girls' faces were sticky and dirty, but that didn't diminish from the pure excitement shining from their eyes as Mrs. Croft handed each a paper cone of candy floss.

Rebecca's heart swelled inside her chest. She loved Ruby City and the folks who'd made it their home. All of them. Ulysses, Dr. Wilkie, and even Cornelia, who now glowed in the awkward arms of Theodore, for whom Rebecca felt an affection she wasn't sure how to define, even if things weren't perfect between them.

Tad moved behind her, brushing her sleeve — an unintentional touch but one that burned through her skin to her marrow and forced her to acknowledge that her affection for him was not the same as how she felt about the others. She peeked up at him, admiring the warm smile he shared with passersby.

Why haven't You taken this from me, God?

It was a good thing that he'd not be coming to Silver City. Then these feelings would fade, as they always did, and she could focus on her choice to marry Theodore —

A new figure sashayed through the crowd, her dark hair cascading around her shoulders, a bandage wrapped over the shoulder of that pink confection of a dress Rebecca had liked, swaying to the beat of the waltz.

Rebecca swiveled back to Tad. "What is Dottie doing here?"

CHAPTER TWENTY-FOUR

Tad didn't hear Rebecca's words. The music, the chatter, the loud, rapid beating of his heart in his ears because Rebecca stood at his side, her eyes soft and dewy, all drowned out everything but his thoughts about how much he cared for her. The look in her eyes wasn't sweet anymore, though. It was shocked. He turned to follow her gaze.

Dottie, who shouldn't even be upright, much less dancing, circled the dance floor, gripping the fabric of her pink poufy skirt and waving it to and fro so that it fluttered in time with the music. Swaying like that, smiling and cheerful with her hair loose over her shoulders, she looked like she had before she left, a young, carefree lass eager to join in the fun. He'd thought he loved that young woman.

He'd been a fool then, but he wouldn't be again. He spared a brief glance for Rebecca.

"Pardon me."

Dottie wanted to make a scene, didn't she? Dressing up, nodding in time to the music, sure to be noticed by all of Ruby City as the sweet gal they all remembered. If he hauled her off to the county offices, she'd no doubt scream and cry to the shocked gazes of the townsfolk — all potential members of her jury. He wouldn't give her the satisfaction.

That meant keeping his actions casual. His thumbs hooked his belt loops, and he was at Dottie's side before the final note of the waltz trilled off the bow of the fiddle. "You seem to be feeling better."

She spun, grinning. "I am, yes. Isn't this grand?"

"Sure is. Say, Dottie, what are you doing here?"

She swayed to the music. "Enjoying the party."

"I'm not sure it's appropriate, considering the sheriff placed you under arrest and all."

"Oh, pooh. He didn't mean that sort of arrest."

"What kind did he mean, then?"

"The kind where everyone knows I'm not going anywhere. If I were, why would I be standing here?" She wiggled her fingers in a wave for Ulysses, who waved back.

"I've got a pretty good idea why."

"Dance with me, Tad. Just like last year."

He'd been right. She wanted to dredge up the past, cause a stir, and give folks the impression of a sweet miss they couldn't convict. Tad shook his head. "Your renewed vigor is a marvel. To think, just a few hours ago you were too sore to speak."

"I had the most refreshing nap. Come on."

"Folks might get the wrong idea, though."

"Why? You're not really married."

"You are."

"Ralph wouldn't mind."

Jealous, bullheaded Ralph? Sure. "What I meant was, if you demonstrate the strength to dance a reel, one might conclude you're also able to, say, get on a horse and lead us to your husband."

"Well, I am a little weary, now that you mention it."

Thank You, Lord. "Where's Jeroboam?"

"Getting more corn bread. I told him I wouldn't go anywhere."

Sure enough, Jeroboam munched away, plate in hand, not six feet behind them. He nodded at Tad, widening his eyes as if to say he watched Dottie all the while. Tad expelled a sigh. "How'd you convince him to let you out of Pa's bedroom?"

"I didn't. The sheriff said the cell would

be ready by eight, and he'd be waiting to lock me in, so I dressed. Jeroboam is escorting me to the jail."

"Some escort." Rebecca appeared at Tad's elbow, hands fisted on her hips. "He abandoned his duty for second helpings of supper."

Johnny moved behind Dottie, his hands flexed as if ready to grip Dottie's arms.

Jeroboam joined them, brushing crumbs of corn bread from the stubble on his chin. "Everything all right, Deputy? Dottie wanted to see the fireworks, and I thought it wouldn't hurt nothin'."

Dottie smiled up at him with her head dipped, that innocent look again.

Rebecca snorted. "The dress is rather festive, Dottie, considering you're recovering from surgery and you're going to be confined to an eight-by-six closet."

"Tad," Dottie whined. "That sounds beastly."

"So was being robbed by you." Rebecca folded her arms.

Tad held up a hand. "Come on, Dottie, let's go."

Dottie tucked her hands under her chin. "Not before the fireworks, Tad. Please?"

"I think you've caused enough fireworks," Rebecca muttered.

Dottie's tight smile evaporated. "Don't be jealous, Rebecca. Tad isn't your real husband. You can't begrudge him showing me a small kindness —"

"My sister showed you a huge kindness by giving you the opportunity to turn yourself in." Johnny folded his arms, his posture exactly like Rebecca's.

At that moment, a blaze of light appeared overhead. Someone had started the fireworks. Dottie turned her face skyward, her cheeks and neck aglow with gold light from above. Jeroboam looked at her with slavish admiration. Mercy, is that what Tad used to look like when he followed after her like a lost pup?

"Enough. Dottie, let's go." Tad had to shout over the *ka-boom* of the fireworks and the cheers of the townsfolk.

"I can take her, Deputy," Jeroboam protested. "Sheriff told me not to bother you 'cause you've had so much on your plate."

Had he, now? Tad took a sharp breath of tangy, gunpowder-tinged air. "It's no bother."

Johnny shook his head. "It'd be my privilege to see she's brought to the sheriff, Tad. You enjoy the fireworks, and you can trust I won't fall for any tricks."

"Thanks, Johnny." It would give Tad a moment to talk to Rebecca privately. "Jeroboam, I appreciate your help. You can get more to eat now, if you want."

Jeroboam wandered back to the food table, his longing gaze fixed on Dottie's sashaying pink skirt as Johnny led her by the arm to the county offices. Dottie turned back to wave good-bye to Tad and Rebecca.

Rebecca turned her back to Dottie, her eyes narrowed in suspicion. "Really, Tad?"

Tad opened his mouth, but another firework exploded overhead with a resounding boom. They'd never get any talking done here. Everyone's gazes turned toward the sky, so Tad grasped Rebecca's hand and tugged.

"What are you doing?" He couldn't hear the words, but her mouth moved that way.

"Getting you somewhere quiet," he shouted. Her brows still knit in confusion.

The fireworks weren't any quieter behind the livery, but the chatter of the crowd wasn't as loud here. Tad let go of her hand and swiped his suddenly damp hand through his hair. "Why are you so angry?"

"You have to ask?"

"Apparently so."

Rebecca shook her head, like her thoughts weren't worth speaking, but then she uttered a mirthless laugh. "Well, for starters, no one in town knows yet that Dottie's a criminal. Why?"

He thought he'd answered that. "She needs to be secured behind bars, not only so she'll be confined, but for her own protection. If folks knew she was in the Gang, someone could take vengeance."

"You weren't in a hurry, though. One look at her in that dress she probably stole, and you sauntered over and chatted instead of hauling her to jail."

Tad gulped. He'd left Rebecca with no explanation, but he could remedy that now. "That's not why I took my time. She wanted me to make a fuss and draw attention. I was determined not to give it to her, so I planned to take her in quietly, and no, I was not going to let her watch the fireworks."

Rebecca's hair turned gold as another shower of sparks glittered overhead, and so did her eyes as they flitted to meet his gaze. "I'm sorry. She just sets my teeth on edge. And when I saw you acting all friendly-like, I told Johnny so he'd step in. I hope you don't mind, but he won't tell until you're ready."

Pops and crackles sounded as more showers of sparks lit up the sky. "I don't mind. And don't ever, for a second, think I'm not long past falling for Dottie's schemes. I wouldn't have married you if I wasn't, and that's no lie."

He only lied to himself, about how much he cared for Rebecca. He told himself all the time this yearning for her would fade, but it hadn't, and it never would.

He loved her, and he couldn't deny it to himself any longer. He wouldn't stand in the way of her marrying Theodore, because it was what she wanted. It was best for all three of them. But every heartbeat pounded her name.

He swallowed hard.

Her gaze caught the jerky motion of his throat. "I know. And she's married, of course."

"So are we."

He shouldn't have said it. His brain scrambled for something to say so she wouldn't think he was going to fight her on the annulment. "I mean, everything's been proper. Just like you won't call yourself engaged to Theodore, I wouldn't flirt with anybody, because we're married."

After a long moment, he realized she hadn't protested. She hadn't said, *Not for long,* or reminded him of the judge's eventual return. Tad realized something else, too. She wasn't immune to him; he'd known that from the start. But right now, the way she looked up at him, Tad could believe it was more than that. Maybe it was the reflection of the golden fireworks in her eyes, but they seemed to glow from an inner fire.

Blasts and pops sounded overhead, one after another, followed by silver and gold shimmers of light, but he couldn't tear his gaze away from her to view the display above. If he were free to do it, he'd kiss her just like he did at their wedding. Not that first, tentative kiss, but the second one, the one that burned to the toes of his boots. And then there'd be a third kiss, and a fourth, and he wouldn't even be counting them anymore by the time he was done.

Maybe there was a way for them to stay married, after all —

Pa-whump. The blast sounded different, like some fool miner lit a stick of dynamite as a way to join in the celebration. It happened last year, setting off a rockslide that endangered Longbeard's camp. Tad should check on him. The timing couldn't be worse —

No, the timing was actually perfect. It hurt, stepping back from Rebecca, but he'd be grateful later that he'd put more distance between them. *Thank You, God, for saving me from temptation.*

"Sounds like dynamite." He forced a

smile. "I should check."

She let out a ragged breath. "I thought a firecracker had gone off close to the ground, the noise was so close."

The moment she said it, Tad's mouth went dry. "You're right."

All the booms and blasts, the pops and crackles, had confused him. So had the wonder in Rebecca's eyes. But if someone was lighting dynamite in town, they needed a stern talking-to and maybe even a night to cool down in the jail cell with Bowe.

"What's that?" She pointed around him, down the back side of the buildings.

He strained to see in the darkness. Now would be a good time for a firework to explode overhead and illuminate things, but all Tad could make out were lumps on horseback. "Come on."

He led Rebecca around the front, not touching her. When they were on the edge of the dance floor, Jeroboam ran toward him, waving a gangly arm. "Deputy, there's trouble at the bank!"

The bank wasn't open for business. Did someone get hurt in front of it, or —

Dottie's warning rose fresh in his thoughts and he ran, pushing past folks until he reached the bank. The door was ajar, a pungent smell hung in the air, and a lit oil lamp illumined the twisted remnants of the safe. Banker Bilson tugged his gray hair by the roots.

Rebecca dashed past Tad. "Oh, Mr. Bilson!"

Jeroboam followed her. "See, I told you."

"Go get the sheriff. He's at the jail." Tad crossed to the banker. "Did you see anyone, Bilson?"

"No, I found the lock picked open. How could they blast open the safe without me hearing it?" Mr. Bilson's hand covered his mouth.

Rebecca helped him sit behind his mahogany desk. "The fireworks were loud enough to cover it."

The thieves weren't too long gone, though. Tad examined the rubble surrounding the destroyed safe. Bills, coins, and bags of what might be gold dust lay strewn about the floor in tantalizing enticement. Anyone could scoop them up in a few seconds. "There's a lot of valuables still on the floor. Do you think your return startled them?"

"What's this?" Sheriff Adkins pushed through the gathering crowd into the bank. "Aw, Bilson."

"What's the hullabaloo?" Ulysses poked his head in the door. "Howdy, Miz Rebecca."

"Where's my money?" Donald Evans shoved inside, followed by Eb Cook.

"I'm back." Jeroboam puffed out his chest. "Make way for the deputy's deputy."

Sheriff Adkins shooed the crowd back out the door. "Everything will be fine, folks."

"I want my money," Donald grumbled.

"Me, too." Eb folded his arms.

Tad gestured to the door. "You know Bilson's good for it. Now, everyone out."

"Not me, too?" Jeroboam's face fell.

"You guard the door." Tad shut it and turned back to Bilson. "Anyone suspicious come in recently?"

"All those mining ne'er-do-wells are suspicious." Bilson's shoulders slumped. "But it could've been anyone."

"We'll find them." Tad clapped the banker's shoulder. Then he turned to Rebecca. "Get back to the boardinghouse and stay there where it's safe."

Rebecca, disobedient creature, poured Bilson a glass of water from the pitcher in the corner. "Where's your broom, Mr. Bilson? I'll get this tidied up in a jiffy."

Mr. Bilson pointed to the back room. Tad's jaw clenched. "Rebecca —"

She disappeared without a glance to Tad. Insufferable. For all her talk of wanting to be safe, she didn't hide behind a locked

359

door like a sensible person. Well, there was one good thing about her being in the other room. She wouldn't hear what he was about to say. "Sheriff, Dottie warned us the Gang was going to turn to bank robbery. It seems she was right. I suggest we form a posse, now, before they get too far."

"Even if it wasn't the Gang, a posse is a good idea. Bilson, clean up as best you can and get yourself a new door lock."

Rebecca returned, a brush and dustpan in hand. Bilson stood, and she waved him back to his seat. "You relax, Mr. Bilson."

"All them people gawking in here, wondering about their money." Bilson's voice held a panicked edge. "Even Bowe Brown, and he don't even got any cash in here."

Rebecca dropped the dustpan with a clatter to the floor. "Bowe's out of jail? But I thought — Tad?"

"We didn't release him." Tad ran to the window. Sure enough, Bowe craned to get a gander at the fuss inside, but once he met Tad's gaze, he vanished. It sure looked like the Anderson brothers chasing after him, too. Tad swung the door open, startling Jeroboam, and ran.

Long-legged Jeroboam caught up at once. "Hey, you fellers there! Stop in the name of the law!"

The youngest Anderson spun to laugh at them, but he'd made a critical mistake. Running backward through the streets normally wouldn't be difficult, but tonight, tables blocked the street. The fellow rammed into a table and flew over it.

"Take him back to jail, Jeroboam."

"Will do, Deputy!"

Tad ran on, following Bowe and the other two fellows around the corner of the street, past Pa and Mrs. Horner at Theodore's table. "Stop 'em!"

He didn't pause to watch but chased Bowe over the thick grass. Tad lunged, getting a mouthful of grass and a fresh stab of pain in his shoulder wound, but he caught Bowe, gripped his wrists behind his back, and hauled him to his feet.

Within moments, half the town surrounded him. Ulysses, Wilkie, and Eb lent assistance as he, Pa, Jeroboam, and Theodore — tie askew — pushed the fugitives along. Mrs. Horner walked alongside, wielding a ladle like a weapon. And then there was Rebecca, her fingers clutching her arms so hard her knuckle bones were white.

"I told you to go home."

"And I don't take orders from you."

"Ain't she your mail-order bride?" Bowe snickered. "I'd send her back."

Tad spared a hasty glance for Theodore, who'd gone red. But it wasn't any use rising to Bowe's bait, so Tad just shoved him into the county offices. "Speaking of being sent back, breaking out of prison is plain stupid. The judge won't view it too kindly."

A sense of dread prickled the back of his neck. He hauled Bowe inside. Sure enough, the back door swung wide, its lock blasted off. Inside the jail, the cell doors hung open, the key still in one of the locks. Over at the closet, the new lock was blown apart by a gun.

The clamor of the fireworks had covered a lot more than the dynamite.

Rebecca looked around, eyes wide. "Where are they? Where's Johnny?"

"The Gang broke Dottie out and set the others free as a distraction, so we'd have work to do before we went after them." He turned back to Rebecca, hating the words even before he spoke them. "And it looks like they took Johnny as a hostage."

Chapter Twenty-Five

Rebecca didn't say a word, not when Mr. Orr thumped her shoulder and said it would be fine. Not when Uncle Giff jerry-rigged locks to keep Bowe and his cronies behind bars. Not when Theodore said he was sorry about Johnny, or when Cornelia hugged her, or when Mrs. Horner suggested they go back to the boardinghouse to wait. But when Tad and the sheriff announced the posse would be riding out in ten minutes, she found her voice.

"I'm coming with you."

Tad, who was issuing orders to Ulysses to guard the prisoners here, turned. "No, you're not."

"It's my brother out there. I can and I will." She spun to Uncle Giff. "I need a horse."

Uncle Giff's mouth opened, but Tad slashed the air with his hand. "Do not give her a horse, Pa."

She waved off Tad's hand. "I know how to ride, Tad."

"This isn't about whether or not you can. It's about whether or not you should, and I say you shouldn't. Everyone does."

But nobody said a word. Not Uncle Giff, not Mrs. Horner, not Cornelia, who pressed her lips together, and not Theodore, who merely watched her. Rebecca's hands fisted on her hips. "I won't slow you down."

"You will, dressed like that." He pointed at her full skirt like it was offensive.

"I'll wear Dottie's trousers." Rebecca lifted her chin.

Cornelia gasped. "Really, Rebecca? Trousers?"

Mrs. Horner hushed her.

Rebecca glared at Tad. "Are you going to waste time arguing, or are we going after them?"

Tad glanced at the sheriff, who shrugged. "Five minutes," he announced. "Have your horses and supplies ready. Even you, Miss Rice."

That wasn't much time. Rebecca paused in the doorway to glower at Tad. "You will not leave without me, Tad Fordham."

Bowe Brown laughed from his cell. "Sounds like a wife to me."

Rebecca rushed to the livery. Dottie's

trousers were where she'd left them, at the bottom of the valise. Rebecca stuffed them under her arm and ran out again, passing Uncle Giff as he tossed a saddle over the dappled horse named Patches. He looked up at her. "She'll be gentle for you, but you'd best hurry. Don't forget a canteen and a blanket."

She paused long enough to kiss his stubbled cheek before running to the boardinghouse. By the time she'd grabbed her medical bag and donned her shirtwaist, coat, bonnet, and Dottie's trousers — an odd sensation, but not an unpleasant one — Mrs. Horner stood at the foot of the stairs, holding a mass of objects. "Food in the dish towel. Canteen's full, and the blanket's thin but enough to lay on if you're out that long."

"Oh, Mrs. Horner —"

"Thank me when Johnny comes home. Now go before the deputy leaves without you. And don't feel bad about going. I'd go, too, if it was my brother."

Several men gathered at the livery, some kissing wives and children, and others already mounted and ready to go. Rebecca recognized a few, like Jeroboam, but didn't pause to greet anyone as she hurried inside, where Patches waited beside the mounting block. Two feet away, Tad tightened a cinch on Solomon's saddle and scowled. She wouldn't dare ask him for help climbing into the saddle. If she did, he'd say she wasn't fit to come along.

She didn't need his help, anyway. She secured the blanket, her medical bag, and food, and then planted her foot in the stirrup. Swinging the rest of her body up and over was easy in trousers. Riding was still awkward, however. It had been nearly six years, and she'd never ridden astride. She bent and patted Patches's neck. "Let's be friends, shall we?"

Tad climbed on Solomon and left the livery without a glance.

Well, she wasn't happy with him, either. Now she knew what people meant when they said rage boiled under their skin. Heat suffused her from her bones and lapped in waves from her chest to her head.

Theodore paused outside, and a fresh wave of something unpleasant washed over her: guilt, because she hadn't even thought to tell him good-bye. She pulled Patches to an abrupt stop. "I'm sorry, Theodore. I have to go —"

"I know. I'll help with guard duty at the jail until you all come back."

To her shame, she'd assumed he'd be

working at the store. "Thank you for helping, Theodore."

"Be careful."

"I will."

She clicked her tongue to Patches and hastened after the men, who'd already ridden away. Her mind stayed on Theodore, though. They'd exchanged no tender words of good-bye, no squeeze of hands. She was left with nothing but remorse, because the truth was, she hadn't wanted more than a hasty, cordial good-bye from him.

Don't feel guilty. After you get Johnny back, you can focus on Theodore. Love will come after you're married. Isn't that what you're always telling everyone?

She had plenty of other things to feel guilty about that were more pressing, though. Like Johnny. He should never have been involved in this mess. Rebecca spurred Patches onward.

They'd traveled a short distance when Tad dismounted to study something on the ground by torchlight. "Broken shoe, just like before."

Mr. Orr nodded. "It's them, all right. No animal comes out of Fordham's with a broken shoe."

"Good. I want my money back." Mr. Cook shifted in the saddle.

Rebecca spun. "We've got people to be concerned with, too."

Cornelia's pa had the good sense to look abashed.

The following hour, Rebecca's molars ground together as she prayed and fumed, angry at everyone. Dottie. The Gang. Even Tad for not wanting her to come along. And at God, too, to be honest. *How could You let this happen to me again? To Johnny? Losing Pa this way scattered our family and left me fatherless.*

God had been her Father, she remembered. But she also remembered being hungry.

As the first glow of pink tinged the eastern sky, Tad turned Solomon and cantered back toward her. "This is the direction Dottie told us to go, and the broken-shoe tracks are still fresh," he announced. "We'll be at the mine shortly."

She appreciated the news but didn't acknowledge it. Instead she stared straight ahead. Tad positioned Solomon alongside Patches and bent toward her, adjusting his Stetson and giving her a view of his furrowed brow and his low-drawn brows. "There are still tracks for five horses. That means the Gang *and* Johnny. They haven't hurt him."

"Oh, he's hurt all right." The words flapped out, noisy and clumsy, like birds escaping from a cage. "They must've incapacitated him somehow, because he wouldn't have gone without a fight."

"You know what I meant, but you're right. The sooner we get to Johnny, the better."

"And Dottie? Is she a captive, too? I doubt it sincerely."

Tad sighed. "I just hope she hasn't told them we know about the hideout's location."

"If she did, they'll be waiting to ambush us. Or they'll hurt Johnny."

"The sheriff and I have already worked out a plan so they won't know we're coming. We'll go around the side of the mountain. There are plenty of trees to hide us, but we'll have to be careful because it's on a steep cliff face. Don't worry, though. There's a sheltered spot in the rocks a quarter of a mile from the mine where we can leave you."

"I will not be left behind. You heard Mr. Cook. The others care more about their money than saving my brother." She spurred Patches onward.

Tad trotted to catch her. "Be sensible." His voice was low, so the others couldn't overhear. "You have no experience bringing in fugitives, and the Gang is unlike anything most of us have ever dealt with."

She stopped then, fully, making Tad bring Solomon around. "Johnny is my brother. No one else cares as much as I do what happens to him."

"I care," he whispered.

Not like she did. How could he? "But this is my fault, Tad. I should've thought of the consequences when I gave Dottie time to turn herself in. If I'd just told your pa before you got home, told everyone in town, there might have been more time to secure her in jail."

"She was plenty secure."

Rebecca tugged off her right glove with her teeth and swiped her damp palm on Dottie's trousers. "Don't try to make me feel better. I'm still angry, Tad, both at myself and at you for wanting to leave me behind."

"I know." It sounded almost like an endearment.

The sheriff wheeled his enormous black gelding around and trotted back toward them. Rebecca took a ragged breath. The time for talking to Tad was over, and just in time. She was angry, so angry, and at the same time — oh, she couldn't deny she was drawn to Tad, too. Relied on him when she felt weak, like right now.

This can't go on, Lord.

Sheriff Adkins pointed. "The hideout is half a mile that away. Should we make some plans, Fordham?"

"Sounds good." He cast her a parting look as he trotted away on Solomon. "You're still hiding while we round them up."

She shook her head. "If someone needs medical care, I can help."

Just like Johnny helped, by putting Dottie in jail for Tad. Just like Pa helped by serving as a sheriff, even though it cost him his life. Just like Tad helps by risking life and limb for the folks of Ruby City. Folks help one another. You're no different.

Rebecca's hand fisted over her mouth. What she did was completely different. Stitching was not the same as what Tad did. What her father had done.

But she held back and prayed while the others formed their plan to sneak up to the hideout.

Fifteen minutes later, after leaving the horses below and directing the group, Tad led the small posse up the slope, around the back of the mine. His feet were steady, but his innards writhed like rats in a meal sack. He was glad for it; fear kept him sharp.

Johnny was in danger. Dottie might be, too. The Gang of Four wouldn't hesitate to shoot Tad or anyone else, not even Rebecca. She shouldn't even be here, and when she refused to wait in the protected alcove, he'd wanted to smack something.

She might be stubborn, angrier than a wet hornet, and bound and determined to marry someone else, but he loved her. He'd be the first to throw the rice at her wedding to Theodore if it meant she'd be safe and sound forever, though.

Tad tiptoed through the brush around the hideout, shoving his emotions down to his boots. He had a job, and right now it entailed a lot less moping about Rebecca and a lot more awareness of his surroundings.

Scrinch. Somebody behind him stepped on a twig. Tad turned back, his forefinger over his lips. Jeroboam mouthed *sorry.*

Tad needn't have worried about being overheard, though. Or about coming to the wrong place. Voices carried from around the curve of the hill, from the direction of the mine's entrance. The Gang of Four was having one beaut of an argument.

Tad couldn't make out the words, but the Gang's distraction offered the posse a distinct advantage. Preparing to wait for the sheriff's signal, the group crept behind the junipers and thickets that overlooked on the abandoned mine. There'd be good cover there, but Tad took Rebecca's elbow and held her back. "Stay here. Please."

The words were mouthed more than whispered.

Rebecca shook her head. He had no choice but to progress into his hiding spot, and she followed after him to crouch behind a scraggly evergreen. He sighed and sidled around her, shielding her with his body. "Could you please try to not get killed?" he whispered.

"I could say the same to you," she whispered back, straining to see over his shoulder.

All four members of the Gang gathered around the entrance of the mine, which was positioned dangerously close to the cliff's edge. Dottie sat against the rock at the mine opening, resting her head. Near her hunched pock-cheeked Skeet Smucker, who shook his head although nobody looked at him except Johnny, who was bound, hands and feet, beside Dottie.

Thank God he was alive.

Ralph White hadn't changed in looks. Still as burly, endowed with the sort of build and face that turned ladies' heads, Ralph positioned himself between his wife and Flick, the fourth member of the Gang. "I should kill you here and now for shooting Dottie, Flick."

Flick Dougherty's head was a little too small for his big shoulders, and his eyes were small, like peppercorns in a large, doughy face. His thick fingers clenched close to his gun holster.

Rebecca tapped Tad's arm. "That's the man I saw in town, all right."

Flick would have had to hurry between his bank visit and the holdup of the piece haulers that day, but it was possible to do. He certainly hadn't needed the two dollars he withdrew for his mother. Perhaps he'd been evaluating the bank's security so the Gang would have an easy time when they returned to rob it.

Flick sneered at Ralph. "Your wife took my horse. That's a hanging offense."

Now that was rich. Tad chomped his lower lip.

Dottie didn't open her eyes. "You didn't treat your pony well, Flick."

"Shut up!" Flick glared at her.

"You shut up!" Ralph loomed over Flick like a standing bear. "You shot Dottie and Tad Fordham, and we decided there'd be no killing!"

"But you want to kill me for accidentally shooting Dottie?" Flick laughed.

Rebecca's breath was hot on the back of Tad's neck. He wished he could turn and comfort her, but any moment now, the sheriff would give the sign to ambush the crooks.

"You've gone too far, Flick." Ralph paced just a few yards from Tad and Rebecca's hiding spot. "Robbin' a few wagons and coaches and scragglers was all we were goin' to do. We weren't gonna hurt nobody, and we weren't gonna steal nobody, neither. Takin' this feller as a hostage was plain senseless."

"It was smart, is what it was." Flick rubbed his block of a jaw. "His sister is the deputy's wife. Or cousin or something. I can't keep track. How does it go again, Dot?"

"She's both." Dottie shut her eyes.

"That don't make no sense, but it don't matter. A posse will let us go in exchange for his safety, if they manage to track us."

Ralph shook his head. "It ain't an *if,* Flick. It's a *when.* Fordham's a good tracker, so we'd best git our goods, let the man go, and git out of here."

"They'll let Johnny go?" Rebecca's whisper tickled Tad's nape.

"No releasin' the hostage," Flick answered for Tad.

Ralph started toward Johnny anyway. "You may be the leader, but I say we're done with him."

"You ain't doin' nothing!"

Skeet's hands curled around his ears. "Let the prisoner go, Flick, and I say Dottie gets the goods so we can skedaddle."

"I can't climb down in that hole." Dottie opened her eyes and gestured to her bandage. "Flick shot me, remember?"

"But you're the only one who can fit down there. Aw, just forget it. We got a good haul from the bank." Ralph bent to gather the canvas bank bag. "I don't want to do this no more, no how. You've changed, Flick, shootin' and kidnappin' folks."

Flick's hands fisted. "You can't quit until I say you can quit."

"You ain't the boss of us," Ralph protested.

Tad exchanged glances with the sheriff. The Gang had admitted to everything, from the robberies to kidnapping to shooting Tad and Dottie. The argument among the members of the Gang was intensifying. It was time to act.

Flick must have thought so, too, because he drew his pistol and aimed at Ralph. "I say when we quit, and I say that time is now, after all. I'll take the haul from the bank, and I'm feelin' generous, so I'll let you all split the goods in the mine. And I take the hostage."

Rebecca gasped, but Tad reached behind him and squeezed her upper arm. *Hold fast.*

Ralph's head stuck out, like he hadn't heard. "What?"

"Hand over the bank bag, nice and slow, and I won't shoot your wife again. And by the way, it wasn't an accident the first time. I was aimin' right at her spine."

Tad didn't breathe. Neither did Rebecca, because his neck went cold. Then Ralph sprang at Flick.

Tad barely saw the sheriff's hand signal. He was at Johnny's side before Ralph and Flick hit the ground. Johnny hopped to his feet, clearly having loosened his bonds without his captors' knowledge. Tad pressed a folding knife into his hand. "Rebecca's behind a tree. Keep her safe!"

"She's here?" Johnny groaned. "Why'd you go and bring her along? I thought you — never mind."

Never mind, indeed. There'd be time for talk later. Jeroboam scooped Dottie, pulling her to the safety of the trees, and two men pinned Skeet on the ground. That left Flick and Ralph, who rolled, kicked, and bit, struggling for possession of Flick's pistol. This wouldn't end well.

The sheriff shot into the air. "Drop the gun and stand up, fellers. You're under arrest."

Flick wrenched his wrist from Ralph's grip and took aim at the sheriff.

Tad lunged. The report of the pistol cracked in his ear, but he felt no pain. Tad smacked the gun from Flick's hand, scrambled to his feet, and kicked the firearm toward the cliff's edge. Flick gripped his leg and yanked, pulling him to the dirt.

Flick hadn't earned his nickname by being slow. He knew he was outnumbered, too, and that made him dangerous. His fists flew, connecting with Tad's lip.

Now that, Tad felt.

He scrambled to his feet. If he drew his gun, Flick would wrestle him for it. He only needed to keep Flick occupied until the others helped subdue him. Even now, the sheriff and two other men reached for Flick, but Flick butted Tad with his head and yanked him sideways.

Tad glanced down. They teetered at the cliff's edge. One wrong move, and he and Flick would go over the side.

Folks yelled. One of the women screamed.

Sure enough, Rebecca had quit the shelter of the trees, gaping beside Ralph, whose hands were raised in surrender. Her eyes were wide, her face leached of color, her hands gripping Johnny's. He hated that he'd caused the pain and fear on her face.

But Tad wasn't finished. He swung his leg and swiped Flick's feet out from under him. They both went down, but Tad leaned forward, away from the cliff's edge. Flick fell backward and reached for his pistol. He managed to curl his fingers around the hilt.

And then he slipped.

Tad dropped to his belly and reached, but it was too late. Flick slid down the hill.

Rebecca was on her stomach beside him before he could expel another breath, gripping his face while dust settled around them in a thick, brown cloud. "Can you hear me?"

Tad grimaced. "Of course I can hear you. You're yelling."

"Your ear's bleeding. I thought he shot it." She stuffed a wadded handkerchief against his head. "I'll stitch it up after I get down to help Flick."

He gripped her hand, the one that pushed the hankie into his ear. "There's no use you going down there, Rebecca. It'll be a recovery, not a rescue."

"Oh." Her eyes filled with tears. Tad

squeezed her fingers. The woman had been terrorized by the Gang, yet she still mourned Flick's passing.

They sat like that for a minute, her putting pressure on the side of his head, him holding her hand there, until Johnny helped them to stand. Ralph, Skeet, and Dottie were all bound, but Ralph and Dottie managed to rub noses.

"I shouldn't have left you," Dottie cooed. "I'm sorry!"

"Me, too, turtledove!"

Rebecca's eyes rolled.

Tad removed the handkerchief. Sure enough, blood sopped it, but his ear was only now beginning to hurt. Maybe the bullet grazed him, or he'd landed wrong. Come to think of it, more of him was hurting now. Scrapes from gravel, the sting of a split lip, and his healed gunshot wound ached like he'd been shot all over again.

Dottie pulled away from Ralph and leveled a gaze at Tad. "I told you I was done with the Gang, and you heard that Ralph is, too. He surrendered, even."

"I sure did." Ralph nodded.

"And I told you where the hideout was," Dottie said. "You remember all of that when the judge gets back to town. You tell him how I cooperated, even though it means I'll

380

be separated from my husband for a time. We'll cooperate so we won't be in prison long, right?"

"We'll tell the judge." Sheriff Adkins folded his arms. "Meanwhile, a few of you fellows head on down and recover Dougherty. We'll meet you down there."

Eb grunted. "What about my money? Do I get it now?"

"Or the goods in the mine?" another fellow asked.

"No money until we've cataloged it and returned it to Bilson, but we should probably get the goods out while we're here." The sheriff peered into the mine.

Ralph held up his bound hands. "We said we'd cooperate, and we are, so I'll tell you Dottie's the only one small enough to crawl down into the shaft. A normal-sized feller can't fit. That's why Flick let her be in the Gang."

"It could be a trick," Eb protested. "She could pocket the goods or sneak out the back way."

Ralph snorted. "Only one way in or out."

The sheriff lifted Dottie by her good arm. "Then do it."

She gripped her poufy skirt, as if showing she wasn't dressed for the part. "I can't."

"I thought you said you were cooperating."

"I was shot, remember? I need two arms, and I've only got the use of one."

She had a point. But before Tad could say another word, Rebecca removed her gloves. "Get some rope and light, then. I can do it."

CHAPTER TWENTY-SIX

Rebecca was ready.

"You don't need to do this." Tad's body was tight, his eyes alert despite split lips, stiff shoulders and hands, which were white-knuckled on her wrist as several members of the posse squeezed into the mine shaft where the Gang had hidden out the past few months.

The mine wasn't deep. A cave-in filled the space not five hundred feet from the opening, but the space offered shelter and a few excellent hiding spots, including one narrow passage that curved down into blackness.

Rebecca planted her feet on the edge of it, gripping the rope tied under her arms as if her life depended on it — which it did. If she separated from the rope, she might not get out again. She tried to smile for Tad, but her mouth wouldn't work right. "There's no one else to fit."

"The sheriff and I will come back with —"

"We're here. I'm even in trousers."

"This mine was abandoned for a reason, Rebecca. It's not safe."

She wanted to be safe, oh yes, but right now, more than anything, she wanted to do this so Tad wouldn't have to come back here again. "I'll be fine."

Johnny held a torch overhead. "I'll try to light the way as best I can."

She nodded and took a tentative step into the shaft.

She had to crouch as she scooched deeper down into the cold, narrow passage, but then the walls closed in and she had to turn sideways to fit. Pa and her brothers had called her bird-legged, and she smiled. If ever there was a time to be small-boned and underfed, this was it.

Her breathing came harder as the air tasted staler. Panic swirled in her stomach as the passage grew tighter. *Help me, God.*

"You all right?" Tad's voice carried down, faint but welcome.

She nodded before she realized he couldn't see her. "Yes." She hoped her voice didn't sound as panicky as she felt.

The shaft ended abruptly into a face of rock, and the light from Johnny's torch didn't reach here well — especially with her body blocking it. She shifted, and the feeble glow landed on something burnished.

Rebecca's fingers patted the ground for objects she couldn't see well, and she scooped the items willy-nilly into the sack at her belt. It felt like stacks of money, coins, pocket watches, necklaces and brooches, cloth and tiny bags. Strange items, too, like Dr. Wilkie's stethoscope, paper, and fur. She shifted, and the pale light illuminated a gold lump that looked like a polished nugget — oh, it wasn't a rock. It was Ulysses's tooth! It was dry and cold, but her fingers still shivered handling it, as if it were fresh from his mouth.

"I'm coming back, and I got it all!" She crouched and slithered up and out, crawling on her hands and knees at one point, never more grateful for the light that grew brighter with each step. How did mining men do this, scuttling into cold, confined darkness, every day, all day? Her lungs ached, as if she hadn't truly breathed since descending into the shaft.

Johnny's relieved face was well lit by the torch, but it was Tad's grave countenance she couldn't look away from. Split lip, bruised jaw, and all, it was the most handsome face she'd ever seen. Without a word, he yanked the rope from her and guided her out of the mine. He didn't remove his hand until they were out in the fresh, sweet air, rounding the hill away from the cliff, down to where their horses waited.

He offered her a canteen. "Drink."

"You need it, too."

He shook his head, brooking no argument. She took a long, deep draft of the water, letting it wash the dust from her mouth. Water hadn't tasted so good since that first cup she'd had when she arrived in Ruby City, just before her wedding. She'd thought she was dirty then, but oh, Rebecca could only imagine what she looked like now.

When she'd drunk her fill, Tad retrieved the canteen, doused a bandanna, and swiped her face and hands, even the one still gripping the sack of stolen goods. She stilled his fingers with her own. "You're the one that needs tending. Your lip is swollen."

"It'll heal."

Most things did. Rebecca wasn't sure her heart ever would, though.

Her shoulder was clapped from behind, and Johnny pulled her into a tight embrace. "Good work, sis."

Some of the men voiced agreement, and Mr. Cook pushed forward. "What's in the sack?"

"Nobody touches anything until I see it first," the sheriff insisted. "We've got to make sure these get back to their rightful owners, if we can."

Then he dumped out the contents, looking a little like Santa Claus.

Rebecca chewed her lip. "Do you suppose these items will be needed as evidence for the trial?"

"We have plenty of evidence to convict the Gang, so I don't think so. Why?"

"I recognize a few things. I thought maybe I could deliver them to their rightful owners."

She pointed out the ones in question. The sheriff lifted a skeptical brow, but then Tad nodded. "I'll escort her."

"Fine by me. Let's break our fasts and then head back. We'll see you back in town."

Rebecca knew Tad would offer to accompany her. She wasn't surprised when Johnny stepped forward, either, just as she was untying Mrs. Horner's dish towel and removing the ham and corn bread from it so she could wrap up the stolen goods she had separated from the rest.

"I'll go with you."

"It's all right, Johnny. I think the sheriff needs your help with the Gang." Ralph and Skeet were tied behind horses, but Dottie had to ride, and Flick's wrapped body draped over one of the spare horses they'd brought. It would not be an easy journey back to Ruby City.

They made quick work of the meal Mrs. Horner had packed in the dish towel, and when they finished, Tad waited by Patches. His hands went around her waist, boosting her into the saddle.

"Where first?" He clambered atop Solomon.

"Where's Longbeard's?"

"Thataway." He clicked his tongue, and the horses started back toward Ruby City.

Tad kept their pace slow, falling back from the rest of the posse, and they spoke of trivial things: the weather, Cornelia's fancy dress, how Solomon got his name from being the wisest horse Tad ever knew. Then Tad pointed up the hill, bringing Rebecca back to the reality of where they were and what they were about. "We fork this way to find Longbeard's claim."

After a spell, the ragged land blossomed with tents and makeshift dwellings. One was marked with rope and stakes that looked newer than the rest. Longbeard stood before a droopy tent, as if he'd heard them coming.

So this was where Bowe Brown stumbled,

almost starting a fight in the restaurant that first night Rebecca was in town. She'd best show respect so Longbeard understood she didn't plan to trespass. "Hello, Mr. Pegg. I have something for you."

Tad helped her dismount, his hands warm on her waist. She inched toward Longbeard, unwrapping the dish towel. "We found the Gang of Four's hideout. I think this might be your mother's collar."

It was a ragged thing, the sandy-brown rabbit fur missing in spots. Rebecca held the folded collar flat on her palm, the way she'd feed a carrot to a horse. In a flash, Longbeard grabbed it without touching her skin and tucked it into his dirty shirt front.

Tad stood at her elbow. "Rebecca wanted to give you your collar personally. Didn't want it to get lost, since it belonged to your mother."

Longbeard glanced at Tad. "Your ear's bleedin'."

Rebecca nodded. "I'll bandage it when we get back to Ruby City, but I wanted to see you first. I owe you an apology, because I knew Dottie was in the Gang of Four, and I let her have a day to tell the sheriff herself. If I hadn't waited, we could have had the collar back to you a day sooner."

"You're wearing pants."

"So I am." What she wasn't sure of was whether he forgave her or not, but at least he wasn't angry.

"Pants don't look right with a girl bonnet."

She loosened the ribbon and pushed the bonnet back to rest at her nape. "How's this?"

His watery eyes scanned her hair. Breeze-blown tendrils swept her nose and cheeks, so it must look a mess.

"Unusual," Longbeard said.

Tad chuckled. Rebecca wanted to take Longbeard's hand, but this was as close as he'd let her get to him, probably. "I'll see you later."

He watched them go. Tad boosted her back atop Patches, and when they were out of the camp, skirting junipers, he shook his head at her. "What you said to him isn't true, you know. If it wasn't for you, Longbeard's collar would still be at the bottom of the mine shaft until we figured out another way, and then it would have been locked in a box in the office until Longbeard claimed it, and who knows if he'd have dared to come do that? You're responsible for making him happy, Rebecca."

Longbeard didn't look it, but he never did.

Tad reached for her reins and pulled them

both up short. "I'm glad you're here, Rebecca, but at the same time, I was none too pleased. I wanted to protect you, but you wouldn't trust me. I thought you knew you could count on me."

She'd known it the minute she first saw him, when he drew on his coat as he hurried to meet her at the stagecoach stop in front of the Idaho Hotel. She'd felt in her bones that he was trustworthy, and she'd been drawn to him. Despite her efforts, she was drawn to him still.

It was his face she'd thought of in the mine. His voice she'd wanted to hear. Not Theodore's, not anyone else's.

She had begged God to uproot that yearning before it spread through her like a wild plant, but it hadn't happened. Now, it seemed she would spend the rest of her life asking His help to weed out every shoot of longing for Tad Fordham that popped up through the cracks of her heart.

He had a duty to the county and the people of this town, and they needed him. But her need for him hurt too much. If she let herself love him and something happened to him, that ache would swallow her whole.

She'd made her decision. Now she only had to see it through.

"Trusting you has never been the problem."

If trust wasn't the issue, what was it? Tad swung down from Solomon and reached for Rebecca. "Come down for a minute."

She slid into his arms, small and sweet. The moment her boots hit the ground, though, her gaze fixed on his temple, not his eyes. "Longbeard was right, your ear is bleeding worse than I thought. It's just a cut, though. Want me to bandage it now?"

"No. I want to talk, and not about my ear. Or what happened at the mine."

She plopped the bundled dish towel of sundries at her feet. "That's the difference between us, because you can stop thinking about it, but I can't. I keep thinking of Flick shoving you to the edge of the cliff."

"But everyone's fine." Surely she understood that today had been a success.

"Flick Dougherty isn't fine, and you're bruised and dripping blood on your Sunday shirt." She tugged her bonnet from her neck, crumpling it in her hands. "I was so angry at you when Johnny was taken."

"The way you're standing, I'm not sure you're over it." Her arms crossed over her chest and her feet pointed toward Patches, not at Tad.

"It isn't you I was really angry at. There are a dozen things sticking in my craw, like my inability to keep my loved ones safe. I'm sorry I lashed out at you, Tad."

"Truth be told, I was angry, too. I wanted you to accept that you can't control everything, and sometimes, no one is to blame." He took a deep breath. "Theodore wasn't keen on you nursing, and you insisted he accept you for the way you are. I can't help but feel you're guilty of holding the same type of grudge against me."

Her dry, cracked lips popped open, but she didn't protest. "You're right, but nursing didn't rip his family apart, it just offended his sensibilities. There's a difference."

True. He dug a divot in the dirt with his toe. He'd been awake for over twenty-four hours now, desperately needed a pot of coffee, and was probably as stinky as a hog in a mud puddle. But all he wanted to do was cup the back of Rebecca's head and kiss those dry lips until she told him she didn't love Theodore and could get over her problems marrying a lawman.

Instead, he returned to his earlier words. "You can trust me, Rebecca."

It was the best he could say, because telling her he loved her wouldn't matter if she didn't trust him.

"I've always trusted you, Tad, even when I didn't really know you yet. But you can do all you can to stay safe, and you could still be pushed off the edge of a cliff by the next Flick Dougherty, or shot, or. . . ." She shrugged. "I can't worry about you anymore. I know it's something that needs healing in me, but I can't promise I'll ever change my mind about someone I love going into the law. If Johnny did, I'd — well, I don't like thinking of it." Her laugh was brittle. "I can't live with this type of fear."

Her admission that she fretted over him pleased a little but mostly burned, because of the finality in her voice. She wanted the annulment, and there was no more discussion about it. He'd heard her words before. His heart just hadn't wanted to believe them.

"Theodore is a good man."

"This isn't about Theodore." She looked down at her boots. "He's always been part of this, but my wound won't be healed by him. I've discovered that loving people, no matter what kind of love it is, is scary, because I can't keep anyone safe. Not even me."

"I've tried to protect you." And failed.

"But nobody can protect anyone. You said

it yourself, remember? Theodore could get hurt. So could Johnny or your pa. Any of us. But I still have to try to be safe, and at the same time I have to let people be who they're supposed to be."

He understood then. If he continued serving as a deputy, she'd be worried sick. If he quit for her — a thought that hadn't occurred to him until this minute — he'd be denying a part of himself and his calling. She feared he'd come to resent anyone who kept him from being who he was.

They stood quiet after that, listening to the chip-chips of birds and the soft snuffles of the horses grazing in the grass. There was nothing more to say or do, short of getting down on his knee and begging her to change her mind and not worry anymore and stay married to him, but that wasn't what she wanted. She'd chosen Theodore.

He wouldn't stand in the way a minute longer. He loved her enough to see her happy.

"Let's finish those errands, shall we?"

Her smile didn't wrinkle the outer edges of her eyes, but she put her hand in his outstretched one and allowed him to help her back into the saddle.

He'd ride to Silver City tomorrow and retrieve the judge. He'd probably also find an excuse to be running errands for the sheriff the day Rebecca married Theodore.

They'd just dismounted at the livery when Ulysses poked inside. "There you folks are."

Rebecca rummaged through the dish towel, withdrew an object, and pressed a yellow lump in Ulysses's dirty paw. "Is this yours?"

He gasped. "It's my tooth!"

"I thought so. Oh my." She jerked back when Ulysses shoved the unwashed tooth into his gums. "Will it stay there?"

Tad wondered the same thing.

"Sometimes. The little prong fits in a hole in my gums." Ulysses smiled, revealing an awkward flash of gold on the lower right side. "Can I give you a kiss?"

She let him, offering her cheek. Tad loved her a little more in that moment, and even more when they searched out the Evanses' tent to return Eloise's five dollars, and then at Mrs. Horner's to ask if the lace was what she'd ordered and lost, and then the barbershop to return Wilkie's stethoscope. Then they stopped in to the county office, where men gathered with talk of burying Flick while the sheriff crammed Bowe and his fighting friends in one cell so Ralph and Skeet could languish in the second.

"I want to be with my wife," Ralph insisted.

"I'll miss you, sweetheart," Dottie called from the closet.

Rebecca strode straight to the first cell. "Bowe?"

He spun around and offered a smooth smile that had probably charmed countless females from here to El Paso. "I like the trousers."

"Keep your eyes on my face, if you please." She pulled the last item from the dish towel, an image of a younger Bowe, his features unmistakable under slicked-back hair, with two women who looked to be a mother and grandmother. "I think this is yours."

Bowe snatched it through the bars. "My carte de visite. I didn't think I'd ever see it again."

Tad would be dunked in a horse trough if Bowe didn't tear up. "Thank her proper-like for saving it for you, after all you did to her."

"Thank you." No flirting. No bravado. Just a whisper.

"You're welcome." Rebecca's hands went to her hips. "Now quit brawling and doing things that'll get you arrested again, Bowe, or you might lose that photograph for good next time."

"You sound like my grandmammy." Bowe chuckled.

Rebecca turned to Tad. "I'm ready now."

Tad guided her away out of the cells and through the main office, his hand inches from the small of her back. His heart beat heavy and fast with admiration for her, and with grief because he knew where things stood between them.

He couldn't put off the inevitable, so once they were outside on the street, he tipped his hat. "Good-bye, Rebecca."

"Good-bye, Tad."

They stood there too long for their good-bye to mean anything but a forever farewell. At last she turned and walked to the mercantile.

She'd be safe there. That was where she belonged.

CHAPTER TWENTY-SEVEN

Rebecca stomped the dust off her boots and stepped into the mercantile. No customers perused the shelves, leaving Rebecca free to take in the familiar sight of the store. Tidy shelves, as neat as the proprietor himself, bespoke order, civility, and comfort.

She wanted those things so badly that it ached.

Theodore popped through the gray curtain and grinned. "You're back. I was on guard duty when the sheriff came back, and heard all about it. Come back and have a seat. I have coffee on the stove. Fresh pot."

"Thank you. It smells wonderful." She followed him to the office. He poured her a mug, and she sat in the spare chair by the desk, taking a sip. "It tastes wonderful, too."

"Pioneer Steam Coffee and Spice and Mills, of course."

Rebecca met his hazel gaze. Such a nice-looking face, on a nice man who was everything she'd ever thought she'd wanted.

But he was not what she needed.

"I can't marry you, Theodore."

"I understand."

Just like that? "Theodore —"

"I care about you, Rebecca. I always have, from the first letters we exchanged." His gaze dropped. "You'd had a tough lot, and even though we won't wed, I'm glad I could help you find a better life."

Why was he being so kind? She'd expected anger or disapproval, not this easy acceptance.

"I'll never be able to thank you enough, Theodore. And I cared about you, too. I loved receiving your letters. They were the brightest parts of my week." She swiped a hot tear from her cheek.

"So you're staying married to Tad?" He didn't sound the least bit upset about it. Instead, he passed her his spotless, crisp handkerchief.

She shook her head, patting her cheek with his clean hankie. "I'd be lying if I said I don't have . . . feelings for him, but this isn't about him. I tried to honor my commitment to you, Theodore."

"We haven't been engaged for a month, as you recall. It wasn't proper for you to be engaged and married at the same time."

Bless him, he laughed. She never thought she'd see the day when he found humor in their situation.

She couldn't quite join him, though. "I never wanted him to come between us, or for me to come between the two of you."

"I'm the one who put you in the middle of my feud with Tad, just like I did with Dottie. I'm sorry for that. I should've treated you better."

"You were kind to me, Theodore."

"But not as kind as I should have been, if you were to be my wife. Over the past few days, I've realized I had ample time to court you while we waited for the annulment. I cared more about expense and convenience than I did about your brother. I wanted things to be a certain way, and it bothered me that they weren't. The truth is, I was more aggrieved over the principle of the circumstances than the events themselves, more frustrated my cousin had a tie to the woman I planned to marry than I was about Tad, who was once like my brother, falling head over heels for a wonderful gal like you. Once I saw that, I realized I'd never developed the sort of feelings I wanted to have for the gal I married, and I knew you and I wouldn't suit. But I wasn't going to abandon you, Rebecca. I made a promise and I would have kept it."

"So you don't want to marry me, either?" When he shook his head, she swiped another tear away. "You're an honorable man, Theodore." If mistaken. Tad wasn't head over heels for her, but that wasn't worth mentioning now.

"I don't know how honorable it is to be relieved that you called it off." He cleared his throat. "In fact, it's quite selfish. Do you know why I answered your advertisement? I wanted a wife, of course, but I wasn't truly grateful for the people I already had in my life. Last night my eyes opened to that, and I realized I never cottoned to you because there was someone else I'd been overlooking. Someone I'd grown close to, a friend, but I didn't realize she was so much more. I'm sorry if that hurts you."

It didn't, not a pinprick. "I want you to be happy. I may not be your fiancée, but I feel like you're my family."

"Well, officially, we're still cousins." He chuckled and then sobered. "He'd stop being a lawman for you, I think."

Tad's face loomed in her mind, and she collected her thoughts while she took a long pull of the strong coffee. "He'd resent me for making him give up something that's such a big part of him. I wouldn't want that between me and my husband."

"What will you do?" Theodore sat forward. "Put out another matrimonial ad?"

Her head shook. "I may have come here believing I could marry without love, but things are different now. I'm not sure what I'll do, other than that. Tad told me not too long ago that God would provide, and he was right."

"You can work at the mercantile, even after I move to Silver City."

"That's kind of you, offering me a chance to repay what I owe you."

"You don't owe me a thing."

"My passage west? Replacements for the items the Gang stole? That silver hairbrush cost you a pretty penny."

"I'm glad I brought you here, Rebecca. You may not be my wife or even my cousin, but you'll always be my friend."

At that moment, a warm flower of love for Theodore bloomed in her chest, not the kind between husband and wife, but something good and healthy. She swiped at a fresh round of tears. "Thank you, Theodore."

The back door pushed open. Cornelia stepped inside carrying a basket and dressed in her old green calico dress, but it had been taken in at the waist, and her hair was pinned in a neat bun at her nape. A flash of something rippled over her face, but in an instant it was replaced by a gentle smile. "I'm glad you're back, Rebecca. I heard all about your adventure from my pa — but clearly I'm intruding."

"No." Rebecca smiled. "We were finished."

At least, their engagement was. Their friendship, free of expectations, was just beginning.

Cornelia still hesitated. "I brought cookies and a pint of cream for your coffee, Theodore."

"Thank you, Cornelia. You know I love those cookies." Theodore carried his mug to the stove. "May I pour you a cup?"

Theodore? Cornelia? What happened to *Mr. Fordham* and *Corny?*

Rebecca had been so dense. Cornelia's initial rough treatment of Rebecca had nothing to do with a fear of losing her job. Cornelia had been jealous because Rebecca was marrying Theodore. When Rebecca talked to her about letting God work, Cornelia's heart changed and she'd allowed God to work things through.

But that wasn't all that changed. Theodore had taken notice of his, what had he called her? His friend? Now, however, he gazed at her with rapt fascination.

Rebecca stood. "Cornelia, Theodore, I've enjoyed working with you. I wish you the best."

Cornelia gaped. "You're quitting the mercantile?"

"I'll let Theodore tell you the details." With a parting smile, she slipped out the back door. She had no idea what the future held for her, much less the day, except for heartache over Tad, but she felt more hopeful than she had since her pa was alive.

Johnny wasn't at the livery or the county office, so Rebecca returned to the boardinghouse, let Mrs. Horner fuss over her, and then bathed and changed into her red skirt and white shirtwaist. She lay on the bed for ten minutes to rest, stiff as the proverbial plank, before rising again. Maybe Mrs. Horner needed help.

Her landlady, however, was tying the strings on her bonnet. "Did I wake you? I tried to be quiet."

"I'm too agitated to rest. Is there anything I can do?"

"Supper's bubbling on the stove, everything's tidy, and you did something extraordinary for me in bringing me my lace, dear. I'd planned to make curtains with it, but I've changed my mind. I think I know just what to do with it," she said with a mysterious air. "Would you like me to make you some tea to help you sleep?"

"Tea won't help, I don't think. I told Theodore I'm not marrying him."

"Oh." Mrs. Horner's eyes went wide. "You do have a lot on your mind, don't you?"

Rebecca briefly recounted their conversation, focusing on her decision that she and Theodore wouldn't suit, without mentioning her feelings for Tad or Theodore's burgeoning romance with Cornelia. "Maybe I should find Johnny. I couldn't earlier."

"I saw him through the window a minute ago. He just left the bathhouse. I'm sure he's at the livery by now. Let's go down there together, shall we? We can chat while we walk."

Rebecca allowed Mrs. Horner to take her arm, but confusion clouded her thoughts. "You don't need to come, too."

Mrs. Horner locked the door behind them. "But there's so much to tell you. Half the talk last night at the party — before Dottie and the dynamite, that is — was about moving to Silver City. I decided I'm going to go, too. It won't be for a few weeks yet, but I want to settle in before the snow comes."

Would anything be left in Ruby City? Rebecca bit her lip. "I understand. You have to do what's best for you."

Mrs. Horner squeezed her arm. "You'll have a room with me, of course, and you'll like Silver City. There are more womenfolk, so Ulysses won't be proposing to you as much."

She couldn't help but laugh. "I can't say for sure yet, but thanks for offering." She needed to talk to Johnny first, although he'd seemed so smitten with Eloise, he might want to marry her. As much as Rebecca wanted to live close to Johnny, she didn't want to be in the way if he married and started a family.

They passed two businesses, their doors wide open and their proprietors moving furniture onto sledges. One hitched mules from the Fordhams' livery to a fully packed sledge, ready to make the trek. Mrs. Horner was right. Folks were leaving for Silver City already, and Ruby City would look far different soon.

In the livery paddock, Madge the mule stood at the fence, as if waiting for Rebecca. Her soft eyes beckoned like the smile of an old friend. Rebecca reached to pat her broad neck. "Hello, sweetheart."

Mrs. Horner chuckled. "You and that mule."

Madge stepped closer to Rebecca, as if relishing the contact, but in an instant her ears rotated toward the yawning livery doors. Rebecca turned. Tad strode toward her, scrubbed, changed, his fresh-shaved jaw clenched tight. When he saw her, his steps faltered.

"Rebecca." He stared at her.

"Hello, Tad."

Mrs. Horner chuckled. "Y'all act like you haven't clapped eyes on each other in days, not hours. I'd say a nap would do you both good."

Indubitably, but fatigue wasn't responsible for their responses to one another. This was the first time they'd seen one another since that good-bye on the mercantile porch that felt so final. Rebecca pressed her hand into Madge's rough coat. It gave her something solid to hold on to, tethering her so she didn't do something foolish, like cry or break her determination to let Tad go and be who he was supposed to be. *Will seeing him get easier in time, Lord?*

Tad's gaze fixed on her hand. "I tried to catch a few winks, but there's too much to do."

Mrs. Horner shook her head. "I imagine so, with a full jail and a busy day at the livery, too. We saw the folks down the street, headed to Silver City. Looked like some of your animals."

It was easier to look at Madge than Tad, so Rebecca smiled at the sweet beast. "But not you, Madge? You didn't much want to go to Silver City a few days ago, did you?"

"She's going now." Tad rested a hand on the gate, clearly intending to enter the paddock. "I'm going to fetch Judge Harris. He should be well enough to travel by now, and there's plenty for him to do here, with the Gang, Bowe and the Andersons, and the annulment."

The way he said *annulment* sounded normal, but it felt as if the word had tenterhooks that sunk into the softest parts of Rebecca's insides and tore at them.

"You didn't know?" Mrs. Horner's hand flew to her chest. "Harris got here nigh on an hour ago. He drove right past my house, sitting up in a wagon bed with his leg elevated on grain bags. No need to make the trip, now."

Rebecca forced the phoniest smile she'd probably ever mustered. "No need to bother him this minute. I'm looking for Johnny, anyway. We have a lot to talk about."

"We all do. Even you, Tad." Mrs. Horner took her arm again, drawing Rebecca into the livery. Inside the barn, she released Rebecca and fisted her hands on her hips. "Giff?"

Uncle Giff popped out of one of the farthest stalls. "Jolene — oh, hello, Becky."

"Hello, Uncle Giff." She should probably stop calling him that, since he would never be her uncle now. "Is Johnny here?"

"He's visitin' Eloise. Sweet on her, ain't he? Must be in the air." Uncle Giff winked. "Tad, you aren't hitching up yet?"

"Mrs. Horner says Harris is back, so there's no need. She also said we have something to talk about?" It came out as a question. Tad leaned against the side of the wagon they'd taken to Silver City the day they found Dottie. The day she'd wanted Tad to kiss her again.

Those feelings rushed through her veins. Rebecca flapped her hot cheek, hoping nobody thought she was doing anything more than shooing a horsefly. "Are you well, Uncle Giff?"

"Amazingly so." He moved to stand beside Mrs. Horner, placing his hand on her shoulder. Both wore grins like toddlers who'd been given cones of candy floss. "Jolene and I are getting married."

Rebecca rushed toward them, arms open. "Congratulations."

Mrs. Horner returned her embrace.

"That's what the lace will be for, Rebecca! I may be too old for a wedding veil, but I don't care."

"You're never too old. I'll help you. When is the wedding?"

"As soon as Orr can do the officiating, I suppose. We want things legal before we move to Silver City." Uncle Giff looked at Tad. "Son? You're awful quiet back there."

"I was just waiting my turn, Pa. Congratulations." He looked tired but happy, hugging his father and Mrs. Horner in turn. "Pa's a blessed man, Mrs. Horner."

"Call me Jolene." She patted his cheek. "I always wanted a boy of my own. Now I've got one."

Tad's smile was sad. Was he thinking of his mother? Or maybe of the coming changes. Either way, he hugged her again. "Thank you, Jolene. That means a lot to me."

Rebecca swiped a tear.

Tad shook his father's hand. "I'm pleased for you, Pa, and I won't be as worried about you being alone."

"What sort of fool talk is that?" Uncle Giff's head hung forward. "You're still welcome in the house."

"Of course," Mrs. Horner insisted. "You're our boy."

411

"Thank you, truly," Tad said. "But I'm not moving to Silver City, Pa. You know that."

Rebecca's stomach tightened as Uncle Giff's expression hardened.

"It's *Fordham and Son,* Tad. This livery is your heritage."

"Pa, let's not talk about this right now. This is a happy occasion —"

"It'll be happier when you come to your senses."

Rebecca and Mrs. Horner exchanged glances. The desire to defend Tad rose hot in her chest, but he didn't need it.

"Pa, let's talk about it later, please?"

"How are you going to be a deputy if you aren't in Silver City? Everyone knows it's a matter of time before the county seat transfers there." Uncle Giff gripped the wagon bed.

"It's a big county, Pa."

"Ranching is too big a risk. It could fail and you'd be up to your neck in poor soil and dead stock. Everyone thinks it's a bad idea. Even Becky here."

Maybe she should keep her mouth shut, but she loved Tad and that meant she wanted his best. Besides, Uncle Giff was incorrect about her opinion. "I'm sorry, but I disagree, Uncle Giff. Tad needs to do this."

Tad folded his arms, but the look in his

eyes was more amused than irritated. "I do?"

"You have to be who you are, Tad. It might be a risk, but so is starting a new livery in Silver City, Uncle Giff."

Uncle Giff's grip on the wagon bed tightened. "If I stay here, I won't have anybody left to rent rigs and animals to."

"True, but I think you understand my meaning. I'm sorry. Please don't let my overstepping ruin your happy day. I'm pleased beyond words for you both, but Tad wants to ranch. I hope you can give him your blessing. And when Johnny comes back, would you tell him I'm looking for him, please? He and I have plans to make, now that I'm not marrying Theodore, and I'm sure neither of us wishes to impose on your family's hospitality anymore."

She rushed outside, imagining the angry looks on their faces. She'd apologize later for expressing opinions that hadn't been sought, if not for the opinions themselves.

Not that she didn't understand Uncle Giff's reasons. She'd wanted Tad to conform to her vision of security, too, but that wasn't fair to him or who he was.

She dashed in Mrs. Horner's house to — what should she do? Clean? Cry? Was Mrs. Horner upset? Would she want her packed and gone? No, she wouldn't be as harsh as all that, but Rebecca still fretted. She needed something to occupy her while she waited for Johnny. Maybe she should bake something to help with supper. What had Mrs. Horner left on the stove? She found a pot of fragrant lamb stew, gave it a stir, and pulled a mixing bowl from the cupboard. A batch of biscuits would be just the thing to accompany it.

When she finished, she scrubbed the sticky dough from her hands, using her fingernails to scrape a persistent splotch from the ring finger of her left hand, bare of Tad's ring. Oh, that ring. She must return it to truly be able to let him go. If she went to bed tonight and found it winking at her from the dresser, as it had for the past weeks, the pain would be horrible. It would be best to hand it over and end things, neat and clean.

She mounted the stairs, put on the ring for safekeeping, and grabbed her bonnet. She'd deliver the ring to the county office, since no one at the livery was probably ready to see her just yet.

Her hand was on the doorknob when a knock rapped on the other side. Johnny? She swung the door wide.

Tad stood on the porch, the brim of his

beloved Stetson Boss crumpled in his hands, his face lined with torment. "Rebecca?"

Oh no. She'd made Uncle Giff so angry he'd collapsed. Or Mrs. Horner was in tears. "What happened?"

Tad stepped closer. "Is it true, what you said? You're not marrying Theodore?"

CHAPTER TWENTY-EIGHT

Tad waited, his heart pounding so hard in his throat it was a wonder it didn't break his neck.

After what seemed forever, she nodded, making her loose bonnet slip backward. "You were right. Theodore and I are not well suited. For all my talk of risks this afternoon, it sure took me long enough to see that I'd taken a few already, and marriage to him wasn't a risk worth taking. We'd have tried, and we might have grown to be happy enough, but —"

"You both deserve better than happy enough."

"Theodore does, at least. I think he'll find it, too." She bit her lip, as if suddenly self-conscious.

"You were on your way somewhere?" He glanced at her bonnet. "Can I take you, or will you do something with me first?"

Her eyes widened. "What do you need?"

"I want to talk to you about what you said at the livery." He stuffed his Stetson back on his head. It probably looked awful, the way he'd shredded the brim in his fingers, but he didn't care. He didn't care about much of anything right now except getting Rebecca out of the house. He shut the door behind her and gestured at the two horses tethered to the porch.

"Whose are these?"

"I borrowed them, since Solomon and Patches are worn-out. Their given names are Old Sardine and Pole-cat, so don't get after me for calling them that." His chest lightened when she laughed.

She patted Pole-cat's neck. "They're nice horses."

"I hope so, because we're going to ride them." He stretched out his arms. "I found a sidesaddle, and Sardine seems the tamer of the two, so I'll ride Pole-cat."

She bit her lip, but then she stepped into the circle of his hands. She fit so well there that he almost forgot to hoist her into the saddle.

"Why are we riding?" She fussed with her red skirt, covering her legs just so.

He climbed astride Pole-cat and nudged him forward. "I thought it might be a better way to talk than sitting on the porch where

417

everyone can listen in. Come on."

She urged Sardine into a trot that matched Pole-cat's, and it wasn't long before they reached a crest of jagged land dotted with sweet-smelling junipers. He dismounted and reached for Rebecca. "We have to walk the rest of the way. It isn't far, but there's something I want to show you."

She slid into his arms, and this time, he didn't let go. Her eyes were wide under the brim of her bonnet. "We rode quite a distance for you to tell me everyone at the livery is upset with me."

"You caused a stir." At her blanch, he groaned inside. "That is, Pa and I came to an understanding because of what you said."

"I shouldn't have meddled in your family business."

"Sweetheart, you've been in the middle of our family business since you stepped off that stagecoach."

She looked down, somewhere in the direction of the place where he usually pinned his deputy badge. "I'm sorry —"

"Don't be. You were right about so many things." He hated to let her go, but he'd brought her here for a reason. His hands dropped from her waist, but then he took her dainty fingers. "Come see why I brought you here."

"Wasn't it to argue with me where no one would overhear?"

"Plenty of people have overheard us arguing already." He laughed.

To his relief, she did, too. The climb was steeper here, and he had to lift her over sharp rocks a time or two. He should've thought about what sort of shoes she was wearing, and the pair she wore now had pointier toes and higher heels than the boots she'd worn with her trousers. "You all right?"

"Quite. The view is stunning."

It was indeed. They looked north over the steep slopes and beyond, miles distant, where a strip of yellow-green valley stretched onward. From this distance, it looked all one color, smooth and flat, but Tad knew up close how the grasses clustered in variegated shades of emerald and gold. A man could stand still among the grass, shut his eyes, and hear nothing but the cluck of quail and the *chip-chip-trill* of black-throated sparrows, and the sound of his own heart. A heart that beat for the woman beside him.

Rebecca pushed back her bonnet, a habit he'd realized came from wanting to cool her neck, and loose tendrils fluttered around her cheeks. He reached to take one delicate strand and tuck it behind her ear. She flinched and spun to face him.

Now that he'd touched her, he didn't want to stop. Ever. His hand trailed her impossibly soft earlobe, down the side of her neck to curl around her nape. He smiled, certain that the love in his heart was there for her to see. "I'm not going to be a deputy anymore, Rebecca."

Instead of smiling, her eyes filled with tears. "Yes, you are."

Tad's hand froze at the back of Rebecca's neck and his lazy smile disappeared, but she couldn't allow him to quit being a deputy. "You heard what I said at the livery."

"Every word." His hand didn't fall from her neck. In fact, he pulled her closer.

"Then you heard me say you must be who you are."

"Your blessing means more than you know." He pulled her into his side so her forehead pressed into his cheek, which made her heart batter her rib cage. "See that grass, a few miles thataway?"

"It's pretty grass."

His chuckle rumbled in her ear. "You want me to be who I am? That's it. Well, not all of it, of course, but several of those acres of grass are my claim, and the cows are on their way to fill it. Old Sardine and Pole-cat

420

are two of the cow ponies that I'm eyeing for purchase. I hadn't ridden them yet, though. So what do you think? Should I buy 'em?"

That made her laugh, even though her heart squeezed with so much pain and joy she could hardly breathe. "You hadn't ridden them before putting me atop one? What if they were neck-or-nothing terrors?"

"Sardine's about as spirited as Patches." He laughed harder. Then he tucked another errant strand of her hair behind her ear. "I want roots, and that land down there is how I'll set them down."

Roots — what she'd wanted all along, but she'd confused them with comfort and material security.

"I even ordered a brand from the smithy, a back-to-back *R,* because I thought I'd call the spread Ruby Ranch after the town where my life changed. It's where I met you and married you — and where I fell hopelessly in love with you, all out of order, but I wouldn't change a thing."

"You wouldn't?" None of the frustration or fights or guilt?

"How could I, when it led me to you? I was drawn to you from the first, but I had Rebekah and you had Theodore, and I wanted to be an honorable man. My feelings for you didn't lessen, though, they intensified — or got worse, as I thought. I fought against it, because of Theodore and your wishes, but somewhere along the way I realized it was too late. I'm yours, Rebecca. I always was. I love you more than my own life."

She couldn't hide it anymore. "I love you, too, and that's why I told you good-bye. I can't let you give up being a deputy for me. That isn't love, dictating what you do and who you should be."

"I haven't finished my speech, sweetheart. See, right now I have everything I love in sight. My land, my future, and you. Not the badge."

"But your pa —"

"Of course I love him, too. But the livery is his path, not mine. Besides, while we were out in the posse, I realized how quickly we'd had to move out. When the county office moves, I won't be accessible to the sheriff unless I live smack in Silver City, which I am confident I'm not called to do. It won't be hard to replace me. Jeroboam has already made himself comfortable at my desk. You should see him, rocking back in the chair."

Her fingers covered her lips. "You'll miss it."

"I'll miss the livery, too, and I'll help Pa

from time to time. I'd like to say the same to the sheriff, if he has need of me, but that's something you and I can work through together, just like we'll have to work through the challenges of starting a ranch. There will be risk, just like you reminded me a while back, but this is what I want: roots, ranch, and my sweet Rebecca Rice. All those *R*s tied up in Ruby Ranch. Will you work with me on every hard thing that comes our way for the rest of our lives? It won't be easy, but I don't want to go through life with anyone but you."

"Tad." Her fingers moved from her lips to his, her thumb a hair's breadth from the split Flick Dougherty had inflicted this morning. The man she loved stood before her, offering her a home, a future, and his heart. When she was in Missouri, she'd prayed for rescue and a home of her own. God had provided so much more. "Yes —"

Anything else she might have said was lost to his kiss. At first she feared hurting his lip, but then she forgot about everything. This was nothing like their wedding kiss. His arms pulled her into his chest, where one of her hands pressed against his thumping heart. One of his hands cradled the back of her head, drawing her deeper into his kiss, and her hand copied his, snaking around his shoulders and gripping the soft brown hair that curled at his nape.

She didn't want to stop, didn't want to breathe, but at length he pulled away, trailing his lips down her chin to the lacy collar at her throat. Then he slid his hands to her fingers and dropped to the rocks at their feet. "The ring's already on your hand."

"I was going to give it back to you."

"You aren't still planning on that, are you?" He kissed the finger, just shy of the ring.

"Not anymore." She laughed.

"We may be married, but I never asked proper-like. I love you, and I'm never going to stop trying to make you the happiest woman in Idaho. Will you marry me? Again, for real this time?"

She tugged him up to kiss him again. "Yes," she said between peppered kisses. "Yes."

Two weeks later

Mrs. Horner — Jolene — and Cornelia stepped back to admire their handiwork. "Go on," Jolene urged. "Take a look."

Rebecca obeyed, stepping up to the barley twist washstand in her room at the boardinghouse to peer at the small looking glass atop it. She couldn't see much beyond her face, but she didn't need to see how she looked in the creamy bridal gown Cornelia had stayed up late to help her stitch. She'd seen that, in the Cooks' full-length mirror. She'd even seen the veil, when Mrs. Horner wore it last week when she married Uncle Giff down in the parlor.

But she'd never seen it atop her pale hair, framing her cheeks. Or the way it made her eyes sparkle at her reflection.

Maybe it was love that did that.

"It's perfect, Jolene." From Mrs. Horner to Jolene Fordham, Rebecca's stepmother-in-law. She spun and embraced her. "Thank you."

"We have to keep these things in the family." Her chest swelled with joy.

Resplendent in her cobalt blue gown, maid of honor Cornelia glanced around the room. "All ready? Is your bag at the livery?"

"Johnny took it first thing." Since Giff moved into the boardinghouse after their wedding, Tad settled into the livery, where Rebecca would join him. Tad promised to start on the homestead in the valley soon, though, so they'd be snug by the first snowfall.

"Don't forget your flowers." Cornelia pointed.

Rebecca scooped up the bouquet of wildflowers lying on her bed, a smattering of fragrant white and yellow posies tied with a green ribbon, similar to her first wedding bouquet.

Johnny waited at the foot of the stairs, handsome in a new broadcloth suit.

"Both Ma and Pa would've been busting their buttons, they'd be so proud. Raymond, too."

Tears stung her eyes, but she didn't mind thinking of her loved ones. Today, their memory brought joy. "I'm glad you're here, big brother."

"And I'm not going anywhere, either." He escorted her, Jolene, and Cornelia into the Fordham livery's coach, which had been festooned with flowers and white streamers and harnessed to Madge. He drove them from the house, along the unusually empty street toward the creek. "I'm the first hire of Ruby Ranch. Tad said I could be the one to tell you."

"Oh, that's wonderful." Rebecca squeezed his arm.

Johnny pulled the carriage to a stop at the bend before they reached the creek. "Eloise's brother got a job at Ruby Ranch, too. Turns out Donald knows a fair bit about cattle. Tad was glad to bring him on."

"And I'm sure you're glad you'll see more

of Eloise," Rebecca whispered in his ear when he assisted her from the carriage.

Johnny's lips twitched as he helped Jolene and Cornelia down.

Jolene stepped ahead. "I'll make sure they're ready for you, Rebecca. Pause at the tree until I give you the signal."

Just as they'd practiced. Rebecca nodded, but she didn't care about making an entrance. She wanted to rush to the creek where Tad would be waiting at the spot where he'd first picked wildflowers for her.

"I should tell you one more thing so you don't hear it from someone else." Johnny's gaze flickered back the direction they'd come. "The judge did some sentencing this morning. He took it easier on Dottie and took Ralph's cooperation into consideration, but they won't be going anywhere for a while. Bowe will serve out his sentence, too, but he told the judge that when he got out, he wanted to be the kind of man his mama and grandmammy would be proud of."

"I hope he will be."

Cornelia tapped her sleeve. "Jolene's waving at us. Let's go."

Johnny led them through the trees. Cornelia scurried ahead, bouquet in hand, for the procession. Then Rebecca turned the corner. Straight ahead, in front of the willows that lined the creek, stood Tad, shoulders stiff, a scab on his ear. Then he caught sight of her and his jaw gaped.

To his side, best man Theodore smiled, as did the black-coated circuit preacher, a young man with bandy legs and a prayer book in his hands.

She reached Tad and took his hands. "Nervous?"

"Not anymore." He kissed her left hand, currently bare of the opal ring. He'd had it sized so it would be a perfect fit today.

"Dearly beloved," the preacher began. This was the wedding she always wanted: a preacher, flowers, friends, and so much love she couldn't stop smiling.

"Do you, Rebecca Mary, take Thaddeus Percival, to be your husband. . . ."

She did. And Tad took her to be his wife, too.

The kiss was far shorter than their first wedding's kiss, but Rebecca received many more from what seemed like the whole town. Theodore and Cornelia, who congratulated them while holding hands. Giff and Jolene. Even Mr. Kaplan, the stagecoach driver, was there, along with most of the town — which explained why the streets had seemed deserted. Johnny and Eloise hugged her, and Eloise's nieces Wilma and

Pauline danced in the aisle.

"Thanks for coming, Doc." Tad shook Dr. Wilkie's hand.

"I'm not a doctor, remember? But I'd be happy to deliver your baby a year from now, if you find yourself in Silver City."

Tad choked.

Longbeard stood off at a distance. Rebecca waved, but he didn't wave back.

"He came, sweetheart," Tad whispered in her ear. "That says a lot."

Only one guest looked sour, or at least, he pretended to. Ulysses stuffed his hands in his pockets and pouted. "I guess I never stood a chance, did I?"

It was impossible not to smile. "You know how brides carry tokens at their weddings, Ulysses? Look at this." She reached into the tiny bag Cornelia had sewn to match Rebecca's dress and pulled out the objects she'd tucked in this morning. "This handkerchief was my mother's. This pin was Tad's mother's."

"And that's my jasper!" His gold tooth flashed.

"It reminds me God gave me friends, like you." She hugged him, gasping for breath when he squeezed her too tight.

"Do I get to kiss the bride?" He looked to Tad.

"Absolutely."

He gave her a loud smack on the cheek.

After the kisses and the feasting and the well-wishing, Tad pulled her behind the crowd. "Everyone's kissed you dozens of times today except me."

"Only Ulysses did it a dozen times."

"Well, I'd sure like to catch up."

Her toes sizzled as Tad lowered his lips to hers.

Their loved ones' hooting and hollering drew them apart. Tad smiled down at her. "The cake's been cut, we've hugged everyone, and we're officially married. What do you say we go home?"

The livery, the house in the valley — anywhere Tad was, wherever God led them. "I'm ready."

No mistake.

ABOUT THE AUTHOR

Susanne Dietze began writing love stories in high school, casting her friends in the starring roles. Today, she's the award-winning author of a dozen new and upcoming historical romances who's seen her work on the ECPA and Publisher's Weekly Bestseller Lists for Inspirational Fiction. Married to a pastor and the mom of two, Susanne lives in California and enjoys fancy-schmancy tea parties, the beach, and curling up on the couch with a costume drama and a plate of nachos. You can visit her online at www.susannedietze.com and subscribe to her newsletters at http://eepurl.com/bieza5.

The employees of Thorndike Press hope you have enjoyed this Large Print book. All our Thorndike, Wheeler, and Kennebec Large Print titles are designed for easy reading, and all our books are made to last. Other Thorndike Press Large Print books are available at your library, through selected bookstores, or directly from us.

For information about titles, please call:
(800) 223-1244

or visit our website at:
gale.com/thorndike

To share your comments, please write:
Publisher
Thorndike Press
10 Water St., Suite 310
Waterville, ME 04901

RUTH ENLOW LIBRARY
OF GARRETT COUNTY
6 North Second Street
Oakland, MD 21550